SILENT CITY

A PETE FERNANDEZ MYSTERY

The following is a work of fiction. Names, characters, places, events and incidents are either the product of the author's imagination or used in an entirely fictitious manner. Any resemblance to actual persons, living or dead, is entirely coincidental.

Cover and jacket design by 2Faced Design
Interior designed and formatted by E.M. Tippetts Book Designs
ISBN 978-1-940610-71-9
eISBN: 1-978-1-943818-08-2
Library of Congress Control Number: 2015957649

First published in 2013 by Codorus Press
Reissued in trade paperback and ebook March 2016
by Polis Books, LLC
1201 Hudson Street, #211S
Hoboken, NJ 07030
www.PolisBooks.com

POLIS BOOKS

For Eva

"There are things that have to be forgotten if you want to go on living."

—Jim Thompson, *The Killer Inside Me*

PROLOGUE

The microwave beep — announcing that her popcorn was done — startled Kathy Bentley for a second. The noise was also enough to jolt her small gray cat, Nigel, from her lap and tip over the little bit of white wine still residing in her glass. Kathy sighed and plopped the glass on the table separating her couch from the television. She paused her well worn DVD of *Eternal Sunshine of the Spotless Mind* and sauntered into the kitchen, where Nigel sat waiting, eyes wide, wondering if whatever was coming out of the microwave could be for him.

"This is Mommy's," Kathy said as she carefully pulled the hot bag of instant popcorn from the microwave. "None for you."

The cat gave out a cry as he saw that the food was, in fact, not for him. Kathy laughed. It was close to midnight and she had been home less than 20 minutes. After a 12-hour shift at *Miami Times*, where she worked as one of the paper's dwindling group of investigative reporters, it took very little to amuse — or annoy — Kathy tonight.

Today had been cluttered with meetings geared toward redirecting the paper's goals and, more importantly, increasing the paper's profits. It wasn't a surprise to anyone that print was dying. With news, opinion, classifieds and pretty much anything of interest available on the Web for free, why shell out any money for something that would get your hands covered in ink? The state of panic there was something Kathy would drown with a few glasses of Chardonnay. Kathy didn't feel productive or fulfilled by her work. As she walked back to her spot on the couch, she glanced at the clock hanging over her too-expensive entertainment center. Javier Reyes, supposedly her boyfriend, hadn't called in over a day. Not totally foreign behavior for him, as he tended to pout after they fought, but troubling nonetheless. Kathy shrugged to herself. She was certain that they'd be texting each other at some point during the wee hours, either to extend the argument — about money, unsurprisingly — or to make the evening more interesting. Javier frustrated her — he was cagey, cheap and she'd caught him in a few blatant lies. Most of the time, these things would be grounds for a break up with Kathy. But for some reason Javier lingered. She couldn't deny there was something that kept pulling her back to him. Maybe the old saying was true — the less they seem to want you, the more you want them. Javier had definitely mastered the art of seeming disinterested. Whether they were fighting or fucking, it was always passionate — dramatic. Feelings that reminded her of being a teenager. Feelings she knew weren't genuine, but whatever. She wanted them to be.

Kathy refilled her wine glass and gulped down a portion of it.

Nigel curled up in his usual spot on Kathy's lap.

She put the movie back on with a quick flick of the remote, but found her mind wandering. She was entering her sixth year at the *Times* and felt like little had changed. She was a crime reporter tasked with writing "enterprise" stories — the kind that require more than a few hours' investigation — at a paper that had no budget or interest in them. The days when she could spend a month chasing a few sources and putting together a 10,000-word series spotlighting corruption in the Miami City Council were long gone, if they were ever there. She was still ostracized, considered an unqualified hire by the veterans on staff, many of whom believed she had snagged the job because her father, with whom she barely spoke, was a long-time columnist for the paper's local news section. Because of the dwindling page count, the number of actual stories she was expected to produce each week had dwindled to where she would not be surprised if she were one of the staffers let go in the next round of layoffs.

But what then? Kathy had never considered a career outside of journalism, much less outside of the comfortable confines of a newsroom. She had little family — a brother in California she never spoke to, a mother and a father she would disown if she could. Javier, a former drug dealer with anger management issues, wasn't exactly a beacon of hope. And the few friends she did have had drifted off the longer she stayed with him. She took a long sip from her glass and stroked Nigel. She wasn't cut out for daily reporting, she thought. The one thing of value she'd been working on — a lengthy, detailed investigative piece dealing with Miami's Cuban drug underworld — wasn't going to be enough to secure her job. And anyway, it wasn't ready, as usual. She still felt the piece needed at least a few more months' work.

She felt she was getting somewhere with the story, though, especially when it came to "the Silent Death," the nickname given to an unnamed enforcer for the Cubans. The killer, who'd left over a dozen bodies in less than a decade, had become something of an urban legend. Some doubted it was even one man. Kathy wasn't so sure. But she wasn't getting much help from the shitty Miami police or her bosses, which meant the story wasn't developing as quickly as she'd like. Still, if she could nail who "the Silent Death" was — so named for his penchant for silencers and a clingy black mask, of all things, over the bottom half of his face — she'd definitely have a job, even if it was one she couldn't stand. But she was getting ahead of herself. She needed to finish the story first, and all she had were a few clues and one theory that was based more on her reporter's instinct than on actual, hard facts. As her editor friend Amy Matheson had reminded her numerous times, "If you want to solve one of the biggest mysteries this town has seen in years, you need more than a gut feeling."

Nigel dug his claws into her thighs as he leaped off toward the kitchen. It was unlike him to just give up on a petting session. Kathy mumbled to herself and returned her attention to *Eternal Sunshine* when she heard a noise. She couldn't pinpoint where it was coming from, but the grating sound put her on edge.

Her one-bedroom apartment, nestled in downtown Miami in the nebulous area between "Little Haiti" and what eventually would become Miami Shores, was not prime real estate. Still, it was close to work and equally close to the beach, two places the tan-and-blond Kathy frequented, only one by choice. She was cautious. She'd been burglarized before. She turned off the television and tried to listen. She was just getting paranoid.

Then it started again. Metal scraping on metal. This time it was clear it was coming from her door — her doorknob, to be specific. *What a time for Javier not to be here,* she thought. She tightened the robe she was wearing around her T-shirt and shorts and headed toward the door, hoping that the sound of someone inside would startle whoever was trying to get into her apartment. The scraping stopped in the seconds it took Kathy to get to her door. She had no way of seeing if there was someone out there.

"Hello?" she snapped. "Who's there? If you don't leave I'll call the p—"

Before she could finish, the door flung open, pushing her back and onto the floor. As she struggled to stand, a man busted in. He was large, muscular, and bearded — a grizzled, Hispanic man with a collection of gold jewelry around his neck and a scar down the whole left side of his face. She got to her feet. The large man grabbed her shoulders and shoved her to the couch, knocking the wind out of her.

The burly man was holding a small pistol. The sight of the gun made Kathy's heart jump. He looked around.

"Hey Kathy. How's it goin' tonight?"

"Wh-who are you? How did you get in here?" Kathy felt separated from her body, wondered how she could even get the words out. He was very close to her now. She could feel his hot breath on her face, cheap rum and Spanish food in her nostrils. His left hand wrapped around her neck. She tried leaning further into the couch, but he wouldn't let up.

"*No te preocupes.* I got in through the front door, remember?"

Don't worry, he'd said. Kathy could glean that much with her bad Spanish. She tried to look around, but his grip tightened, forcing her eyes to meet his. "Gotta get you a better lock. This one here was too easy for me to pick."

Kathy's eyes darted around, looking for something, anything that could get her out of this. What did he want? Her money? There wasn't any. Her stuff? Possibly. Her body? Likely. The burly man seemed to read her thoughts in the inch of air between them.

He raised his other hand and wagged his index finger in her face. *No. You're not going anywhere.* She began to shake. She felt warm tears collecting in her eyes and choked on desperate sobs.

"Don't go doing anything stupid, ok? No one knows I'm here." He was whispering now. Her neck, still being held in place by a firm grip, was starting to hurt. "I've just got a few things to ask you, is all. Simple enough, no?"

Kathy tried to speak. Nothing came out. She nodded.

"Now, where does a smart reporter like you keep her notes, eh?" He said "reporter" with a sneer, dragging out the last syllable, English clearly not his preferred language. She could barely breathe through the heat of his body.

This is it, Kathy thought. *This is how I die.* Someone must have tipped him off about her article, but why? She'd spoken to only a handful of people. And they'd all been trusted sources she'd built up over time. What had she done to lead the burly man here?

"M-m-my notes aren't here," Kathy stammered. "My story's done. I've already turned it in to my editor. Lots of people have read it."

Kathy was interrupted by a slap. The sharp pain took an extra sting through the tears coating her face. The burly man was no longer whispering. His breath slammed against her as he yelled, "You had better be lying." Kathy felt herself being lifted, his grip closing off her throat. "Because if you're not, this is not going to end well for you."

Kathy began to speak, but felt a knee slam into her midsection. She couldn't breathe. She heard her ribs crack. His grip loosened as Kathy fell to the tiles, her knees crashing hard, followed by her body and then her head.

She ran her hands over her face and body, trying to will them to work, when she saw the man take aim and slam his boot across her face. She couldn't make out what he was saying. Everything had gone dark. For a second or two, it felt like the ground was moving. Then the tile was scraping against her skin. Something was yanking at her hair, no, pulling. She wasn't sure if she was still crying. She thought she heard Nigel.

CHAPTER ONE

The bright red numbers on the nightstand stood out in the darkness of Pete Fernandez's bedroom. Some sunlight crept into the space between his hastily drawn blinds. Two-thirty in the afternoon. Pete groaned and scanned the room with his bloodshot eyes. Clothes scattered on the floor. Mail at his feet on the bed, black messenger bag tossed near the door. He covered his eyes with his palm. The throbbing in his forehead was bad. Not as bad as earlier, at four in the morning, when he'd relived the bottle of red wine and peach schnapps shots he'd consumed over the course of a few hours in his bathroom.

Pete seemed to recall the bartender, Jesus, being generous last night. Most of the evening was clinked glasses, slurred conversation, and a foolish drive back home on Biscayne Boulevard to his Little Haiti apartment. His usual nighttime ritual of three glasses of water and four Advil — plus whatever seemed edible in the fridge — had done little to prevent this anguish. Pete wasn't even sure if he'd managed to get one glass down before passing out.

Before he could decide whether he would get up or try to finagle an extra hour of sleep before work, Pete heard the familiar pounding on his door. It was Costello, his four-year-old black cat, alerting him that, yes, it was time for breakfast, hangover or not. Costello had become very methodical in his requests for food. Thump. Thump. Tortured meow. Thump. Thump. Questioning meow. It was cat jazz, Pete thought, and then laughed out loud. Yeah, he was still drunk.

His dry mouth and all-over ache made it clear to Pete that he wasn't getting up just yet. This didn't deter Costello, who Pete had named after Elvis — not Lou — during a particularly obsessive period that had never really disappeared. The case of records near his desk could attest to that. The only Costello albums collecting dust were recent stuff. And "Goodbye, Cruel World," too. He leaned over, found an errant shoe, tossed it at the door. The racket stopped. For now.

Pete fell back into bed, trying to block out the sunlight by closing his eyes and letting his mind wander. Bits and pieces from the night before flooded back, between the throbbing of his headache and his aching body. He remembered talking to Mike Carver, one of his few remaining friends since he'd returned to Miami, after a stint as a sports reporter in New Jersey had gone up in flames, and drunkenly thanking him. For what? Pete wasn't sure. There was a girl, too, at some point. He hadn't gone home with her, as he was in his own apartment. Pete groaned again. Every time he awoke like this — feeling like shit, hazy on what he'd said or done the night before and usually embarrassed by what little he did remember — he'd promise himself it'd be the last time. So far that hadn't worked. He rolled over in bed, facing the wall. He could still sneak in an hour or two of sleep before he had to head to the *Miami Times* newsroom. Back to the grind of his life now. Copy editing the stories he used to be tasked with writing. A paper pusher in a time when paper — and newspapers — were dying.

Then the phone rang.

Pete rolled back and reached for his cell phone, which was blaring a scratchy, digitized version of the Replacements' "Waitress in the Sky" as its ringtone. *Great song,* Pete thought, *but not now.* The sloppy, shuffling delivery Westerberg gave the ode to flight attendants wasn't what Pete needed. The sad, pleading lyrics only reminded Pete about how sad and pleading he'd been the night before. The alarm clock's red numbers taunted him as he checked his phone. It was Mike. He wondered what kind of details he'd find to fill the gaping holes in the memories from last night.

"Yo." Pete half coughed his first word of the day.

"You still asleep, bro?" Mike let "bro" drag out for a few extra seconds, an old college joke that wasn't funny anymore but had become a habit. Pete could hear that Mike was on the road, probably heading back to his apartment up in Fort Lauderdale from his girlfriend Tracy's house. Mike, like Pete, had been pretty tanked in the wee hours of the morning. Unlike Pete, though, Mike knew when to stop.

"Nah, I've been up for a while," Pete lied. "Have fun last night?"

"It was good. Good to see the crew. Too many shots, though," Mike said. "How'd you get home? You were still with that chick when I left."

"Which chick?" Pete asked, instantly regretting it. *Shit. What chick?*

Mike laughed. "Never mind. I didn't know who she was. It seemed like you guys knew each other, though."

Pete thought back. He remembered the girl now. Stephanie — a former coworker from Pete's time in Jersey. She was also friends with Emily Blanco, formerly Sprague, also formerly Pete's fiancée. After the breakup, Emily had done a stint as a designer with the *Miami Times* before settling down with her new husband, Rick, down in Homestead. Pete liked to think they were friends now, in that weird, stunted way people tried to be friends with someone that broke their heart. He liked to think that, at least. Pete grimaced. Stephanie was in town covering the Miami Book Fair and just happened to be at the same joint where Mike, Pete, and a few other friends were imbibing: Kleinman's, a narrow sports bar nestled in a half-empty condo building just a block away from the *Times*. Pete only got back bits and pieces of conversation, but he could see Stephanie's face. A sad, pitiful look. Not for her, but for him. Maybe it was better that he didn't recall what they talked about.

"You're lucky you just had to drive a few blocks, bro. D-U-I . . ." Mike sang the dreaded three letters.

He was right. Pete had been stupid last night, could barely remember anything after that last shot of schnapps. Not anything clear, at least. But being such a creature of habit helped. Pete could stumble home pretty capably from anywhere. Or so he told himself. What was the term for this — "Functional alcoholic"? Best not to think about that.

"Yeah, I remember now," Pete said. "She was a friend of Emily's from Jersey. I don't really remember what we talked about. I'm sure she'll tell Emily all about how wasted her almost-husband was. Great."

"Eh, fuck it. I wouldn't worry about it too much," Mike said. "Who cares what Emily or her idiot friends think?"

Mike was always good for this kind of support. He was a coworker and a good friend. Always loyal, always forgiving, he helped Pete come to terms with his own failings. Or at least ignore them. Pete wondered if this would all be easier if Emily had stayed in New Jersey, allowing Pete to create this idea of her in his mind as an evil person, so he would not have to cross paths with her regularly, only to be reminded of why he fell in love with her in the first place.

"Anything going on tonight?" Pete asked, more out of habit than anything else. The last thing he wanted was another drink. But he was kidding himself if he thought he wouldn't have one or two before the day was done.

"You nuts? Nothing, man. I'm just going to chill at home," Mike said. "I need to do some shit around the house."

"Yeah, I should do the same," Pete said. He gave his bedroom a quick once-over. "You work tonight?"

"Nah, I'm off. Unless Vance calls me in. That dick." Mike laughed at his own profanity. "Alright, I'm out. I'll talk to you later." *Click.*

The abrupt ending to the call, much like the beginning, didn't faze Pete. It's how he and Mike communicated.

He returned to bed, eyes on the ceiling. Headache was better, Pete thought. He couldn't help thinking of Emily, and he groaned aloud at the thought of what Stephanie — a girl he'd met once at a random dinner party — would tell her about their encounter. Knowing Emily, though, she'd never mention it to Pete. She'd made it clear that she was no longer going to try to fix him. It wasn't her responsibility anymore.

After a few minutes, he dozed. In that cloud between sleep and wake, Pete found himself dreaming. He was younger, probably in high school. He was riding shotgun in his dad's old blue Ford Fairmont, down 87th Avenue, in Westchester, the Miami suburb that young Pete had called home. He was smiling. The sun was out. The leather seats of the car felt hot on his arms and his back. His father had the oldies station on. The Beatles were playing, Pete thought. "Hey Jude"? His dad was wearing his usual short-sleeved business shirt, tie, slacks, and thick glasses. He was still working. A homicide detective for the Miami PD. He looked good, healthy. He was smiling, too. It was summer in Miami and all was good. A leggy Dominican girl crossed the street in front of them and Pete saw his father motion with his chin. "*Está rica, no?*" *Isn't she lovely?* Pete shrugged and looked out his passenger-side window. In his dream, he wasn't sure why he did that. His father looked away. Pete could tell his disinterest hurt his father. The dream fizzled. Pete awoke sad. His cat had gone quiet.

CHAPTER TWO

P ete's battered black Toyota Celica wheezed its way up into the Times' main parking garage. While working nights at the paper allowed him to sleep off the most brutal of hangovers, it never guaranteed a parking space. The broiled meat smell wafting from the McDonald's bag resting next to Pete in the passenger seat made him retch a bit. Too soon for a double cheeseburger and fries.

After some swerving around, Pete snagged a space on the garage's top floor, open to the elements, which meant his car would still be a sauna when his shift ended, around midnight. Summers in Miami were brutal. A tropical paradise most of the year, Miami became unbearable from late May until about mid-September. For Pete, who wasn't much of a beach guy, that meant a lot of time indoors, in cars, and in bars. Pete winced. Sweat was already through his black polo.

He stepped out of his car, snatched the *Times* ID badge hanging from his rearview mirror, and collected his grub. He sighed as he walked toward the Times building, nestled between a vacant strip mall and the expressway.

The newsroom was in its early stages of life. People were still shuffling in for the evening shift, and the unluckies forced to work weekends were already gone, desperate for some semblance of a normal schedule. Pete nodded here and there as he made his way across the Features cubicles toward Sports, where Pete found his desk in the same shape he'd left it two days prior — disorganized and funky. He tossed his food to the side, sat down, and logged on. Pete had the dubious role of "duty officer" on weekends, meaning he had to represent the *Times'* sports section at the nightly news meeting and oversee the pages being sent to press throughout the night. It also meant Pete had to come in at least 30 minutes earlier than usual to familiarize himself with what was going on in the sports world. His hangover and junk food run had eaten into any chance for prep. Pete was barely on time.

He hadn't bothered to listen to the sports talk stations on his way in, nor had he scanned the wire last night — too busy moaning into his toilet bowl. He began to unpack his dinner-for-breakfast as he waited for his archaic computer to boot up.

To say he wasn't in good standing with his bosses was an understatement. Pete had eliminated whatever reputation he'd built up as a basketball beat writer for the *Bergen Light* in his first few months at the *Times*. He was consistently late, mediocre when he was actually working and, while pleasant to be around, not terribly interested in his work. Pete knew this. He did little to change it. He found the job of copy editor boring. The drudgery made his last job — covering Jersey's pro hoops team — seem like a vacation, even though by the time he'd gotten that gig he was already spinning his wheels. He had his reputation to thank for this job, though. A few years out of college, Pete had used keen sourcing and a knack for analyzing records to uncover a small-scale gambling operation involving the assistant basketball coaches at Hamilton University. The story vaulted Pete from small-town general-assignment reporter to hotshot sports writer. That's when things got fuzzy, Pete remembered. Instead of being picky and waiting for the right job to come around, he'd jumped at the first chance he got to cover a big-league team, and that was his undoing. The travel, hotels, hotel bars, and expense accounts mixed a little too well with his thirst for drink, and soon he found himself unhappy, almost married, and in a cold-weather state that lacked the appeal and draw of New York.

Then his father died.

That's what brought Pete — and at the time, Emily — back to Miami. The plan was to stay for a few months and get his father's affairs in order. His mother had died in childbirth and Pete was the only son of Pedro Fernandez Sr., respected and retired Miami homicide detective. Pete had no choice. Three months had turned into a year. The *Bergen Light* refused to give him any more paid leave, Emily had left him, and he'd settled for an editing job when he had previously been one of the nation's rising writing stars. The full scope of Pete's career collapse was still just an abstract idea in his head most of the time, but days like today, when the mundane reality of his new life stared right back at him, he felt a great sense of loss—and really wanted a drink. Pete's screen flickered to life in yellow on black.

P ete barely noticed Chaz Bentley walk into the newsroom. It was well past 11, and he was putting the finishing touches on a late Marlins game recap while looking over proof for an inside page. Pete, despite his general disregard for his duties, was proud of his headline writing and took some pleasure in making sure there was something there that would pull a reader in. The page was already covered in red marks from its first pass through the copy desk, and Pete envisioned a few more rounds before the night was through. As on most nights, Pete had his headphones on, trying to drown out the usual newsroom din as he focused on the words and sentences forming on his screen and on the pages the printer spat out with alarming frequency. Pete had a Pixies mix going, the opening, deceptively melodic bassline of "Debaser" pulsing into his ears, when he felt the tap on his shoulder at the moment the song kicked into sonic apocalypse. Pete took off his headphones and wheeled around to face Chaz Bentley, the *Times'* local news columnist. In his early sixties and inching toward retirement, Chaz was one of the guys that had been around forever, worked every job, and inhaled every part of the city. At least that's what the *Times* brass wanted readers to think. Pete didn't buy it. Chaz had seen better days. He was kept on the payroll mainly for his name — which still seemed to rate with the huge senior citizen readership. In reality, Chaz barely wrote more than his required weekly puff piece, and even that was a product of heavy editing and lots of hand-holding. Pete felt sorry for him. He'd only spoken to him a handful of times in person. It was odd for a columnist to be in the newsroom at this hour, unless there was an urgent rewrite needed. Why he was in the Sports area was doubly baffling.

"Hey, uh, you got a sec?" Chaz was rubbing his hands together. Pete looked across the room. The clock was ticking. The paper was inching close to the deadline for the final edition.

Chaz looked around the newsroom. Everyone seemed deep in his or her respective tasks. The loud bustle of a few hours ago had been replaced by a hum.

"Sure," Pete said. "But I'm a few minutes from deadline and I've got three stories in my basket. Did your column get shifted to one of us by accident?"

"No, no, nothing like that," Chaz said. "I — uh — look, I know this may sound strange," he trailed off. He could smell whiskey on Chaz's breath. A glance back at his monitor indicated a growing number of messages blinking at Pete from colleagues across the newsroom. More than half of the messages were probably screaming "WHERE ARE MY PAGES?" Pete slid his hand through his short dark-brown hair and leaned back, eyebrows raised.

"Well, I think Kathy's missing."

"Kathy?"

"Yeah, my daughter," Chaz paused again. Pete thought back. Kathy. The news reporter. She was friends with Emily. They'd bonded soon after Emily had returned to Miami with Pete and had done a stint as a designer for the news desk when it was clear they were not going back to New Jersey. They'd all hung out together a handful of times. Kathy was pretty, blond, thin, and relatively friendly the few times Pete had spoken to her. Flirted with her was more likely. He'd considered asking her out a few times, but never could find the right moment. It also didn't help she was friends with his ex.

"Missing? What do you mean?" This time Pete made his glance at the clock obvious to Chaz. *I am late now,* he thought. In a few minutes, Steve Vance would be calling to see why the pages hadn't been released to the plating area, where they were then put on the actual presses. Pete knew that was the last call Vance wanted to make on his day off, close to midnight.

"Listen, can we meet up and talk about this?" Chaz said, his face now sleek with sweat. "I just need a few minutes of your time."

"Sure, sure." *Anything to get back to work,* Pete thought. If he hurried, he might avoid the Vance call and get the pages out under the gun. They'd be full of errors, but they'd be done. "Just let me know when. I'm free tomorrow."

"No, it has to be tonight."

"Where?"

"Do you know the Abbey?"

"Yeah, yeah. Hole in the wall on Alton?"

"Yes," Chaz said, his voice clearer and in control now. "Near the beach. Next to the McDonald's."

"I should be out of here close to one. That too late?"

"No. Let's meet there at a quarter to two. That work?"

"Sure. See you then."

Chaz walked off. Pete turned back to his monitor. He had felt the stares from his fellow sports editors, stuck waiting on him, as he chatted. Pete tried not to think about how odd it would be to sit with Chaz, who was around the age his father would be if he'd lived, at a bar at two in the morning, no less. Pete tried to focus on work. There were still a few late West Coast baseball games tonight. The scores wouldn't be in for at least an hour, if then. He'd have to blow them off to meet with Chaz. *The website guys could post them,* Pete thought.

Despite his lingering hangover, the idea of another drink appealed to Pete. It had taken Pete a minute to even make the connection between Chaz and Kathy. Kathy, the investigative reporter all the editors lusted after. Daughter of the surly "columnist" who never dared show his face in the newsroom unless he had to. Something was really weird.

Still, there was work to be done. Pete pushed Kathy, Chaz, and everything else to the back of his mind and dove into the pile of proofs and e-mails that had converged around and inside his computer, the clock taunting him. Had the Sports team — or, better said, Pete — managed his time better, the final section would be more complete. He said a silent prayer in the hope that he wouldn't hear about this tomorrow. Sometimes it worked. The newsroom bustle filled his ears, the faint sounds of the Pixies' "U-Mass" tinny from the headphones he'd set aside, Black Francis yelling "It's educational!" as the newspaper skidded toward deadline.

CHAPTER THREE

Pete sat down at the far end of the Abbey's bar, close to the speakers. He usually avoided bars that didn't have a jukebox — being part music nerd and part control freak — but the Abbey boasted a fairly solid, iPod-run sound system. Not every song was a winner, Pete thought, but they batted a pretty healthy average. Now, they were blasting the Buzzcocks' "What Do I Get?" — a power-punk plea for attention that only the best bands could pull. The track took him back to his college days, when his love of music had helped him discover a love for writing, and his nights consisted of rock shows by bad-to-great bands in seedy bars on the edge of downtown. The nights usually produced some overly-stylized reviews that consisted of Pete's best imitation of Lester Bangs or fluffy features for his college paper on the few bands that dared pop down to Miami for a show. He'd even been in a band — the foolishly named Dancing Violence. Pete hummed the melody to one of their songs but couldn't remember it past the first verse. He didn't even own a guitar anymore. Pete rubbed his eyes, sore from staring at his monitor for nine hours. It'd been a long night. It wasn't over.

The bartender, a thirty-something stoner named Nick, was wearing a rumpled Smiths T-shirt and sported the requisite blond stubble. He hovered at the other end of the bar. Pete motioned for him and ordered a Delirium Tremens. The bartender served him a glass with the trademark pink elephant on it and returned to his post, talking to a thin, bespectacled man. From what Pete could overhear, they were debating the Dolphins' chances in the coming football season. As much as Pete loved football, specifically the Dolphins, he was in no mood to get involved in heated sports debate. Not tonight.

Pete sipped his beer slowly, aware from many past experiences that the selection of brews at the Abbey was not only diverse, but also highly potent. It was close to two. Pete was early.

The bartender looked over as he wiped off a pint glass with a rag that hung limply from his waist. A few minutes passed and his first beer was gone. Pete ordered another. He pondered a shot, but remembered the Abbey was beer and wine only. Probably for the best.

Chaz walked into the Abbey at a quarter past two. Wisps of blondish-gray hair framed his thin face. He reminded Pete of a sitcom dad after a three-night bender. Pete pictured Chaz sitting him down on the couch for a heart-to-heart about the perils of premarital sex. Pete chuckled under his breath. Chaz wore a plaid, short-sleeved, button-down shirt and worn light-blue jeans. Like Pete, Chaz carried a notebook in his shirt pocket. Chaz had been working at the *Times* for over 25 years. Despite his recent nosedive in quality, he still had an impressive résumé that Pete could only dream of matching. He appreciated Chaz's old-school ethic. Too many reporters had lost themselves in the technology, using it as a crutch to mask bad journalism and weak writing. Despite their difference in age, Pete felt some kinship with the elder reporter.

Chaz looked around the empty bar until he noticed Pete at the far end. Pete was on his third drink and feeling it. He forced himself to focus.

The bartender looked at Chaz as he took a seat next to Pete, nodding politely. Pete slid over the drinks menu.

"What'll it be, man?" the bartender asked Chaz.

"Rogue." His voice was hoarse, but cleared up a bit as he spoke.

The bartender nodded and walked over to the taps near the center of the establishment. Pete and Chaz were the only people in the bar, aside from Nick the bartender.

"Good to see you," Pete said. "Though, I can't say I really know what this is about."

"Thanks for coming. I appreciate it." Chaz's eyes were tired and empty. Pete could still smell whiskey on his breath. "At this point, I feel like I need to take any help I can get."

"Well, what can I do?" Pete said. "I don't really know Kathy that well. So, she's missing?"

"I don't really know. She was fine a couple weeks ago, but I haven't seen her since."

"Well, OK. How does that mean she's missing?" Pete asked. "Has she been to work?"

"I only realized she was gone yesterday," Chaz explained. He trailed off a bit as the bartender served his beer. He took a hungry gulp. Most of the beer was finished with one lift. Pete felt like he was getting a glimpse of what he might look like in 30 years. Or was he just being melodramatic? Chaz closed his eyes for a second and then looked at Pete. "Sorry. It's hot as fuck outside. I hate this city. Even at night it's hot. No breeze, just heat, sweat, and smell. Too much. It's too much sometimes."

"I guess," Pete said. He looked up at one of the muted TV screens. Repeats of the evening news. A gator found in Homestead. He'd have to call Emily to see if it had crawled through her yard. Or not, he thought. Pete could already hear her laughing on the other end of the line.

Chaz slid a finger over his glass. He didn't respond.

"Why don't you go to the cops?" Pete asked.

"The cops don't think she's missing."

"Doesn't that count for something?"

"They think that she's just not talking to me, since we don't have much of a relationship." Chaz looked away from Pete and finished his beer in one pull.

"Maybe she's on vacation? I don't know," Pete shrugged. His buzz was fading and he was getting bored.

"She's been off my radar for a few weeks. She usually calls once a week, on Sundays," Chaz said. "To chat, to say hello, to ask for money. The usual routine. The last time we talked she sounded frazzled. Just . . . I dunno . . . off. She's been seeing this guy, Javier."

"Javier what?"

"Reyes. You know him, right?"

"Yeah, I know him. We went to high school together," Pete said. He hadn't thought of Javier in years. He vaguely remembered Emily or Mike mentioning something about Javier and Kathy. The few times Pete had hung out while Kathy was around, the topic of Javier never came up. Neither did her having a boyfriend. He felt slightly disheartened to discover she wasn't single. Javier and Pete had run together in high school, back when Pete wasn't much more than a wannabe street thug — petty theft, minor dealing. If it hadn't been for Pete's dad and his discipline, he'd more than likely be doing time or struggling to get back on his feet after doing time.

"Early thirties — about your age. Kind of a smartass. Acts like he's hot shit but still talks like he'd just pulled his raft off the beach. Has the same '¿Que Pasa USA?' accent all those new Mexicans or Cubans have." Chaz stopped himself, realizing he was drunk and not in control of his tongue. "Aw shit, sorry. I didn't mean that."

"Don't worry about it," Pete sighed and slid his empty glass toward the bartender. His system could probably handle one more. But his patience was wearing thin. This was going nowhere. He still felt the residual pounding of the morning's hangover.

The proverbial collision of two worlds — his misspent youth and his misspent present — had taken him by surprise. Of all places to find Javier, he would have never expected it'd be at the Abbey with Chaz Bentley.

"So they were dating?" Pete was surprised at the directness of his own question.

"I guess so," Chaz muttered. "They're always together when she comes over, all wide-eyed and chatty, hopped up on who-knows-what."

Pete scratched his chin, rubbing against his four-day stubble. The bartender poured him another. He closed his eyes and let his mind drift back to a decade before, when he couldn't think of anyone closer to him than Javier. Best friends that never acknowledged it. Strumming guitars in Pete's bedroom, hustling students with a few weed sales here and there. They weren't bad kids. Sure, they cut class, drank and smoked, listened to loud music, snuck out late at night to see the few punk acts with enough cash to make the trek down to Miami — but there were always other kids doing worse. Pete often found himself getting nostalgic for when the biggest problem was how to get to the mailbox before your dad did, to prevent him from finding that form letter from the school informing them his kid hadn't bothered to show for class in a few weeks. Before Mike and Emily, there was Javier — his literal partner in crime.

Those years, his first few at Southwest Miami High, were glorious times, fueled by cheap beer, weed and great music. He could almost feel the summer breeze whipping at his face as he and Javier sped down Bird Road in his dad's battered red Mustang, well after midnight, listening to the title track from *Let It Bleed* on loop. Mick's put-on drawl reminding the listener that we all need someone we can lean on. The words meant so much then. Pete hadn't played that record in years.

It had ended abruptly, like those things do. A few beers too many one night and they'd decided they were invincible. Strutting into a desolate 7-Eleven on Coral Way with nothing to lose. Both of them wearing big coats that screamed "We're shoplifting!" on a humid Miami evening. They thought they were the shit as they slid a few forties of Olde English into their pockets, trying with little success not to giggle. They stopped laughing when the old man behind the counter pulled out a shotgun and ordered them to put their hands up. Extreme? Sure. Javier gave Pete a look that said, "Let's go, he won't shoot." But for Pete it was over. This was farther than he ever thought he'd get, and he wanted no part of being an actual criminal. Pete would never forget the look of betrayal in Javier's eyes. He didn't know it at the time, but that's when their friendship died. Later that night, Pete's father — looking more shamed than he'd ever seen him — walked into the police station, hat in hand, and dragged Pete back home. Pete remembered the cloud of guilt that hovered over him for weeks. Knowing that his father was already working himself to death chasing after a pile of unsolved cases, only to find his biggest problem was his own son. Pete resigned himself to his new life, more out of sheer embarrassment and shame at disappointing his father. By their junior year their friendship was nonexistent. Pete ran into Javier outside a party and Javier brushed off his half-baked attempts at reconciliation before driving off in the same Mustang that had been basically his, too, just a few months before. One of the last times Pete remembered seeing Javier was during freshman year in college, when he found Javier leaning against a fence for support outside Pete's newly discovered hangout, the Gables Pub. He looked older, gruffer, his shirt wet with vomit. It had taken him a few moments to even recognize Pete. His words only cemented what Pete should have known years ago: "What, Pete? Come back to slum with the losers you left behind?" He remembered a shove and Javier was gone.

Chaz's words snapped him back to reality. "He's not a bad guy, I guess. He seems to treat Kathy OK, from what I can tell."

"I have a few questions before this conversation goes any further," Pete said, lifting his glass. Chaz nodded.

"First, what is it exactly you want me to do that the police can't do?"

"Well, the police aren't doing anything."

"Be specific." Pete was growing weary of the conversation.

"I called the cops, but they said they can't really do much until they get more proof that she's missing and not just avoiding her dad," Chaz said, his eyes on his drink. "We don't have a great relationship. Sometimes it's close to normal; other times, she acts like she wants me dead. I . . . I wasn't much of a father to her when I was with her mom. I feel like it's too late for me to go back and fix that. I just want to make sure she's OK. Alive. Somewhere."

"OK, fair enough," Pete turned his barstool to face Chaz. "Why me, though? Kathy and I aren't friends. I mean, we've hung out from time to time. She used to be friendly with some friends of mine, but that's it."

"Kathy has had some trouble fitting in at the *Times*," Chaz said. "It's hard to come in and not be considered some kind of golden child when your dad's worked at the paper for years, so that made it hard for her to make friends."

Chaz took a quick sip from his beer. It was kicking in, Pete thought.

"You know my daughter, and you're smart," Chaz said. "Before you came here, you had a pretty solid rep as reporter. A reporter known for finding things out, digging for information. You were good journalism. It's not like I can afford a private eye. Not on my salary."

Pete tried to not let the compliment go to his head. He reminded himself that the Chaz Bentley sitting next to him was not the same one he'd read as a kid with his breakfast each morning.

"There isn't much to it," Chaz said, looking at him. Pete could see that Chaz's eyes were already bloodshot. "Everyone in that place resented her. You were nice and chatty a few times. She said you guys had some good conversations when you all went out. Whether you were trying to get her into bed, I don't know. It doesn't matter. What matters is you didn't just hate her because she had my last name."

Pete paused for a second before responding, both of his hands on his pint.

"I don't know — I don't buy it."

"What?"

"Kathy's a nice girl," Pete said. "I like her. But I know she has friends, I know some of them myself. Just because I was nice to her at work and over a few drinks in the last year or so doesn't qualify me to find her — if she's actually missing, and not just avoiding you."

"You don't think you can?"

"That's not what I'm saying," Pete said. He felt himself beginning to ramble slightly. "I feel bad for you, and I want to help, I just don't know why you'd come to me."

Chaz sighed and finished his beer. The bartender had lowered the music slightly and put on CNN.

The usual mix of bad news and puff pieces was creating a buzz of background noise Pete was finding hard to avoid.

"I don't know anyone else," Chaz said. "I don't know who my daughter hangs out with. I barely know her boyfriend. You know both of them, might know some other people in their circles. You're not a novice. You know how to follow logic and formulate theories — maybe for a newspaper article, but it's the same ballpark. You could probably check her files — see if she was working on anything that might be worth reading or is alarming. That gives you more of a head start. I'm really just looking for someone to make a few calls and find out she's fine. If after that, you've got nothing, I'll have more reason to pressure the police. It's not complicated."

"Fine," Pete said.

"What?"

Nick the bartender walked over and refilled Pete's glass. Chaz declined another beer with a quick nod as he waited for Pete to respond. Pete was tired of this conversation. Tired of talking to Chaz. Tired of the memories that it dredged up. Of a friend left behind, his father's disappointment, his youth growing smaller in the rearview mirror. Maybe this was a chance to reconnect with a friend he'd thought lost forever. Or, at the very least, a chance to do something, anything again. He thought about Kathy, her flirty smile over a few drinks, when their eyes would meet across a crowded table. What was the harm in helping this sad, old man if it meant he would have something to do aside from drinking himself to oblivion each night before waking up in time to stumble into his car and go to work again? He couldn't deny he was curious to see what Javier was up to. Not surprisingly, he was more curious to talk to Kathy. He blamed the beer.

"OK, I'll do it," Pete said. "I can do some basic research through the paper, but I'm not going to break the rules and get fired over this."

"That's fine. I understand. Thank you."

"Do you have keys to her apartment? I'll need to look around her place to see what's up. Get a better idea as to whether she left recently or what."

"Yeah, sure," Chaz didn't hesitate, and rummaged through his front pocket before handing Pete a set of keys. *He knew I would say yes*, Pete thought. "I can't guarantee they'll work, though. She's been known to change the locks — on me, ex-boyfriends, whatever."

Pete shrugged.

"She lives around Little Haiti — small place off Biscayne." That was relatively close to his apartment, he realized.

Pete nodded before taking his latest swig. He was past the point of being drunk and was now coasting toward being just plain fucked up. Still, he was enjoying the misleading moments before pure drunkenness struck. He would be of no more use to this guy tonight.

"I can pay you — a little bit. Obviously, I'm not flush. I'm just not sure what this kind of thing costs," Chaz said, reaching for his wallet. It was now half past three in the morning.

Pete waved him off. "Put your money away, man," he said, leaning on the wall now. Pete's legs hung loosely around his barstool, his left hand still gripping the goblet-like glass. He'd barely touched his new beer. It felt like the previous ones were hitting now, all together. He wondered if he'd had five or four. The stereo had shifted to Modest Mouse. Was it "Float On"? Pete wasn't sure. Emily loved that song.

"Let me find Kathy," Pete blurted out. "Then we'll worry about money."

"I can't explain how much this means," Chaz looked close to tears. That was the last thing Pete needed tonight. A grown man sobbing at the bar.

Pete felt his vision begin to blur. His stomach churned. Hungry, or about to get sick? He had to slow down. Night shift or not, there was work to be done tomorrow; Pete mumbled something in response to

Chaz but wasn't sure what. Something about not worrying about the tab. Chaz slipped him his business card, his number and address on it.

Pete looked over at Nick, who was staring up at the television. There'd been another gang-related murder near the beach. The country was at war. The Marlins were playing the Dodgers. Pete was reminded of the West Coast scores. Chaz left. Pete leaned his head back and let his eyes close.

CHAPTER FOUR

Pete felt something grab and shake his shoulder. His eyelids were heavy. He could still taste the alcohol and he had a bitter, bile taste creeping up in his throat. Had he thrown up? He gave himself a quick once-over and determined he hadn't. He turned his head slowly and saw Mike standing beside him. Pete was still at the Abbey. He'd been leaning on the wall. He was used to this scenario: Mike comes to collect Pete after a bender leaves him splayed out somewhere, usually at a bar. Mike had a list of places to check. The Abbey was not far from the top.

"You alive, man?" Mike was half-joking. Pete could tell this routine was getting tiresome for him. He was starting to worry. Pete hated this.

"Barely," Pete coughed, and then straightened out his shirt. Nick the bartender met Pete's eyes briefly, and then he returned to cleaning. The bar was closed. It had to be past five.

"Nick said he'd let you sleep it off, but he's gotta close up," Mike said. "You want a ride home? We can pick up your car tomorrow."

Pete let his head hang down for a second. Mike was like a brother. They'd been in the trenches together. Good moments and terrible ones. Their bond was strong. They'd met in college and became fast friends — going to shows, staying out late, working for the paper. They had been inseparable for a while. Mike leaned on Pete and vice versa. But lately, it seemed more like Pete depended on Mike to keep him from falling off the edge. He was pushing Mike to the limit. One day, he'd just say "Fuck it" and let Pete fall.

"Nah, I'm OK," Pete said. "Just tired. I had a few drinks with Kathy Bentley's dad, it got late, and you know how strong these drinks are."

Mike sat down, a glass of water in front of him. Pete thought for a second. Had he called Mike to come by? He felt a pang of guilt. The Abbey was a 45-minute drive for Mike. Pete's hangover had already kicked in — the headache, the dry mouth. He groaned slightly and looked at Mike.

"Let's go eat," Mike said. "You need to sober up, and I want to know what you were doing drinking with Chaz Bentley, of all people."

Pete nodded, and soon they were out of the bar and walking down Meridian, toward David's Café. David's was a 24-hour Cuban restaurant. Cheap eats for the post-bar crowd, tucked away amid the neon lights, dance clubs, and dingy hotels that littered South Beach. The ideal spot for someone looking to preempt a hangover.

They both ordered medianoche sandwiches — marinated pork, ham, cheese and pickles on Cuban bread — with fries on the side. Simple, filling and tasty, Pete thought. The pair ate in silence, Pete regaining some clarity as he plowed into his food. He was still drunk, but at least functional. If Mike allowed him to, Pete was certain he could make the 10-minute drive home. Sort of.

Pete brought Mike up to speed quickly, between mouthfuls of food and large gulps of water.

"So," Mike said. "You're basically going to play detective because Chaz can't afford a real detective? Chaz, a guy you only know from work and don't really like one way or the other?"

"That's not exactly what I said, but yeah."

"And you're going to do it?"

"I told him I would."

Mike finally looked up from his food, a confused look on his face. "Why?"

"I was drunk, I guess. I dunno. It made sense at the time."

"So did having another beer."

"Come on. Don't judge." Pete wasn't in the mood.

"Why you, though?"

"He said Kathy knew me and that he knew I was a good investigator, I guess," Pete motioned to the waitress for the check. He was no longer that drunk, but he did need sleep. He turned to Mike. "I figure I'll check her out in the system, visit the apartment, see if anything jumps out at me. When nothing does, I'll go back to her dad and suggest he go to the cops."

Mike picked at his fries, eating the small ones first, organizing them by size. He popped another in his mouth, chewed, chewed, swallowed, and looked at Pete from across the table.

"What if something does jump out at you, though?"

CHAPTER FIVE

Pete winced as the coffee burned his tongue. He put the extra-large cup of Dunkin' Donuts Hazelnut back in the cup holder of his Celica. He was off. Despite getting a few hours of sleep, he still felt sluggish and hung over. He was parked outside of Kathy's apartment complex. It was close to three in the afternoon. He had about an hour to check out Kathy's living space and use his very unrefined eye to determine if Kathy was just avoiding her father, or something else. Then, back to work. He hadn't woken up early before work in months. And while he hadn't woken up early for work, exactly, Pete felt a tinge of pride at being a semi-functional member of society.

He looked at his rearview mirror reflexively. Ever since the encounter with Chaz, Pete had felt an unease slip over him. Not just his usual post-drinking jitters, either. Pete wasn't really even sure what he was doing, wandering around near someone's apartment.

He decided to let the coffee cool for a bit and got out of his car. He slipped on a cheap pair of Fila sunglasses over his bloodshot eyes and scanned the handful of apartments. Kathy's apartment was one of four, on the west side of the small building's second floor. Of the three cars parked in the complex's tiny lot, none was parked in Kathy's assigned space. Though he had no idea what Kathy drove — and mentally kicked himself for not asking Chaz that — he figured this meant she wasn't home. Or, at the very least, her car wasn't. *Quite the detective*, Pete thought.

He walked up the west stairwell and reached Kathy's apartment, number four. He knocked on the door a few times and couldn't discern any noises coming from within. Feeling sheepish, Pete looked around and pulled the key to the apartment out of his pocket and set it into the lock. He tried turning the key, but no luck. He tried again before realizing that Chaz either had provided him with bum keys, which made little sense, or Kathy had changed her locks recently, as her father suggested she sometimes did. Neither possibility let him into the apartment.

Fortunately, the front door had a tiny cat gate. Unfortunately, crouching down and sliding his arm through the gate was more overt and prone to arousing suspicion than just opening the door with a key. Normally, Pete would give up by now. He took a quick look around and, determining the coast was clear, got down on one knee and wove his arm through the cat door and up toward the inner doorknob. With some painful stretching and a few seconds of jostling around for the best position, Pete found his hand on the lock. He unlocked it and turned the knob slowly with his fingers. He felt a jolt of excitement run through him as pushed the door, something he hadn't experienced in a while.

Pete walked in and immediately caught the strong odor of a cat box left unchanged for days. He looked at the door from inside the apartment and saw it was equipped with a few other locks and latches. They'd have prevented Pete from entering, had they been in use. Why would someone who'd gone to the trouble of having so many locks on their door leave them unused? He heard a weak meow coming from near his feet. He looked down to see a small gray cat, clearly hungry, pathetically rubbing his face on Pete's feet, begging for food. Pete scratched the creature behind the ears and continued to look around. The cat could wait a few more minutes before he refueled. The apartment was small — a one-bedroom with a tiny kitchen and medium-sized living/dining room area. The television was on — the menu screen for *Eternal Sunshine of the Spotless Mind*. An almost-empty wine glass rested next to the remote and a tipped over bowl that once held popcorn in it sat on a table near the couch. There were dirty dishes in the sink and a grocery list tacked onto the fridge. All this suggested two things, Pete thought: Kathy hadn't been around for a few days and she hadn't planned on going anywhere. Both could mean nothing. For all Pete knew, Kathy could just be an irresponsible pet owner and prone to leaving appliances on. But something gnawed at Pete. This wasn't right. He didn't know much — if anything — about Kathy, but she didn't seem like the type to up and leave without telling anyone. If Kathy had gone somewhere, she wasn't planning on being gone for long.

He gave her bedroom a quick once-over and didn't find any telltale signs of a trip — no missing luggage or clothing, all her toiletries seemed to be in the bathroom, cell phone charger plugged in. The apartment was sparsely decorated, with few personal items. Pete found a framed photo of Kathy and Javier on her nightstand. They were drinking wine at a bar in Hollywood — Pete recognized it. Le Tub. Outdoor seating. Good wine list. Best burger in America, apparently. They seemed happy.

He opened the top drawer to Kathy's nightstand and found her address book, which didn't feature many names. He flipped through the pages and noticed a few he recognized. Turning to the front flap, he saw Kathy had jotted down "kbentley" and "nigel" hastily. He guessed it was a password of some kind. Kathy's handwriting was florid and legible, mixing the colorful penmanship of a high school teen with the structure and control of an adult. Pete flipped to Javier's name and found his number. Instinctively, he pulled out his cell phone and called him. It rang three times and went to voicemail. Pete didn't leave a message, but slipped the tiny address book into his back pocket. Considering the light layer of dust that was on the black book, he didn't think Kathy would miss it much.

He was running late. There wasn't enough time for him to swing by Javier's apartment on the way to work, assuming the address Kathy had for him — somewhere in the Design District — was still valid.

He made his way back to the kitchen and searched a few cabinets before he found a can of cat food. He opened it up and watched as Kathy's cat stuffed his face desperately, barely stopping to breathe between gulps. Considering the cat was still alive and hadn't fully abandoned the apartment in search of food, Pete guessed it hadn't been more than a day or two since his last meal, but couldn't be certain. He also realized he couldn't just leave the animal here, unless he wanted to make Kathy's apartment a stop on his way to work each day. Then again, if Kathy was just at the grocery store, could he just walk out with her cat? Pete decided he would. Costello could use a new attraction.

Pete felt his phone vibrating in his pocket. He pulled it out and read the display. Work. Pete cursed under his breath and scooped up Kathy's cat. He ignored the call and let it go to voicemail. But it was time to go. He felt a pang of regret. He wanted to spend more time looking around — piecing together what had happened, if anything. But he couldn't. He headed for the door with his new sidekick.

"No time for pleasantries, bud," Pete said to his new adoptee, who was busy licking a few remaining globs of food from his mouth. "If I don't drop you off and get to work in the next 15 minutes, we might all go hungry."

Pete locked the door from the inside and closed it quietly, hoping no one would notice the strange man walking out of Kathy's apartment with her cat fidgeting in his hands. He gave the place a quick glance and caught the DVD screen of *Eternal Sunshine* flash on and off one more time.

CHAPTER SIX

The second Pete dropped his bag at his desk, he sensed something was wrong. Ideally, he'd hoped to ease into the workday 15 minutes before, well, starting to work. The blinking red light on his phone meant that wouldn't be the case.

He was already running late, and even Pete wasn't inclined to push his luck that far, no matter how intrigued he was by what was going on. And, by the way, what was going on?

He picked up his desk phone slowly and tapped in his message code and waited. It was Steve Vance, the paper's managing editor for special projects. A fancy title that just meant he oversaw the sports department. Pete's usual boss, Angel Menendez, was out indefinitely on medical leave, which meant Vance was in charge. This was not good for Pete. He missed Menendez, who had been kind to Pete during the trying two years he'd spent at the *Times* so far. He wasn't a

42

mentor — Pete felt like that bird had flown for him — but Menendez was certainly someone Pete could look up to. He was gruff but considerate and always put others ahead of himself.

Like Menendez before his health issues began, Pete was pretty no-nonsense when it came to work. He wasn't prone to double-talk or getting mired in daily newsroom politics. He ran a relatively loose operation on the nights he was in charge, relying more on skill and independent thinking than procedure. Steve Vance was the opposite. Everything he said or did was calculated, and he catered to the *Times'* corporate masters. Pete pictured the fifty-something Vance, with his slicked-back gray hair and tailored suit, speeding into the Times' executive parking lot in his cherry-red Mini Cooper from his SoBe condo, where Pete was certain he had a black French bulldog and cougar second wife. A message from Vance was not good.

"Hey, Pete . . . it's Steve. It's around three in the morning. Just hopped online to check a few things and wanted to pick your brain. Call me when you get a chance. Thanks."

The West Coast scores. Shit. That had to be it, Pete thought, as he got up, rubbing his temples. He needed a soda or something before he called Vance back. He looked across the newsroom and saw Vance's office. The door was open. It was a Sunday and Vance was there.

Vance usually worked Monday to Friday, 10 to 6. A normal schedule, which was considered the Holy Grail for all newspaper employees. The kind of thing you dreamed of and realized you'd never get, after a few years. It had to be a big deal for Vance to violate his sacred schedule to come into the newsroom on a Sunday.

Pete walked over to the bulletin board area outside the kitchen, a few paces west of the main elevators, and scanned the duty roster.

Usually, he wouldn't bother. He knew which days he was running the show and which days he wasn't. Today was one of the days he was slated to be the duty officer. He focused on the hastily tacked-on piece of paper. There he was — Pete Fernandez. But not under "duty officer." He was listed as one of the five copy editors working the shift. Pete cursed under his breath.

As he walked over to Vance's office, Pete could feel a few stares from the other editors. He made eye contact with Mike, who, being a page designer, was seated closer to the bay windows of the building, where the light was better. Mike's eyes widened with concern. He knew something. Pete considered detouring and talking to him first for some — any — kind of hint as to what was coming, but thought better of it. He'd rather jump into the fire and get it over with than delay the inevitable.

The newsroom knew something was up. Steve Vance liked to talk. He liked to cement things before he made any kind of move. He was more politician than manager, and Pete wasn't much of either. This could be very bad, Pete mused, before rapping his fingers lightly on Vance's slightly open door.

"Strange to see you here on a weekend," Pete said, trying to sound as casual as possible.

"Hey, P. Come in, have a seat," Vance said, stifling a yawn. Pete tried to force himself not to grimace. He hated when anyone called him anything other than Pete or Peter, or even Pedro, his given name and the one he shared with his father. Vance was in his "casual" clothes — a University of Florida T-shirt and long, khaki shorts. He had a few days' stubble. His entire look screamed, "I was enjoying my weekend until you went and fucked something up!"

Pete waited for the line that would seal his fate and confirm that he was in trouble. "Close the door."

Pete sat down facing Vance and braced himself.

Vance didn't hesitate.

"What happened with the West Coast baseball scores?"

"What about them?"

"Well, why weren't they in the paper? I checked the system and it said the pages were closed at around one. The results came in at two. You didn't wait?"

"No, I guess not."

"You guess? The other paper had the results. We look stupid."

"We had them online. We were one man down, and everyone was worn out. I made the call to let it ride."

"Not good. Not a good call. You chose convenience over effort. Pete, this isn't the first time we've had this conversation. It's become a problem. A real problem."

"OK."

"I know you like to be the boss everyone likes, the weekend editor who lets guys get away with murder, since it's a pain in the ass coming in on a Saturday."

"That's not true. I'm just not a hard-ass." *Like you,* Pete wanted to say.

"Neither am I," Vance responded sharply. "But there are certain things that need to be done. This was one of them. I'm going to have to write you up."

"Are you kidding me?" Pete paused for a second, then continued, "Go ahead."

Vance stopped, surprised by Pete's response. Pete could tell Vance didn't expect there to be much argument here.

"This was a serious lapse in judgment and I'm concerned about your ability to continue to manage. I'm sorry."

Pete felt himself losing his cool.

"Are you reading that from an HR manual?"

"Excuse me?"

"Never mind. Do what you think you have to do."

"That's not the point," Vance said, sliding out of his chair and standing up. He began to pace around his desk. "We have to leave this discussion having learned something — I have to be confident it won't happen again. Can you assure me of that?"

Pete gritted his teeth. He was watching what little was left of his career slip through his fingers, and he couldn't muster up the energy or nerve to do the basics — accept the reprimand, promise to do better, be conciliatory in some way. None of it was coming out of his mouth. Instead, he felt himself seething. He could imagine Vance on the phone earlier with someone from Human Resources, discussing the proper protocol for disciplining an errant drone. Steve Vance was a smarmy memo come to life, and Pete could do nothing about it.

"No, I can't."

"You can't?" Vance said, unable to hide the shock in his voice.

"I can't assure you that I won't think of the people working extra hours for free, because they're not allowed to take overtime. I can't assure you that I'll just suddenly change my entire managing method."

"I'm not asking for that."

"Well, you kind of are, to be blunt," Pete literally spit. "Is it really the end of the world if we don't have a few game scores in a print edition that fewer and fewer people are reading? We had them online. People use the fucking Internet." Pete instantly regretted his use of profanity. Now he'd emotionalized the discussion. It was lost.

"You're missing the point, and I'm not pleased with your tone. I don't need to remind you that in Angel's absence, I'm the de facto sports editor. And this is unacceptable. Whether you realize this or not, one more mistake of this level and we're going to have to make some tough decisions. Your opinion is noted but irrelevant in this situation. Understood?"

Pete stopped. He was done. If not now, then in the next month or so when he made another mistake. There was no win in prolonging the exchange. All he really wanted to do was get back to his desk and put his headphones on. He looked out to the newsroom, through the glass window Vance had facing the staff. He saw Mike trying to sneak a peek. Some editors were less discreet, but turned away when they met Pete's eyes. He'd been in Vance's office for over 20 minutes. They'd seen Vance pacing around, Pete hanging his head dejectedly. They'd heard the raised voices, surely the sign of a problem to those trying to get the day's work done nearby.

After a few awkward seconds of silence, Vance cleared his throat.

Pete spoke first. "I understand. I'm aware of your role. You're in charge. You want it done a certain way; I have to do it that way. And I will."

"Thank you," Vance sat down and leaned back a bit in his chair, his hands behind his head, as he looked Pete over. "Now, that wasn't too hard, was it? Let's just try to work together on this. We'll be alright."

"Ok," Pete said as he stood up. "Are we done?"

Vance stood again, ignoring Pete's question, and extended his hand, which Pete took with some reluctance. Pete felt a shiver shoot up his arm as Vance's cold fish handshake met his own. Vance walked Pete to the door, holding it open for him, placing his hand on Pete's shoulder and holding him for a second too long.

"And, well, I still have to write you up. Company policy and all that. No hard feelings?"

"Right," Pete said, and walked out.

Pete felt his hands scrounging through his pockets to prevent himself from lunging for Vance. At his desk, he pulled out a wrinkled coaster from the Abbey and the useless keys to Kathy's apartment. Pete closed his eyes for a second. He could feel his breathing and the blood pulsing through him. Everything was coming apart, he thought. Everything was coming apart. He sat down and jammed his headphones onto his head.

CHAPTER SEVEN

The light clicking sound of his fingertips on the computer keyboard seemed louder as the Talking Heads live album in his headphones shifted from "Psycho Killer" to "Heaven." The quiet break between David Byrne's beat-box-fueled solo rendition of the first track allowed the sound of the newsroom to creep into Pete's head. He felt some calm return to him as he realized the office was humming at a normal volume. The initial drama of the day had been momentarily forgotten and people were hard at work getting the paper out. Pete felt some relief that he wasn't in charge this evening. He was happy to just be one of the editors, churning away at story after story and able to leave when the shift was over.

It was midnight, and close to the end of his reduced workload. Vance had left around dinner, his dirty work complete. With his departure the staff seemed to loosen up, and Pete could almost forget that his career — what little was left of it — was on the ledge.

Feeling a tap on his shoulder, Pete took off his headphones and turned around to find Mike leaning on his desk. They'd reached the end of the line for the night — all the pages were designed and only copy tweaks were left, meaning designers like Mike had very little to do. The perfect time for some newsroom socializing.

"How you doing?" Mike asked, keeping his voice a little lower than usual.

"Eh, fine," Pete said. "It is what it is. I just need to cut down on mistakes, you know?"

Mike nodded. "Yeah, you'll handle your shit. You just can't let people get to you."

Pete sighed and typed a quick response to the slot editor about the sidebar to the main baseball game story. The reporter had misspelled a player's name. Pete quickly typed back the correct spelling for "Renteria."

"Yeah. That's tough. I don't want to rip on the guy. I just need to do my thing and know what will set him off."

"You seem distracted lately, though. You were almost an hour late."

Pete wheeled his chair around. "I had stuff to do."

Mike raised his arms in mock surrender. "I'm just saying you were late. That probably didn't help your cause."

"Nah, it didn't," Pete said. "I had to do some stuff. I only have time to run errands before work."

"Since when do you run errands before work? You're usually sleeping off the night before."

Pete couldn't help but laugh. A dry, empty laugh. It was true. He didn't like it, but it was true.

"Well, I told Chaz I'd look into this Kathy business, so I did."

"So, you're actually doing this thing? I thought you'd sleep that off, too."

Pete looked up at Mike and sighed. He didn't feel the need to respond. His fuse was short tonight, and the last person he wanted to go off on was his best — and probably only — friend.

Mike folded his arms and looked around the newsroom. Sports was the last section to go to press, and the building was slowly emptying out.

"I don't like it."

Pete shrugged and turned back to his computer. The word was out — the slot editor had messaged everyone to alert the newsroom that sports was sent and ready to go.

"I get you don't like it," Pete said. "It's a distraction. Once I convince Chaz Kathy's missing, he'll take it to the police. It's pretty clear she's not on some kind of pleasure cruise."

Mike straightened up, clasped Pete on the shoulder and began to head toward his own desk to shut down his computer.

"I hear you, man. Whatever you think works," Mike said. "What are you up to tonight?"

Pete thought for a second. "Nothing, but I need to get some other stuff done here first."

"Oh yeah?"

"Yeah. You wanna grab a drink later?"

"It *is* later, man," Mike said. He was as literal as they came, Pete thought.

"Let's hit the Pub, in the Gables," Pete said. "We haven't been there in forever. I'll meet you there in an hour or so."

Mike shrugged and laughed. "Sure, why not. I don't have anything better to do. I'll call up Emily and see if she wants to join us."

Emily. He hadn't seen her in months. Not since she'd left the *Miami Times* and moved south to Homestead with her new husband, Rick, a well-built and well-meaning clod of a man. She'd worked a few uncomfortable months as a designer at the *Times* after breaking up with Pete, and before settling down with Rick. Even then, Pete had seen little of her. The wounds were too fresh, he thought, and he was too immersed in drinking his sadness away to even consider trying to build — or rebuild — any kind of relationship with Emily. After she'd left him, they made a few feeble efforts at becoming friends, but Pete didn't have it in him. She'd left him, and in her place was a creaking emptiness. Pete suspected that she'd strayed from him toward the end, and he could never really forgive her for that. He'd never be certain. The nights out without a call. The way she'd dress up more than usual for happy hour with her friends from work. He'd never gotten the nerve to call her out, too busy spinning around in his own depression, his father recently buried and his career soon to follow. But he knew. Still, he also didn't want to hate her. So, they'd talked from time to time — terse e-mail exchanges or drunk dials in the middle of the night that usually involved her hanging up on him. If one's definition of friendship was loose and based on familiarity between two people, then, sure, they were friends. But they weren't friends by Pete's definition, and that's what mattered. Their relationship now had become one of resignation—Pete resigned to the fact that this was all they'd ever be to each other and Emily resigned to dealing with Pete, sneaking glances and sidestepping his random, almost unintentional advances. He loved her; she would never love him again.

The idea of hanging out with her tonight sounded less than appealing, but he did want to talk to Mike. And he did want a drink.

"Sure, that sounds good," Pete said in a monotone. Mike knew as well as anyone what their history was, but he was friends with Emily and wasn't about to choose who he hung out with based on Pete's bruised heart. "Haven't seen her in a while," Pete added.

Mike slid into his backpack and shook Pete's hand. "Alright, I'll see you there, then," he said, walking toward the elevators. "Don't stay too late, whatever the fuck you're doing."

CHAPTER EIGHT

Pete waited a few minutes after hearing the elevator doors close to be certain Mike was gone; then he began logging back into his computer. He had been desperate to do this earlier, but after his war of words with Vance kicked off the shift, Pete couldn't risk being caught doing something other than work. He looked around and saw only the web editors and a few custodians.

He logged into the *Miami Times*' employee network and hit the "home" button on his Internet browser, which took him to the company Intranet, which housed a number of basic reporting and editing tools and databases, including an electronic newspaper archive, access to the Associated Press archives, and a variety of personal search engines that were meant to be used by enterprising young journalists looking to find sources or connect the dots on their next story. Pete wasn't sure how closely his movements when using these programs were tracked, but he knew he was leaving some footprints. He only hoped they weren't big enough to be noticed. The thought struck Pete as odd. He was now officially violating his job, arguably threatening it, and clearly going against his ethics as a journalist. Still, he wasn't moved to stop. Something was tugging at him, the same spark of excitement and energy he had felt years before in New Jersey when he was chasing a story or looking for the perfect turn of a phrase to close out a profile piece on a new player or coach. He was hungry for information. He didn't know Kathy enough to really care about her well-being. But he did feel like something was happening, and he wanted to be doing something for once, instead of just sitting around feeling bad for himself. He typed Kathy's name in the search field.

A quick scan of the *Times'* database only pulled up Kathy's actual work for the paper: cop beat pieces, crime stories and the occasional police profile. He noticed that, of late, Kathy'd been spending a lot of time writing about Miami's criminal history—specifically, about the Cuban gangs and their ties to the drug trade. One headline jumped out at Pete: "Who is the 'Silent Death' of Miami?" He clicked on it and got a rather lengthy, speculative piece about the killer who'd haunted the dark side of the Miami streets for years, working as an enforcer for the Cuban mobs. Kathy's story suggested that the Silent Death was responsible for a string of murders involving the Cuban cartels and that it was one man, a previously unheard-of hypothesis. Understandably, she had little concrete information to go on. Pete found himself engrossed in the reading, reeled in by Kathy's staccato writing style. The story ended on a hypothetical note, wondering when the Silent Death would strike again. Pete checked the date on the story — it was from a few weeks before. He sent it to print, hoping there'd be something of use in it, and went back to scanning Kathy's clips. She was a prolific writer, and she was good. She covered the cops beat with aplomb and seemed to generate a wide range of pieces, not limited to the usual police report rehashing and publicity-seeking pieces. He found the historical pieces — which had increased in frequency lately — the most interesting. She knew about the criminal history of the city, the drug lords, the gangs, and corrupt cops, and could weave a compelling narrative. Could this be what got her in trouble? He wasn't sure. She had never been the story herself. Pete did a quick background check on Kathy and also found nothing out of order — she paid her taxes on time, and, at worst, had two unpaid parking tickets from earlier in the year. Otherwise, she was a model citizen. Why hadn't Chaz mentioned anything about the stories Kathy had written? Why hadn't he done a basic search any *Times* employee could do if he was so worried about his daughter? The thought troubled Pete.

Kathy's boyfriend was another story, Pete realized. Not only did Javier Reyes' name pop up a handful of times in the electronic archives — small news briefs reporting on petty robbery or arrests — but his actual arrest record was spotty at best. Pete scanned Javier's rap sheet quickly, starting at age 18 — a few misdemeanor arrests, a DWI about five years prior, and one charge for possession with intent to distribute. He'd been nabbed on the last charge a few years back and was currently on work release and serving probation, meaning he worked at a sanctioned job for five days a week and then served the remainder of his sentence under house arrest.

Pete felt a sharp jab in his stomach. This is what Javier's life had become. Pete knew he himself was fucked up — desperately in love with a woman who had cheated on him and left him, on the brink of being fired and drinking away his sorrows and hopes nightly. But Javier was inching toward becoming a career criminal, if he was not one already. *Where would Javier be,* Pete thought, *if he'd had a father like Pete's?* He remembered the new world order after the 7-Eleven incident. His father drove him everywhere. No outings after school. Monitored homework sessions after class. On days Pete didn't have school, he'd go to work with his father, to the station house at the Miami Dade PD. Pete was resentful and angry for years — it took even longer for him to forgive his father. But his father had made the right decision. What little of a life Pete had, he owed to his dad's firm hand. Javier had gone down another path, though.

Could he have done more to help him? He was his friend. He'd failed him. Pete sighed. His eyes drifted back to the work-release information. *Interesting,* Pete thought. Pete didn't immediately think of Javier's neighborhood as a place for ex-cons. And from what the report was telling him, Javier was working 30 hours a week as a busboy at a restaurant in Westchester — a suburb of Miami where both Pete and Javier grew up and where they met and became friends.

Pete jotted down the restaurant's name—Casa Pepe's—and began to close down his computer when, on a whim, he did a quick search for the restaurant in the *Times'* article archive. A few classified listings and ads popped up, as expected, but Pete was surprised to find an actual story appear as a result, a puff piece community news story, but a story nonetheless. Susan Frey, a reporter close to Pete's age, wrote it. She'd moved to Orlando a few months back to take a business editor gig. He scanned the story, which profiled the restaurant's owner, Jose Contreras, a Cuban refugee who, after coming to Miami during the Mariel boatlift of 1980 and spending a year in a Miami jail for assaulting a fellow refugee, had toiled in the kitchens of various restaurants before finally cobbling together enough money to open his own.

It made him laugh. Did Miami really need another Cuban restaurant? The story went on to paint Contreras as not only a capable businessman, but also a good citizen, noting he had set up part of the Casa Pepe's workforce as an approved work-release program for convicted felons in an effort to help them get back on their feet. *Probably got a healthy tax cut, too,* Pete thought as he finished the story. He printed out a copy of the story and jotted down the restaurant's address after collecting his pages from the printer. This was something, Pete thought. He wasn't sure what. He stuffed the folded paper in his back pocket and hooked his bag over his shoulder. Something to do tomorrow, he thought. Talking to Javier, if that happened, would shed a different light on the situation. But now it was time to cut loose a bit. As Pete walked toward the elevators, his screen flickered off, asleep.

CHAPTER NINE

The Gables Pub was a shitty dive off Le Jeune Road, on the edges of Coral Gables, one of Miami's swankier neighborhoods. The Pub reminded Pete of college and the dozens of nights spent drinking in the bar's patio area, closing the place down, being politely—and sometimes not so politely—asked to head home by the patient waitstaff. His memories of the drives home were a little blurry, and Pete was grateful to still be in one piece. It had been a destination not because of a particularly great ambiance, but because they were notoriously lax about carding students and the bartenders mixed the drinks strong—an attractive combination for Pete and his friends at the time. Back when drinking a Long Island Ice Tea was a good idea because it fucked you up quickly, the Pub was where Pete and his buddies hung out. Pete, Mike, Emily, and a few others willing to risk missing class the next morning made the bar their salon, where they'd talk about their lives, the news of the day, or argue about whether Radiohead's *OK Computer* was historic or hype, and when Weezer was going to come out with a new record as good as *Pinkerton*. Pete didn't care about either band anymore.

Before he'd moved to New Jersey to take the *Bergen Light* job, before he'd fallen for Emily and decided to go from friend to lover, he'd lived in a tiny apartment less than three blocks away from the Pub, making it all the more obvious a destination for him. It also made driving between the lines less of a worry when he was trying to decide between going home and having one more. It may have even been one of the reasons he moved downtown when he returned to Miami, as opposed to settling into Coral Gables. Not much had changed. In his new neighborhood, he had just found another bar down the street.

He walked toward the double doors that led into the Gables Pub. Blondie's "Dreaming" was playing low on the jukebox as he walked in, looking around for Emily and Mike. The Pub was dark and empty. Aside from Blondie, the only noise came from the middle-aged, long-haired bartender whistling to himself as he wiped down the bar. He stopped abruptly as Pete entered, recognition flickering in his eyes. It'd been a few years, but Pete remembered him, too. Pete slid onto a stool near the end of the bar.

"Hey Jimmy," Pete said, realizing the bartender couldn't place his name. He leaned over the bar and extended his hand. "It's Pete. Pete Fernandez. I used to basically live here a couple years back."

Jimmy the bartender smiled and nodded, shaking Pete's hand drowsily and speaking in a hippie/surfer drawl that took Pete back to simpler times, when his biggest concern was being able to roll out of bed at noon to get to class.

"What can I get you, dude?"

Pete hesitated for a second. It'd been a shit day. Normally, that'd call for a serious drunk. But he needed to think. "Just gimme a Bass," he said.

Jimmy's eyes widened slightly at the request.

"Damn, dude. No shot this time?" Jimmy said, puzzled. "Shit, I remember you closing this place down more than I did, and I fuckin' worked here, man."

Pete looked around. Emily and Mike probably stopped to get a bite to eat or decided to go somewhere else. He stood up quickly and scanned the patio area. Nothing. He took his seat at the bar. That was fine. He wasn't in a hurry to see her. Not yet.

Jimmy walked over to the other end of the bar and began pouring Pete's beer. Jimmy pointed at the Jägermeister machine next to the tiny Red Bull cooler and nodded toward it. Pete groaned to himself as he gave Jimmy the thumb's up. *Fuck it*, he thought. The reminder that he'd be seeing Emily soon made the decision that much easier.

Jimmy returned with a full pint and a shot of Jäger—a healthy shot, too, not a plastic, sissy shot. As Jimmy walked away, Pete downed the purple liquor in one swift motion. He winced as it slid down. He coughed, gagging a bit on the drink as it coated his stomach. Pete gripped the bar.

He took a small sip from his beer and pulled out the small notebook he carried in his back pocket, a remnant of his reporting days. He started jotting down notes. Kathy. Javier. Jose Contreras. Kathy was missing, Pete decided. He wasn't sure if it was the Jäger giving him clarity, but she didn't seem like the type to leave her cat unattended or her TV on for days. Her apartment did not seem like its owner had left on vacation, either. And if she was missing, she was most certainly in trouble.

He was certain he'd missed something at Kathy's apartment. Had he planned better, he'd be able to figure out where Kathy went, and if she'd left with Javier. Pretty unremarkable work, Pete thought, as he took another sip from his pint glass. Yet, for some reason, he felt energized.

He was fuzzy on why he was helping Chaz, beyond his inherent need to be liked and to be helpful. Something still bothered him about Chaz's request. He could have done many of the things Pete did today—basic info hunting, visiting Kathy's apartment—but he'd passed the buck to Pete instead. Odd.

His thoughts drifted back to Kathy. They worked opposite schedules. She was a day-sider, which was standard for most local reporters. He worked nights and weekends. They'd only exchanged workplace pleasantries before she came out with Emily to meet him and Mike for a drink a few months back. Pete was smitten, but also drunk. More drunk than usual, because Emily was around. Kathy seemed accepting, and their conversation was breezy and funny. He didn't have to work hard to make her laugh or keep her interested. The random bar outings didn't translate into much else. The times they'd see each other were few and far between. She hadn't crept into his thoughts until Chaz interrupted him at work the night before. He also didn't know much about her. What was she like? What were her hobbies? Was she a happy person? What were her goals in life? Pete shrugged. He made a short list of things he needed to accomplish the next morning. Well, maybe afternoon. He motioned to Jimmy for another beer. No shot.

Pete straightened up in his seat at the bar. It was close to two in the morning, no sign of Emily or Mike. He shook his half-filled pint glass at Jimmy and tried a smile. There were a few people in the bar now, none of them sitting next to Pete. He recognized a girl he'd dated briefly in college sitting close to the jukebox with two dudes that were probably fraternity alums trying to relive their heyday. What was her name? Lisa? Linda? He didn't know. Had it been a few years earlier, Pete would have felt the need to say hello, or make some small talk. Not tonight. He'd had at least three beers on top of that shot — nothing destructive by his standards, but still enough to have him feeling fuzzy.

He thought about his life in New Jersey. The cramped two-bedroom apartment in Hoboken with Emily and Costello. The miles he'd racked up flying. The myriad hotel rooms, locker rooms, and meeting rooms that came with the job. He loved it, or so he told himself. He had started drinking heavily then. Started ignoring Emily, ignoring their problems. For the first time, they weren't talking. And yet, even that life sounded appealing. But Pete had no clue how to get back there. If he continued to spin out at the *Miami Times*, there was no chance he'd catch on anywhere else.

He thought about Emily's expensive perfume—some kind of Chanel. He'd forgotten the name, but he could pinpoint it if he smelled it on someone else. He thought about how her eyes would squint, almost close when she was focusing her gaze on Pete in mock anger. How her lips would pout. Moments flashed at him like a highlight reel during a sitcom reunion show. Flowers, anniversary dinners, concerts, mix tapes, bars and restaurants. All painted by the brush of his memory. Except she wasn't gone. He still had to see her.

He wasn't strong enough to shut her out of his life, although she'd given him ample opportunity. He had come to terms with still being in love with her. It'd been just a few months back that he and Mike had sat outside the Pub, Pete cross-legged on the floor, drunkenly explaining to his patient friend why Emily was the only thing he'd ever wanted. How nothing was worth his time anymore. They never spoke of that night again, but Pete saw pity in Mike's eyes for the first time, and that was heartbreaking. Loving Emily was all Pete had after his father died, and he'd let it slip away without fighting for it.

It was always work, though, Pete realized. Even at their best. Still, the memories flooded his mind constantly. He tried not to think about the bad ones, but those popped into the beer soup of his brain, too. The arguments. Her disappearances. The dozen times or so she'd gotten up and left him sitting alone—at a restaurant, bar, or visiting friends. Those memories, unlike the idyllic ones he'd started with, still stung. He found himself back on his father's lawn, a few weeks after the funeral. Realizing that he couldn't return to New Jersey, that the life he'd created and wanted to continue with Emily was close to collapse. He'd been staying at his father's house—the smallish three-bedroom where he'd grown up—with Emily while they got his father's affairs in order. It had been surreal, but also strangely comforting.

He remembered pulling into the carport slowly. He had stopped at La Carretta, a chain Cuban restaurant on Bird Road, for a few beers. He moved slowly. They'd been fighting lately. It took him a second to notice the suitcases by the porch. A few more to catch Emily as she brought out another bag. She saw him first and stood at the top of the steps, waiting for him to speak. A cab pulled up. Pete stood there.

"Please, don't try to call me. This is the decision I've made and I need you to respect that."

At the foot of the steps, Pete shook his head, to clear the cobwebs partially, but also on the off chance that this was just another bad dream in a series of nightmares.

"You're doing this now, of all times?" The words spilled out of his mouth.

She walked to the cab, dropped the remaining bags in the trunk and got in the car. Pete remembered walking up to her window. She didn't lower it. She was looking straight ahead. He rapped his fingers on the window. Nothing. She looked back at him for a fleeting moment and then the cab was moving. Pete was tempted to chase after her, like in the movies. All that he had left, though, was dust.

The memory disappeared as quickly as it had popped into his head. Pete made himself cough in an effort to explain away his red eyes to anyone that cared. He noticed Paul Westerberg was on the jukebox now. "As Far As I Know."

"How long have you been here?"

Pete turned around slowly to see Emily, her dark brown hair in a tight ponytail. She was in a T-shirt and jeans, but still looked great—scrubbed and fresh-faced. He felt a pang of guilt for lusting for her so quickly after taking a rollercoaster ride through their failed relationship. Emily looked concerned. She stared at Pete, which made him realize that a few seconds had passed and she was waiting for an answer.

"I dunno, couple of hours?" He tried to not sound as buzzed as he felt. "Where were you guys?"

"Don't get me started," Emily let out with a dry laugh. She was a little annoyed, Pete could tell, but it wasn't worth getting angry over. "Mike wanted to go all the way to his neighborhood to eat, so it took forever to get here. Then we walked in and went straight to the patio. I just came to the bar because our dumbass waiter went home and closed his bill with us."

"Ah, shit," Pete mumbled. "I checked outside and couldn't see you."

"Don't you check your phone, Pete?" Emily said.

Pete could smell the Chanel. "It's gonna rain in a bit. Lemme go out and get Mike and we'll meet you here."

She darted out, shaking her head. Emily was, like Pete, usually in a state of annoyance. She rarely got enraged or very angry, but it took very little to get under her skin. Pete pulled two stools closer to his. He was glad she was here, though. And that Mike was here. Whatever he'd been through, with or without them, made more sense when they were near him. Whenever he found himself alone for too long, things got dark very quickly.

CHAPTER TEN

"**D**o I need to use the bridge example?" Emily said, staring right at Pete, more frustration than humor in her voice. "Kathy's a fuck-up. She's a great writer, I consider her a friend, but she's totally unreliable and a mess. I'm surprised it took this long for her to go AWOL."

"Bridge example?" Pete asked, knowing where she was going.

"Yes."

"What are you talking about?" Mike asked. Emily turned to look at him with the same annoyed surprise she'd already served up to Pete.

"Maybe it's time to cut you both off." She slid her glass an inch away from her grasp. "I was just saying that just because someone asks you to do something, it doesn't mean you need to do it. What if Kathy's dad asked you to jump off a bridge?"

Pete laughed. Mike joined. Emily smiled as she took another sip of wine. The three of them had been friends for over a decade, so ribbing and sarcastic exchanges were par for the course. Pete wondered, as he took a quick sip of his beer, if they'd ever make it back to being real friends, or if they were forever cursed to this weird purgatory. When Emily was a Features designer at the *Times*, she had had plenty of contact with Kathy. The two of them would hang out from time to time, before Emily got married and Kathy found Javier. Pete wondered why Emily was even out at this hour.

"I just think it's stupid," Emily said, pulling out her cell phone and checking it quickly. "And as someone who actually knows Kathy—which you don't—I think she's more trouble than she's worth. Smart girl, very pretty and cool to hang out with, that's it. If it was me or Mike, then yeah, of course you should come find us."

"I'm not risking anything," Pete said, annoyed. "This'll be over in less than a day. I'm calling Chaz tomorrow, once I check out a few more things."

"What are you going to check out?" Emily asked.

"Well, I need to check with her friends and neighbors . . . stuff like that," Pete stammered. "And I checked out her boyfriend Javier's record."

"How'd you check his record?"

Pete scratched his head. He'd painted himself into a corner. Luckily, this was Emily, and awkwardness aside, she wasn't going to get him in trouble. She would rib him about it, though.

"You used the *Times* database? Right?"

"Yeah," Pete said.

Emily took a long sip from her glass. Mike nodded absentmindedly.

"Well, whatever, everyone does it," Emily said. "Chaz is going to pay you, right?"

Pete put up his arms defensively. "I just said I'd make a few inquiries. This is a one-off thing. I may not even accept any money from him if I don't find his daughter."

"She probably went on some trip with this dude," Emily said. "Anyway, what did you find?"

"Not a lot, really," Pete admitted. "Javier's got a rap sheet. I was going to swing by this restaurant where he works and talk to him, see if he's there."

"Where does he work?" Emily asked.

"Casa Pepe's, a Cuban joint near my dad's house," Pete said. He noticed Emily's eyes softening slightly at the mention of his father. She'd loved his dad. Emily would sit with Pedro for hours, talking and drinking, when she and Pete visited from Jersey. She was shattered when they got the news. Pete had come home haggard and drunk. It didn't click for her immediately—that sad, empty look in his eyes. He'd often come home wasted after covering a late Nets game. But he looked different that night, or so she'd told him. "You looked like you'd died," she had whispered to him, a few nights later, as they shivered outside the Caballero Funeral Home in Miami, drenched in a rainstorm and not caring.

Pete shook his head and looked at his watch. It was late.

"So Javier works there?" Emily asked, pulling Pete out of his thoughts.

"Yeah," Pete said. "Seems like it. I have to check to be sure."

"That place is odd," Emily said, looking at her hands as she fiddled with a matchbook. "Hardly ever see anyone in there. Pretty nice looking for a Westchester Cuban place, though."

"The food sucks, too," Mike chimed in, after finishing his beer and sliding the glass over to Jimmy.

"Yeah, it's not amazing; but you don't like much food," Emily said, looking at Mike. "The servers are totally rude, too. But people seem to go there."

Pete nodded. It was almost three in the morning. He was more tired than hammered. Talking to Emily and Mike had leveled him out. He could drive home, he thought. He snapped to attention as Emily quickly stood up.

"Shit, I have to go," she said, putting her cell phone back into her purse. She leaned in and gave Pete a quick peck on the cheek and an automatic hug. "Rick isn't a big fan of me being out late, and he's home with the dogs."

Pete wondered how married life was treating her. He wondered how married life would have treated them.

"Come on, you can't do one more? Rick'll watch the dogs," Mike said.

Emily ignored the belligerent Mike and stood by Pete, still seated in his stool. She put a hand on his shoulder. "Be careful, OK? This whole situation sounds odd."

Pete's heart jumped at her concern. He fought an urge to grab her hand. "I'll be fine, but thanks."

"OK," she said, her hand lingering on Pete's shoulder. She was a little drunk, too, Pete realized. Her hands felt familiar still. Her eyes focused on his for a second and she snapped her fingers, shattering whatever drunken connection Pete felt. "Shit, you know who you should talk to? Do you know Amy Matheson?"

"The news editor? She handles cops, no?" Pete responded.

"Yeah, her," Emily said. "She's Kathy's best friend—well, her only friend at work. They talk all the time. If Kathy's not talking to her, then something is shady."

"Yeah, definitely," Pete said. "I'll check with her tomorrow when I get in." He felt himself leaning in to Emily more than he normally would. He was drunk. She was drunk. She looked at him.

"Stephanie says she saw you a few nights ago," Emily said, letting the statement hang out without any context.

Pete cleared his throat. "Yeah, we chatted for a bit," he said, refusing to fully engage. "She seemed OK."

"That's good," Emily said, her eyes meeting Pete's. In the past, she would have pressed the issue—asked why he'd been so wasted, why he'd embarrassed himself in front of someone they both knew. She didn't do that anymore. They were quiet for a few moments before she spoke again. "How's your new place?" Emily asked. The question came out of left field and didn't at the same time.

"That was random," Mike commented. Emily didn't turn to respond.

"Uh, it's fine," Pete said. "Not really that new anymore." He stopped himself. He could have continued—noted how long it'd been since she'd left in that cab. He could mention the piles of unreturned e-mails, phone calls, and letters that further confirmed for him that Emily wanted nothing to do with him. That it was over.

"Yeah, sorry," Emily said.

Pete could see pity in her eyes, and that made him feel worse. He moved back slightly. She moved her hand from his shoulder. An awkward silence lingered. He thought it'd gone so well, but now his mind was spinning. He hated to think about her like this. He hated how his heart — in a second — could show him that nothing had changed. He coughed quickly and offered up a humorless smile to Emily.

"OK, I really have to go." She kissed him quickly on the cheek again before turning to Mike and shoving him. "You idiots get home safe. Have some water before you leave."

Mike giggled. Pete laughed in response. He was rarely more sober than Mike. Jimmy hovered over them, looking a little worn out after a long night of serving underage college students and depressed thirtysomethings.

"Hey guys, last call," he said, wiping around their respective glasses. "Can I get you something else?"

Pete started, then turned to look at Mike, whose eyelids were half shut as he leaned on the bar. He looked at Jimmy and shrugged.

"I think we're good for the night."

Pete fumbled with Mike's keys as he tried to open Mike's apartment door. Mike, relatively useless, was leaning on the opposite wall. Pete smiled. He considered how bad Mike — and he — would be had they let themselves do a few more rounds at the Pub. It was dangerous enough that Pete drove up to Mike's house, a good 45 minutes away, after the half-dozen drinks he had in his system. He managed to get the door open and they walked in.

Mike's apartment was decorated sparsely. Lots of white space, little clutter. Pete marveled at the OCD of it all. He motioned Mike to the couch, where they both plopped down with a thud.

"I am fucked up," Mike said, as if by vocalizing the situation, he could remedy it.

"Nah, you're alright," Pete said, grabbing the remote, looking at it in an attempt to figure out how to get to ESPN. "We were just there too long, you know?"

"Yeah, bro," Mike said. "I hadn't seen Emily in a while. Always nice to check out that rack." He laughed.

Pete stayed quiet. He wasn't sure if he should sleep over and avoid another risky drive late at night or leave Mike alone and head to the comforts of home. He was leaning toward the latter.

"What, you're offended now?" Mike said, turning to Pete.

"No, man," Pete said. "I'm just tired. It's been a long few days."

Mike leaned his head back and closed his eyes. "That's for sure. I'm not feeling ok at all."

"Emily seemed to be in a rush at the end there," Pete said. He would only make such a comment when Mike was drunk and prone to ramble.

"Hm, yeah," Mike said, looking at the TV before taking the remote from Pete's hands and turning it on. "I don't think she's that happy with her life. You really derailed her, you know?"

"What do you mean?"

"You went off — and you took her with you," Mike said, his voice clearer. "The only way she could get her shit straight was to leave you behind. But you guys keep dancing around each other. It's sad."

Pete stayed quiet.

"And yeah, she seems out of it," Mike said. "She barely talked about Rick or her new job. She just kept asking about you and the paper. She sounded almost nostalgic."

"Who'd be nostalgic for the *Times*?"

"You might be, if you get fired," Mike said, no trace of humor in his voice.

Pete bristled. "What's that supposed to mean?"

"Nothing, bro," Mike said. "You know what I mean. As for Emily, I don't know. Something's going on there. She's not acting like herself. All nervous and jittery. It's weird."

"She seemed OK," Pete said.

"Yeah, sort of," Mike said. "But she seemed off. Everyone seems a little off lately."

Pete wasn't sure how to respond. They both watched ESPN highlights silently until Pete could hear Mike snoring softly. He eased off the couch and wandered into Mike's room, returning with a comforter. He draped it over Mike and shut off the TV. He hit the main apartment light and walked out, locking the door behind him.

CHAPTER ELEVEN

Pete turned off his noisy Celica's engine. He looked around his car. It was a mess. Papers everywhere, fast food containers and CD cases strewn all over the backseat. After realizing his car was on its last legs a few months back, Pete had given up on upkeep. Now he felt a pang of guilt as he got out of the car. Then something caught his eye in the back seat. A large cardboard box peeked out from under one of his winter jackets—now pointless since he wasn't planning on returning to New Jersey anytime soon. Pete slid the driver's side seat up and moved his coat. He remembered what the box was instantly, and regretted finding it. It was a box of his father's old paperwork. Probably receipts and expense reports. He hadn't thought of the box since he tossed it in the backseat the day Emily left. He groaned as he picked up the box—heavier than he'd remembered—and closed the car door with his hip. He walked up the stairs to his second-floor apartment slowly, trying to shift the box's weight after every four or five steps. His arms hurt from the strain.

"Come on, Pete," he said under his breath. "Don't embarrass yourself."

He managed to open his front door without much trouble and let the box thud on his faded brown couch. He sank into the couch and let out a disappointed sigh as he realized the remote control was not within reach. He sat, waiting for his breathing to steady, and looked around his small apartment at his posters. David Byrne's *True Stories*, a ratty Marlins inaugural season celebratory poster and an Edward Hopper *Nighthawks* print that Emily had given him on their anniversary summed up the last few years of his life. Costello sauntered into the main room with a yowl, followed by his new gray sidekick. Realizing no food was in the offing, Costello rolled over slowly and went to sleep. The gray cat mewled and walked off.

He flicked on the light near the door and turned to face the box that rested next to him. Inside were a series of file folders and a brown paper bag, scrunched tightly behind the stack of manila folders and paperwork. Pete skimmed the titles of each. His father, unsurprisingly, was very organized. The folders were in order by year, and most contained your basic police info — reports, crime scene breakdowns, witness comments, and his father's own notes coming out of interrogations. Pete wasn't sure his dad was even supposed to have this level of info, retired or not. Carlos Broche, his father's longtime partner and closest friend, had probably turned a blind eye to the copying.

"Old man couldn't put the gun down," Pete said to himself.

Most of the cases seemed relatively routine, as far as homicides went. Robberies gone bad, spousal abuse escalating to murder, jealous lovers, vengeful coworkers. The files made for interesting reading and Pete felt himself energized and awake. This was his father's life, he thought. He dealt with the scum of the earth on a daily basis and still remained a strong and gentle soul. Pete pushed the papers away and leaned back on the sofa. He was staring at the ceiling. He wasn't sure for how long. It was time for bed, he thought, returning his eyes to the box, now less organized thanks to Pete's meddling. Beneath the manila folders Pete found another — this one a faded red — with two staples holding it closed. Pete's father didn't really want to open this, he figured. The tab, which had featured years and case numbers on the other folders, just read "The SD." Pete knew what it meant: The Silent Death.

From the few times his father had mentioned it, Pete knew it haunted him. It was his white whale — the one that got away. Pete popped the staples off and watched them bounce onto the dirty brown carpet.

The file folder was sparse and mostly contained dated notes in his father's handwriting. Pedro could point to at least twelve murders that bore the signature of the Silent Death. Mostly noted mob figures and other criminals. They all had little to no evidence to offer a seasoned homicide detective on the scene. As Pete flipped through the notes, he could feel his father's growing frustration.

> *They're all connected. I know this. Broche thinks it's a few people — I know it can't be. Not sure why this case is sticking to me more than the others. It's not like we don't have work to do. The early one troubles me. The count is close to eleven now. Probably more.*

Whoever's doing this has to be living somewhere in secret — not a hermit, that's not possible in a city like Miami. Too many people would need to reach him. He has to have a front. But where? Why? I'll think on it tonight. — PF

That was the last entry in the folder. Reading his father's notes felt more reassuring than sad. It was like peering into Pedro's life and catching a glimpse of him. Pete knew these opportunities would come less and less often as time passed. He retired a few weeks later, Pete thought. He died months later. Pete slid the folder back in the box and organized the folders in his best imitation of his father. The Silent Death was still out there.

He pulled out the crumpled brown paper bag and knew from the feel what it was without peering inside. He opened it slowly and pulled out his father's police weapon—a Glock. Standard issue for most police officers in Miami. It was surprisingly light. Black and bulky. The gun felt strange in his hand. He remembered it—or its type, at least. He checked the weapon and noticed it wasn't loaded. His mind veered back to his youth and the detailed sessions with his father at the shooting range, where Pedro Fernandez taught his only son how to load, reload and sometimes—when he could see the boredom in his son's eyes and felt a pang of guilt—fire his weapon under his watchful eye. Always careful. He shook the bag and found a few stray bullets. He held one up to the light. His head was throbbing now. He was still drunk. The clock above his entertainment center told him it was well past five in the morning. He had to work later. He should go to sleep. He should move on and hope the rest of the day was going to be—if not better—at least a little more bearable.

"Fuck it," he said.

He slid the bullets into the gun, loading it slowly and meticulously. He remembered the procedure. He had touched this gun before. His father's gun. His father's life. In a box next to him on the couch. Pete finished loading the gun and pointed it at his television set. He saw his reflection through the coat of dust on the screen. He could smell his father's cheap Varadero pharmacy brand cologne on the handle. He put the safety back on the gun and laid it down on the small table between the couch and the television.

His father had been a hero. Perhaps only to a handful of people, but to more people than most. Pete slumped back in his seat. What did he have to show for himself? Not much of a job, no wife, a half-empty apartment, and a sense of fading opportunity.

His gaze didn't move from the gun on the small, cheap IKEA table. It used to have magazines like *Cosmo* and the *New Yorker* mingling with his copies of *ESPN* and *MOJO*. The gun had spun slowly after Pete placed it on the table, stopping mid-cycle; the barrel of the Glock 34 stared at Pete.

CHAPTER TWELVE

The Miami sun beat down on Pete through the booth window at Casa Pepe's as he sipped a large glass of Diet Coke. The giant plate of picadillo — seasoned ground beef with white rice and black beans — that he'd just devoured had helped somewhat, but didn't fully eliminate his hangover. Usually around this time he'd be rushing to get to work, not sitting in a restaurant in his old neighborhood savoring Cuban food and staring out at another beautiful Miami afternoon. But he didn't feel any particularly strong motivation to be at work early today. The encounter with his dad's files — and his gun — had left Pete more shaken than he'd anticipated. The sight of his father's things and the memories they brought up left Pete not only nostalgic, but distraught about the present. The last thing he felt like doing was sitting at his desk.

Then why was he at Casa Pepe's, of all places? Pete couldn't come up with an answer. It was an unexpected longing for his friendship with Javier that first motivated him to start looking for Kathy, so it wouldn't hurt to try and look him up. Or so he told himself.

A normal person would have gone to sleep long before toying with an old weapon between bouts of feeling bad for himself. *Not me,* Pete thought. No, his night ended with a long, presumably rambling call to Emily. Pete only knew this because he'd checked his outgoing calls when he woke up this morning. What he'd said to his former fiancée was probably best left undiscovered, he mused to himself. So much for trying to be friends again.

The waitress, a pudgy, tan girl who was probably a few years younger than Pete, politely asked if he needed anything. He responded slowly, his Spanish rusty from lack of practice. The waitress—Maribel according to her name tag—seemed to notice Pete's plight and switched to English. Her accent was strong, but she managed.

"Can I get you anything else?"

"Sorry," Pete said. "I haven't been speaking much Spanish lately."

"It's OK," she smiled. "How was the picadillo?"

"Oh, great," Pete said. "Can I ask you a question?"

Maribel seemed slightly taken aback and confused.

"Yes, sure. Do you want dessert?"

"Ha, no," Pete said. "I'm looking for a friend of mine, I think he works here. Javier Reyes?"

Pete noticed Maribel's bubbly demeanor visibly shift upon the mention of Javier, and she hesitated before saying anything.

"Javier's not here today."

"I figured as much," Pete said. "But do you know when he'll be in? We went to school together, and I wanted to say hi and maybe catch up with him."

Maribel looked around the restaurant and turned back to Pete.

"Did you want any dessert?"

"No, I'm fine," Pete said. "But do you know about Javier? Is there a manager I can speak to?"

Maribel nodded and stepped back quickly.

"Yes, I'll have him come by here," she said. "And I'll bring the check."

"OK, thanks."

Pete took a final sip of his Diet Coke and began to take some money out of his wallet when a stocky bearded man approached his table, wearing a beige guayabera and black slacks. He was fairly unremarkable looking, except for the long scar running down the left side of his face. Pete wondered how a restaurant owner got a wound like that. The man reached out to shake Pete's hand.

"Hello, I'm Jose Contreras," he said, clearly not comfortable speaking English. "I own Casa Pepe's. I hope you enjoyed your food here."

"Pete Fernandez," he responded. "Yeah, the food was excellent. I used to come here, years ago. I was actually wondering about a friend of mine. I'd heard he works here. Javier Reyes?"

Contreras seemed to be straining to keep up his jolly demeanor at the mention of Javier's name.

"Ah, yes, Javier," Contreras said. "He was a smart kid. He doesn't work here anymore. You know how it is. I get a lot of employees. They come and go."

"Oh, that's too bad."

"Yes, yes," Contreras said. "You know how things are in the restaurant business, my friend. It is very flowing. He was a good employee, but people come and go."

Pete placed some money on the table and stood up next to Contreras.

"That's a shame," Pete said. "Did he tell you where he was going? Is he still on work release? I'd imagine he'd have to report where he's working, no?"

Contreras forced another smile, this time more visibly annoyed. It was clear that he had hoped Pete would've dropped it by now. He tucked his hands behind his back and leaned into Pete slightly.

"Look, Javier was a good kid, a hard worker, sometimes," Contreras said, looking around him and smiling at the customers who probably couldn't hear what he was saying. "But he doesn't work here anymore, OK? Now, stop asking my employees questions, OK? If you want dessert, it's free. If not, go."

Pete was surprised at the venom in Contreras' response. Pete dropped an extra dollar on the table. As he did this, he noticed something scrawled on the back of his receipt. He couldn't make out the message, but he stuffed it into his pocket and turned to Contreras, a forced smile on his face.

"No, that's fine," he said. "Thank you for a lovely lunch."

Clouds had weakened the sunny day, so Pete walked out of Casa Pepe's to a gray sky. Once he was clear of the front door and walking toward the small parking lot behind the restaurant, he pulled out the crumpled receipt. Written hastily on the back of the small piece of paper was a quick message: "Dessert at Denny's in 20 minutes. — Mari." Pete slid the paper back into his pocket. He didn't notice that someone was behind him.

"Looking for me?"

Pete turned around quickly and saw Javier—or, at least, an older, gruffer version of the kid he used to pal around with—leaning against an employee exit, taking a drag from a cigarette, surrounded by trash bags and empty boxes. He was in a cook's attire—white smock and apron, white pants—each one sporting its own palette of food and work stains. It took Pete a few seconds to process that it was really Javier standing in front of him.

"You alright, man?" Javier said.

Pete realized he'd been just staring at his old friend for at least 15 seconds. He coughed awkwardly. "Yeah, yeah," Pete said. "I'm fine. Your boss said you didn't work here anymore."

"Well, I don't," Javier said, scratching around the stubble on his face, letting out a long lungful of smoke. "Not on the books, at least. You probably made him nervous. He has everyone trained not to rat me out."

"Why would you need to pretend you're not working here, though?"

Javier dropped the cigarette butt on the asphalt and ground it out with his shoe. He took a few seconds to respond. He was scanning Pete.

"Aren't you going to say hello? Or ask me how I've been?"

Pete felt a pang of guilt. Javier was part of the reason he'd even started looking for Kathy. He wanted to find his friend more than he wanted to find her. And here Javier was, clearly down on his luck, struggling to make a living, and all Pete could think about was minutiae. He stepped closer to Javier and extended his hand.

"It's good to see you, man," Pete said.

Javier took his hand and pulled Pete in for a hug. It lasted a few seconds longer than Pete would have expected, but that was fine. Javier smelled like a kitchen. Mixed with nice cologne. Pete stepped back.

"It's been a while, huh?" Javier said. "You look good. Lost some weight?"

Pete didn't think so, but took the compliment.

"You too," Pete said. "We're all getting old."

Javier laughed. Pete recognized it. Javier was being polite. Despite the novelty of seeing each other again, they were not friends. They hadn't been for some time.

"So, what's happening with you? Do you want to get a cup of coffee?" Pete asked, pushing Maribel's note to the back burner in his mind.

"Nah, I can't," Javier said. "My break is almost over. But I saw you from the kitchen and I wanted to catch you before you left."

"Your boss is a piece of work," Pete joked. "Guess I won't be welcome here anytime soon."

Javier tensed up slightly. He looked at Pete for a split second, then turned away.

"He's just a paranoid old man," he said. "My work release is done and he doesn't want to pay me the regular wage, so I'm working for him on the side, under the table. It's a weird, backward compliment, I guess."

"I don't follow."

"Well, he liked my work so much he wants me to stick around," Javier said, pulling out another cigarette from the pack in his shirt pocket. "He doesn't have the money to pay me a regular wage, but I owe him. He let me get back on my feet after my last fuck-up."

Pete thought back to the files he'd scanned from work. Javier's life had not been easy. He felt bad for him. His father had been out of the picture for years, and Pete couldn't remember Javier mentioning his mother often. He'd been a latch-key kid who survived on street smarts and the kindness of relatives. Always asking to borrow some money and very rarely offering to lend any.

Javier took Pete's silence as a cue to keep talking.

"I have to run soon," he said. "So, while I'm happy to see you, I'm wondering why you came to find me now, of all times. How did you even know I was working here?"

Pete paused. What could he say? That he misused the *Times* database to find out about Javier's criminal career in a haphazard effort to find his girlfriend, who was possibly missing according to her alcoholic dad? Probably not.

"Well, it's a long story," Pete said. "But I'm actually looking for Kathy Bentley."

Javier's eyes narrowed slightly and he took a long drag from his cigarette, his look locked on Pete's face.

"Kathy? Why?"

"Her dad thinks she's missing."

Javier's nose scrunched up for a brief moment and he sighed.

"Chaz thinks she's missing? How would he know?"

"Not sure," Pete said. "Honestly, the whole thing feels strange. It doesn't seem like they have the best relationship."

"They don't," Javier said, looking at his watch. Pete noticed it was a relatively nice one—the silver band shining in the little bit of sun that was still around on the gloomy afternoon. "And it's weird for him to ask you, of all people, to find her. No offense."

"None taken," Pete said. He felt relief wash over him. It was good to talk to Javier. It'd been so long. Just like before, he was bringing logic into their discussions. Why was Pete even doing this for Chaz, a person he barcly knew? At least it had helped him find Javier. "Like I said, the whole thing is strange. Have you heard from her lately? I figure I'll just tell him I've spoken to you and she's fine."

"She is fine," Javier said quickly. His eyes widened slightly. Pete could tell he was getting annoyed at the entire exchange. Not at Pete, but at the idea that his girlfriend's father was sending an old friend of his digging around for her. "She does shit like this all the time. She'll go to visit her mom, or she'll just stop answering her phone. I'm used to it by now."

Pete started to respond, but stopped himself. It wouldn't help things to mention he'd been in Kathy's apartment. If Javier said she was fine, she probably was. Javier straightened his apron and half-turned toward the door before extending his hand. Pete took it.

"I have to get back to this," he said, disappointed at having to leave the conversation incomplete. "But let's keep in touch. We were young before. Now we're old. We're supposed to be smarter."

Pete shook Javier's hand and smiled. "Yeah, definitely," he said. "I'll talk to Chaz and let him know Kathy's fine."

"Cool," Javier said. "Let me know if you hear anything else. Let's grab a beer one of these days. It's hard to catch up when one person is covered in rice and beans."

Pete let out a quick laugh and nodded. Javier waved awkwardly and walked back into the restaurant's kitchen. Pete stood in the half-empty parking lot after the door closed. He looked at his watch.

Denny's was a few minutes away. Pete turned and walked toward his car, his head still buzzing, but no longer from a hangover.

The Denny's on Galloway was your typical chain diner — bright lights trying to mask a coat of grime, mediocre food, bad service, worse coffee. Pete remembered many a late night ending at Denny's, less than a mile from the house he grew up in. Nights and early mornings spent drinking coffee and eating Grand Slams in a futile effort to sober up, or at least to mask the effects of a night out with friends.

He found Maribel sitting at a booth near the back of the restaurant, sipping a chocolate milkshake and looking around nervously. He nodded at Maribel and slid into the seat across from her, giving her a "Well? Let's get on with it" look. The menu made an unpleasant sticky sound as Pete opened it up to scan the desserts, giving Maribel a moment to speak.

Before she could, a waitress came by the booth and took Pete's order — a slice of apple pie and a black coffee. She smiled politely and walked away.

"So, here we are."

"Javier still works at Casa Pepe's."

Pete was surprised at Maribel's sudden mastery of English, but pressed on.

"Yeah, I figured that," Pete said. He decided to keep his encounter with Javier to himself for a bit longer.

"He's an asshole."

Pete nodded, hoping she would continue talking. After a few

moments he spoke again. "Look, I know Javier. He can be a dick. I'm just looking for him."

"Why do you want to talk to him so bad?"

Before Pete could answer, the waitress was sliding a plate of apple pie in front of him, along with the coffee he'd ordered. He thanked her and waited for her to walk off.

"It's been a while since I last saw him," Pete lied. "And I'd heard he was working there, so I thought I'd stop by."

Maribel took a long sip from her milkshake, her eyes locked on Pete. "He's not a good person," she said, looking down at her lap. "He's a liar. He doesn't work as hard as the rest of us. Sometimes he doesn't even show up. I'm not sure why Jose even keeps him around."

Pete took a moment to digest the information. This was new territory for him. He took a bite of pie. It was dry and not very flavorful—about right for Denny's.

"Why would Contreras keep him around if he was such a terrible employee?"

"No idea," Maribel said, becoming more comfortable with the exchange. "Jose always had him running errands outside the restaurant. I'm not even sure what he was doing half the time. He was hard to keep tabs on."

"Were you guys dating?" Pete surprised himself with his own question. Maribel absentmindedly pushed her milkshake away.

"Javier has a girlfriend," she said.

"That doesn't make my question invalid."

Their eyes met briefly and Maribel sighed. "Javier is a good-looking guy," she said. "Sometimes we worked late and went out after. Stuff happens in those kinds of situations. But he was smart about it."

"Smart how?"

"He knew when to pull back," she said, a wistful tone in her voice. "He gave me enough information and affection so I'd want more. He knows how to read people and situations."

"That sounds like him," Pete said. "How did he get along with Contreras?"

"He's close with Jose," she said. "So he's got more security there. I don't think he's even on the books as an employee. Whatever work release he was doing finished a long time ago. I'm not sure how he makes enough to live the way he does, though."

Pete's interest was piqued. He wasn't expecting this. He noticed Maribel's mood darkening. She seemed more annoyed, despondent. He felt he was on the cusp of learning something, but he wasn't sure what — or if he wanted to know.

"Money from where, though?"

"I don't know," she said, getting defensive. "Maybe his family? He's a charming guy and he knows how to make friends quickly. I don't really know much about him, and we've worked together for almost three years now."

"What about Kathy?"

"His girlfriend?"

"Yes," Pete said. "Did he ever talk about her?"

Pete looked at Maribel. She was worried. She cared for Javier, in her own weird way. Maybe she even loved him.

"Sometimes," she said, slowly. "Not a lot. It wasn't exactly something I wanted to hear about."

"That's understandable," Pete said. He wasn't sure what to say, so he let the conversation breathe a bit.

"They weren't the best couple," she said. "He cheats on her, she's cruel to him. It's strange. Their dynamic is weird. But he really cares for her. He talks about wanting to move away with her. Whatever."

"Move? Where?"

"Contreras has a house in the Keys," she said. "We were supposed to go there a few weeks ago, just to get away from all the bullshit — work, his girlfriend, the city. But then he mentions he wants to move there with her. It's weird."

"Key Largo?"

"No, Key West, it was a bungalow near this bar, Willie T's," she said. "I've never been, though. Why are you asking about his girlfriend? Is she in trouble?"

Pete fought the urge to write the info down immediately, thinking that would look a little odd.

Maribel stood up and looked around, realizing Pete wasn't going to answer her question, or didn't have an answer. "I have to go." She tried to drop some cash on the table but Pete waved it off. His mind was straining to find the next question to ask her before she left. He dropped a twenty on the table.

"You're not a very good cop," Maribel said.

"What do you mean?"

"I mean, you know, going undercover and pretending to be friends with Javier from way back. You're not the first person to ask about him like this." She was bordering on angry, possibly at herself for revealing too much. "I could tell you were a cop. Why else would I talk? I don't want any trouble. I just hope Javier isn't in too much. El pobre. He's not a bad guy. Not all the time."

"What do you mean, not the first one?"

She looked away from Pete. The conversation was over.

Pete stood up. "I'm not a cop," he said, scanning her face for surprise. "But thanks anyway."

He walked off. He felt Maribel's eyes boring into the back of his neck. The Denny's hostess gave him a dry smile as he pushed the front door open.

CHAPTER
THIRTEEN

ete glanced at his watch. He was running late for work. But, for a change, he was in the *Miami Times* building, just not in the fifth floor newsroom. He was on the third floor balcony area, a haven to the smokers forced to find refuge to feed their nicotine habits. Pete wasn't smoking, but sipping a Diet Coke. He sat on a bench on the far side of the large, open-air, roof-like area, hearing the cars on the expressway speed by to and from Miami Beach. He found his feet tapping anxiously. The smokers' zone was mostly empty, as people were just getting started with their night shifts or heading out, able to smoke on their way home. Pete took a final swig from the soda and tossed it toward a nearby trash can, making it in. *Of course, a swish without anyone around to see*, he thought to himself.

He turned at the sound of slow footsteps behind him. Chaz Bentley looked around anxiously as he scanned the balcony, finally stopping as his eyes discovered Pete. His pace quickened and soon he was standing over Pete.

"Aren't you late for work?" he asked, skipping pleasantries.

"A bit," Pete said. "Don't worry about it."

Chaz sat down to Pete's left, looking around before settling in. He seemed nervous. Pete chalked it up to the old man having the alcohol jitters. Pete wondered what he himself would do if there was a drink in front of him now, late for work or not.

"So, you called," Chaz said. "What's the latest? Did you get in touch?"

"No," Pete said. "Not directly. But I spoke to Javier, and he says she's fine."

Chaz coughed awkwardly and looked away from Pete for a second, his hand rubbing his chin quickly.

"Oh, OK, how did that go?"

"Fine," Pete said. "I caught him at work. Casa Pepe's. Cuban joint in Westchester. Ever been?"

Chaz didn't answer. He stood up abruptly.

"Are you alright?" Pete stood up as well, backing away from Chaz slowly. The older man was running his hands nervously through his thinning gray hair, his other hand buried in his pants pocket.

"Yeah, yeah," Chaz said. "Don't sweat it. Keep going. So, you spoke to Javier at Casa Pepe's? No one else, right?" His eyes told Pete that's exactly what he wanted to hear.

"I spoke to the owner and a waitress," Pete said. "That's it. I didn't really get much information, but you said you wanted me to keep you updated, so . . ."

Pete felt himself being pulled and slammed into the bench.

The motion and shock at hitting it startled him. Chaz hovered over him, his hands on Pete's shirt as Pete was splayed awkwardly, half-standing, half-sitting.

"The fuck?" Pete said, surprised at the old man's speed.

"What did you tell the owner? Tell me. Don't skip a beat, son."

Pete pushed Chaz away and backed up. He kept his eyes on Chaz, who was shifting his weight from one foot to the next, probably expecting Pete to take a swing at him. Pete supposed that's what most men would do in this situation.

"What the hell was that for?" Pete said.

"Look, forget it, I'm just curious. I want to know what's going on with my daughter."

"I told you — she's fine. I heard it from her boyfriend," Pete said, his brow furrowed in anger, his hands slowly balling into fists. "Why are you so bent out of shape about this?"

"What did you tell Contreras?"

"How'd you know his name?"

"Whose name?"

"All I said was I'd spoken to the restaurant owner," Pete said, taking a step closer to Chaz. "I never said his name."

"I've been there a few times, is all," Chaz said, his voice cracking slightly. "What did you say? Just tell me."

And in that moment, Pete felt very sorry for Chaz Bentley. He was a beaten man. Pete wasn't sure if he really did care for his daughter, but whatever it was that he was involved in that also involved Contreras, the angry man with the strange scar, was much more frightening to Chaz than any cruel possible endgame for his only child.

"What the fuck is going on?" Pete said.

Chaz began to back away from Pete, his gaze still with him.

"Look, don't worry about it," Chaz said, his voice a low, frightened hiss. "This is not your problem. You said Kathy's fine? Great. Thanks for checking."

"What? That's it?"

"Yeah, I don't need your help anymore," Chaz said. "I'll give Kathy a call and take it from here."

Before Pete could say anything else, Chaz had turned around toward the entrance to the building. For a moment he considered following, but by then it was too late. The seconds he'd sacrificed to surprise and shock had cost him a chance. Why had Contreras' name sent Chaz into a frenzy? He wasn't sure. He looked at his watch. What he was sure of, though, was that he was late. He straightened his shirt and headed for the door, a humid wave of Miami heat slapping his face as he opened the door.

CHAPTER FOURTEEN

Pete instinctively looked at the time on his computer after its seemingly endless boot-up, but he didn't need to check to know he was close to an hour late. He groaned audibly. The encounter with Chaz had left him confused and curious. He wanted to keep digging for information. What did Contreras have to do with anything? Was Kathy really OK? Why did Chaz seem more concerned about who Pete spoke to than with news of his own daughter?

He cracked his knuckles. The last thing he wanted to do was show up for another mindless shift at work. A bottle of wine and a dark room sounded ideal. This worried him in its own way, too. He needed to think. Something was happening, and he wasn't happy about it. He looked around the newsroom. People were focused on their assigned tasks, as he would be, had he shown up at the appropriate time. Steve Vance was gone for the day, but Pete would be mistaken if he thought he wasn't going to hear about it. Pete was usually supposed to be here before Vance's exit on a Monday, and he hadn't been. Not ideal on any day, but right after a terse warning from the head of Sports? Doubly bad. Pete wondered whether he should be momentarily relieved or more worried. He opted for quick relief, sure that he'd regret it later.

As he logged into the paper's design and editing system, Pete wondered what his father would think of him. His father, a man who'd never been drunk a day in his life, who worked nights, weekends, and holidays to make ends meet and never complained. What would he expect Pete to do in a situation like this? The question hung over him as he looked across the newsroom. The day-side local news editors were milling about, rushing to relay information to the night-side editors and reporters before they could amble home to their DVRs and empty apartments. *How novel*, Pete thought. For Sports, it was a good night if he was out of the office before one in the morning. An early evening exit seemed like a luxury. As his mind wandered, he noticed a fifty-something redheaded editor hastily shoving copies of the *Miami Times* and papers into an oversized handbag. Amy Matheson. Kathy's best friend, according to Emily. If Kathy hasn't talked to Amy, Emily had said, then Kathy's in trouble. Pete felt himself getting up and walking across the newsroom. Before his mind fully registered what he was doing, he was softly tapping Amy on her shoulder. She turned around abruptly, her hand still in her bag.

"Hey, uh, it's Pete, I work in Sports."

Amy sized him up. She was older, but fit and with a grace Pete hadn't immediately noticed.

"Hello. I'm about to head out, so if this is about the 1A teases you're going to have to talk to Greenberg. He's . . ."

"No, no, that's not it," Pete responded. He waited. She finally made eye contact with him, shaking her head slightly in confusion.

"Um, OK," she said. "What's up, Pete from Sports?"

"It's about Kathy," Pete said quickly, his voice lowering slightly. "Kathy Bentley?"

"What about her?" Amy said. "Have you heard from her?"

Pete's heart sank slightly. Her question had answered his.

"No, I haven't," he said. "I was hoping you had."

Amy sighed and slung her bag over her shoulder. She seemed dejected at Pete's answer. "Why are you asking? You realize she's seeing someone, right?"

"That's not why I'm asking."

"Oh? Why else would an editor who doesn't even work in her section wonder about her?"

"Her dad is worried about her."

Amy let out quick, dismissive sound. "Chaz is suddenly worried? How convenient. Why doesn't he call her? She's his daughter. Listen, I really have to go."

Amy walked past Pete toward the elevators in the middle of the newsroom. He followed a pace or two behind her.

"Look, I know this is random," Pete said, trying to keep his voice quiet so only Amy could hear. "But I've reason to think she may be in trouble."

Amy turned to face him, clearly annoyed. "You're right about one thing," Amy said, meeting Pete's eyes. "This is very random. Why the hell are you looking for Kathy? What makes you think she even needs to be found?"

"Did she come to work today?"

"What?"

"She works on weekdays. Did she come in today?"

Amy paused, her eyes still fixed on Pete. "What's your angle?"

"Angle?" Pete asked.

"Yes, angle," she said. "Why should I talk to someone who I've never met, asking about a friend of mine, taking orders from a father that she's never said anything nice about?"

Pete slid his hands into his pockets and looked around. People were starting to take notice of the exchange happening outside the elevator bay. "Can we talk about this somewhere else?"

"No, we can't talk about this somewhere else," Amy said, her voice forceful. "I don't even know why you're asking; so as far as I'm concerned, this conversation is over."

She turned and started toward the elevator. Pete saw her punch the button and head in. Again, without much thought, he darted into the elevator after her. The doors closed behind him. She let out a surprised yelp.

"What the fuck is wrong with you?" Amy said, now more worried for her own safety than about any questions Pete might have.

Pete put his hands up. "Look, just hear me out," he said. Amy's features softened slightly to reveal her own concern. "I don't know her very well, but talking to Chaz got me to thinking that she might not be OK."

"OK," Amy said. "Go on."

"I know you and Kathy are close," Pete said. "And, at this point, I'm not sure what Chaz's game is. But, for my own peace of mind, I want to know if you've spoken to her, so I can either stop worrying and get on with my life or go to the cops and let them know she might be in danger."

Pete took a breath and continued. "So, did she come to work today?"

"No. No, she didn't. I haven't heard from her in almost a week."

The elevator reached the main lobby and opened its doors.

"OK," Pete said. "Has that ever happened before?"

Amy hesitated and looked Pete over quickly one more time. She was calculating. Should she trust him? Pete hoped she found his face to be trustworthy enough, despite the stubble and slightly bloodshot eyes.

"Do you have time for a cup of coffee?"

Amy and Pete sat across from each other at Kleinman's. In the brief moments when they had debated where to go, Pete discovered he only knew of bars in the area. Amy, a recovering alcoholic from what Pete had heard through newsroom gossip, seemed reluctant, but they both knew options in that neighborhood were limited. The bar was your usual generic pub, with dark brown and dingy décor and the requisite pool table and electronic jukebox. If it weren't for its proximity to work and thus a quick post-deadline nightcap, Pete wasn't sure he'd frequent the bar as much as he did.

Amy ordered a coffee, black, and Pete felt compelled to do the same. Considering that he was already an hour late and logging in was his only work-related accomplishment of the day, he wagered that returning to the office smelling of alcohol wouldn't do wonders for his employment status.

Amy took a cautious sip of her coffee and looked over at Pete before speaking. "Ok, spill."

"Spill?"

"What's this all about? Does Kathy owe Chaz money? Why is he so desperate to find her?"

Pete moved to drink his coffee but hesitated. It seemed like it was too hot. He could let it sit for a while. "Honestly, I'm not sure," he answered. "I just know he was worried and he asked me to find her."

"Do you always do favors for bumbling, drunken strangers?"

Pete was slightly taken aback by Amy's retort, deciding a humorous aside wouldn't be the best idea. He pressed on.

"Honestly, no. I don't really know Chaz or Kathy," Pete said. "But I am a little worried, and if anything, I'd feel worse about this if I just let it go without at least figuring out she was OK. I'm not overly concerned with her issues with her dad, or work, or whatever."

Amy frowned and took another sip of her coffee. The bar, which saw most of its business happen after sunset, was mostly empty.

"Kathy is a very needy person," Amy started. "She needs constant reassuring, constant attention, and constant coddling. She's also one of the smartest people I've ever met, which is why I tolerate her. She's a great writer, sharp as hell, and funnier than that. She's the closest friend I have." She paused, as if for emphasis. "We've never gone this long without talking."

"Have you reported this to the police? Has anyone noticed she wasn't at work today?" Pete felt his phone vibrating in his pocket. Someone was calling. He chose to ignore it.

"No, I haven't talked to anyone," Amy said. "It's not my place. I will now, though. If you're her only hope, then we're in trouble."

"What's that supposed to mean?"

"There's no nice way to ask this, so whatever," Amy said. "But do you look in the mirror when you wake up? For all I know, you were in this very bar before you came to work."

Pete shrugged off the insult.

"Chaz asked me to try to find her — why? No idea," he said. "At this point, I'm not sure who to trust. I'm also not sure I'm the person for this job. I'm going to the cops."

Amy nodded. She seemed relieved.

"Well, that's a start," she said. "Has anyone heard from Javier?"

"I spoke to him. He said she was fine, that she does this kind of act all the time."

"To him, she does," Amy said. "He's a prick."

"Do you know if anything was going on with Kathy lately?" Pete asked, looking down at his coffee. "What was she working on for you? She does long-form stuff, right?"

"Yes, she's an investigative reporter," Amy said. "She's been busy, I don't know—nothing out of the ordinary. She's been piecing together this one story on gang murders. That's been taking up most of her time."

"What kind of gang murders?"

"The mob kind," Amy said. She seemed exasperated, as if the conversation was going nowhere. "Ever heard of the Silent Death?"

Pete nodded.

"It's some kind of weird, pseudo-urban legend," Amy said. "One dude. Killed a dozen or so gangster-types. Ranging from bosses to low-end thugs. Same method: two bullets in the head from a silencer. The one or two witnesses that have ever seen him say he comes totally dressed in black — hat, overcoat, scarf, glasses. Real spooky, I'd guess."

Pete took a long sip from his coffee.

"Anyway, if it is one person—and I don't really think it can be—this guy kills for the highest bidder," Amy said. "He's murdered on all sides and no one has any clue who he might be. He's been doing this for the last five or six years and no one has any idea who he is or where he comes from. So, Kathy's been trying, bit by bit, to figure it out."

"How close is she?"

"Close," Amy said, her eyes meeting Pete briefly. Concern flashed across her face. "At least she thinks she's close. I'm not convinced yet."

Pete felt the wheels turning in his head. He wasn't sure what to make of Amy's information. He wasn't a big believer in coincidences. His mind flashed back to a few nights back, rummaging through his father's files. Had he missed something that could help him now? He'd have to revisit them, to at least get a better sense about this Silent Death.

His thoughts were interrupted by Amy clearing her throat.

Amy gently put her mug down and put a few dollars on the table. She looked down at Pete.

"I don't want to seem ungrateful, because I'm not," she said. "But you're in a little over your head. Your timing is way off and from what little I know about these kind of missing person situations, time is imperative. I think the best thing you can do for Kathy — and for me, and that idiot father of hers — is to make sure the cops get on this as soon as possible."

"Yeah," Pete said, staring at his folded hands on the table. He felt almost ashamed.

The precinct— nestled downtown off the expressway—brought back some memories of when he was in high school and his dad was a detective on the force. He remembered many a visit to the station. To bring his father coffee. To keep him company on a late case in the hopes of borrowing the car. It wasn't always by choice, either. If high school was his second home—and, after Pedro set him straight, it was—then the downtown Miami Police Department building was his third. He walked up to the desk slowly. He didn't recognize the officer manning it—a chubby, older woman with a fading perm and frazzled, burnt-out look about her.

"Yeah?" she blurted.

"Hi," Pete said hesitantly. "I'm here to see Detective Broche."

Pete had determined the lady's last name was Ramirez from her badge. She gave him a dazed look. "Do you think we just let people come in and meet with detectives?"

Pete smiled at Gladys as politely as he could muster. "*No, señora, of course not*," Pete said, already noticing her smile at his formal greeting. "*Claro que no.* I'm an old friend of Detective Broche. He used to work with my father, Pedro Fernandez."

Her eyes widened slightly. Was she blushing? Pete wondered.

"Pedro Fernandez?" she almost exclaimed. "*Bueno, hijo*, wait right here. I'll get Detective Broche myself."

Pete watched as she labored to extract herself from her chair and waddled over to the back. He looked around the waiting area one more time. The place still smelled the same—a mix of cleaning liquid and sweat, like a boys' locker room. Pete was here to resolve this situation. After his talk with Amy and Vance's call, it was clear he was in over his head. What had served as a momentary distraction

---

"Kathy, as wonderful as she is, has the habit of running with the wrong people," Amy said, getting up. "Things may have caught up with her. And if that's the case, none of us may want to see the results."

"What do you mean?" Pete asked.

"You see the pieces, don't you?" Amy said. Pete noticed her eyes were reddening. "Either she's dead or she will be soon. She's not on vacation. She hasn't moved to New Mexico. She is in some serious shit. And if you think for a second Chaz Bentley came to you because he thought you were the best chance he had at finding his daughter, you're more delusional than I thought you were."

Pete watched as Amy turned and left the bar. He realized she was right. This was a case for a professional, not a washed-up journalist looking for meaning in his life. He looked at the empty seat across from him and sighed. His eyes drifted to the bar. He could probably swing a quick vodka soda or shot before heading back to work, right? Pete pushed the thought out of his head. If he was going to disconnect from this, he needed to talk to the police as soon as possible. But first, he needed to get back to work. He pulled out his phone and saw that whoever called him had left a voicemail. He clicked to check it. The second Pete realized who it was, he knew his day had gone from bad to terrible.

"Pete, it's Steve Vance. I'm going to get to the point to save us both some time. You're on paid suspension for two weeks. After which you'll be evaluated by a Human Resources rep. It's as bad as it sounds. I thought our talk would be enough to motivate you to show the promise we've been waiting on since we hired you, but it wasn't. I don't need to list the reasons for this call. Your stuff will be boxed pending the review. Your access pass has been blocked. Please call HR with any other questions."

Pete heard the last bit of Vance's message as his phone landed on the table. The bartender looked up from the day's sports section to see Pete slam his fist down on the table, cursing himself.

CHAPTER FIFTEEN

Pete winced as the police station's fluorescent lights beat down on him. It was early in the afternoon and he'd been awake for less than an hour. The night, not surprisingly, had been a blur. After the call from Vance he decided the best way to deal with his impending career change wasn't by taking a walk over to his job to confront the problem, but by a slow and gradual obliteration at Kleinman's. He vaguely remembered stumbling to his car, only to be awoken a few hours later by the Times' night security, who found him passed out and drooling in the driver's seat. Luckily, the security guard didn't seem concerned about Pete's driving the five or six miles back to his apartment. He felt defeated. He no longer had the grim walls of the *Miami Times* hovering protectively over him. There was also the issue of money. But Pete knew there would be some severance. He hoped it'd last him.

from his regular life couldn't be treated as such. Even hung over, Pete realized he had bigger issues to deal with beyond looking for Kathy Bentley. But he couldn't shake the lingering feeling that the Miami PD — known for lax detective work and not exactly the most honorable institution — wouldn't give the case the attention it deserved. Still, what could he do?

Detective Carlos Broche had been his father's partner in Homicide for almost two decades. He had been a constant presence in Pete's formative years, and Pete had as many memories involving the gruff, mustachioed Cuban as he did of his father during the time. Conversations over coffee while his dad had a suspect "in the box" being interrogated and junk food runs during another late night when his father couldn't come home but wanted to keep tabs on his errant son were etched into Pete's memories. He could almost taste the strong Cuban coffee shots, cold from being out for hours, still potent and delicious.

Pete felt a strong hand on his shoulder and turned around to find Broche, burly and powerful but a bit grayer and chubbier, pulling him into an emotional bear hug.

"Pedrito," Broche said, calling him by a name he hadn't heard since he was a child. "Why in the hell has it taken you this long to come visit your uncle?"

Pete found himself hugging Broche back, feeling a jolt of nostalgia.

They backed up a pace and looked each other over. Broche was overweight—less like the bull of his earlier days and more like a sleepy bear. Still, he commanded attention. He kept his left hand on Pete's shoulder, his other hand gingerly slapping Pete on his cheek.

"It's been too long, *hijo*," Broche said, smiling, proud. Pete wondered just how closely he'd followed his old partner's son. "Let's go sit down in my office. We have a lot of catching up to do."

Pete dutifully followed Broche down a short hallway and into a smallish office, decorated with photos and an unused bulletin board behind Broche's tiny black desk, where he slowly sat down. Pete took a seat across from him.

"It's good to see you," Pete said, speaking slowly, slightly overcome by the energy in the place and the rush of memories each step gave him. "It's funny to be back here after so long."

"Yeah," Broche looked around. "This place doesn't change, little man. Same shit, different day, you know? We had a gas station owner in here last night — beat up real good. Said two guys burst into the station and wiped him clean. Carrying shotguns and shit. This town is going to hell. Always has been."

Pete let out a dry laugh. Broche was always the pessimist to Pete's optimistic dad. They were opposites but also meshed well together. Pete shifted in his chair a bit, unsure how to begin.

"So, what's the deal?" Broche said, cutting through the bullshit. "Your dad dies a few years ago, you don't even visit? I haven't seen you since the funeral, man. How've you been?"

"I've been OK, trying to keep busy," Pete said. He hated small talk.

"You still with that pretty girl? What's her name? Emily?"

"Nah," Pete said, not elaborating. Broche shrugged.

"Eh, whatever," he said, waving his arm dismissively. "There's always another woman waiting around the corner. Fuck her. How's work? You at the *Times* still?"

"Yeah, yeah, it's good," he said, wincing at the lie. "Pretty busy with all the layoffs and stuff like that."

Broche nodded along, paying attention, but thinking of something else. He leaned back in his chair.

"You look like shit," Broche said. "You know that, right?"

"What?"

"I'm telling you like it is," Broche said. "Same way I'd talk to your dad when he'd come into work looking like he'd just gone 10 rounds with Roberto Duran after a week without any sleep. You smell like liquor, too. Went out last night?"

This wasn't the conversation Pete was looking to have.

"Only a bit."

"Big bit, then."

Pete remained silent and let his eyes wander around Broche's tiny office. It was part workspace and part relic — Pete could point to the photos that hadn't been touched in years. On Broche's desk was a framed picture of himself with Pete's father, high-fiving in the middle of the squad room. A photo Pete had called "cheesy and forced" as a kid. *What a brat I was*, Pete thought.

"*Bueno*, enough giving you shit," Broche said. "You obviously came here for something, not to hear me do my best imitation of your dad, right?"

"Yeah, I actually need a little advice."

"With the ladies?" Broche laughed at his own crude humor. Pete pressed on.

"No, actually, it's police-related."

Broche perked up. "Are you in trouble?"

"No, no, nothing like that," Pete backpedaled. "I'm doing a favor for someone I work with. They asked me to help them find someone and I figured I'd check with you."

"Why would this person ask you to help them find someone?" Broche asked, his brow furrowing. "What qualifies you to find anyone? No offense, but who is this guy?"

Broche was done with pleasantries and was cutting to the heart of the issue, the same issue that Pete had grappled with this morning. He was out of his element. If Kathy had any chance of surviving, it would be if the police took over.

"It's his daughter—Kathy Bentley. Her dad thinks she's missing."

Broche rubbed his chin and sighed. "Did this guy file a report?"

"He said the police didn't believe him."

"How long has she been missing?"

"He said he wasn't sure, that they'd not talked in a few days."

"Fathers and daughters don't talk for a few days all the time," Broche said, turning to face his desktop computer. "I'm guessing this girl is your age or older? You said Bentley, right?"

Broche began to type before Pete nodded to confirm. Pete watched the older cop squint as he scanned his computer screen.

"OK, here's the deal," Broche said. "We have zero calls on file from anyone named Bentley. What's your friend's first name?"

"He's not my friend, he just asked me to help him."

"Do you do this a lot, help people you barely know?"

"Chaz. Chaz Bentley."

"Chaz Bentley?" Broche said. "You're fucking kidding me. The newspaper guy? I used to read his column all the time. When it was good. Guy's a drunk. Gambles whatever he has away. Your dad took him in a few times. We did, I mean."

"Yeah, that's him," Pete said. The idea that his dad had arrested Chaz Bentley stuck out. The fact that Chaz had lied about calling the police worried him.

"That's it," Broche said, still looking at the screen. He turned his chair to face Pete. "Look, this happens all the time. Parents lose contact with their grown kids for whatever reason and they think they're in trouble when they're really just pissed off and don't want to talk to mommy or daddy. Unless there's strong evidence of foul play, or this person isn't showing up for work or church group or whatever regular activities they partake in, we usually don't call out the big guns."

Pete could feel Broche looking at him, even as his own gaze rested on the photo of his father, taken years before.

"This is what you're going to do," Broche said, his voice clear and forceful.

"Ok."

"You need to tell this Mr. Bentley that unless he has more proof that his daughter is missing, we can't do anything. I hate to say it's down to manpower, but that's part of it. We just don't have enough cops or detectives to go chasing after every lead."

"She hasn't been in her apartment for a few days," Pete blurted out. He was nervous. He felt like a kid bringing home a bad report card. He fought a desire to wince in anticipation of Broche's response. "And she was working on a story about the Silent Death." Pete let the last few words hang in the air.

"How the fuck would you know those things?"

"Because I was there, OK? She hadn't fed her cat, the TV was on, there were dishes in the sink . . ."

Broche stood up and pointed at Pete. "So now you're fucking Miami PD? You have the authorization to break into someone's place to confirm if they're alive or not?"

"No, of course not," Pete said.

"You are out of your mind," Broche said, his voice lowering to a whisper. "Do you know how much trouble you could be in? If this girl ends up dead somewhere, and we do, God forbid, have to go into her apartment and investigate—do you have any idea how bad it would look if our forensic guys find your fingerprints at her place? Or anywhere in relation to her?"

A drop of sweat slid down Pete's back. He could feel his heart beating in his chest. No, of course he hadn't thought of any of that. This was some wacky adventure that was going to pull him out of his rut. He hadn't stopped to consider real lives were involved. Broche was now leaning over, his palms flat on the desk. His face was red.

"And what the fuck do you know about the Silent Death, kid?" Broche said, his voice now a strained whisper. He looked at his open door, as if expecting the assassin to waltz in and smoke them both any second. "No one works that case. No one. It doesn't exist. You know as well as I do what the deal is. This department has two or three good cops. The rest answer to the wrong sergeant. Understand? I do what little good I can, bide my time until I can retire, y ya. That's all I can do. This is a silent city when it comes to him, Pete. The sooner you realize that, the longer you'll live. No one talks about him. The ones that do end up dead. No one knows shit."

Broche glared at Pete.

"Do you realize what an awkward position you've put me in?" Broche said, his voice a seething whisper. "You broke the law. If I ignore this now, and it comes back to bite me in the ass, it could cost me my badge, my pension." Broche shook his head and straightened up. Pete said nothing.

"I'm going to pretend this conversation never happened," Broche said. "You should, too. You need to tell this asshole Bentley that if he really thinks his daughter is missing, he needs to come down here and explain why. Then we'll send an officer with him to check out her place. Then, and only then, a professional—not some half-assed amateur—will determine if she's missing or if daddy's being a paranoid *pendejo*. Understand?"

Pete felt like a kid again, being lectured for yet another fuck-up. Another suspension at school, another fight after class. He felt ashamed. He got up quickly and headed for the door. He turned to Broche at the last second.

"Look, I'm sorry," Pete said. "I realize I fucked up."

"Just go," Broche said. He seemed dejected, slumped in his chair, no longer looking at Pete. "Do exactly what I told you and never involve yourself in police business again. Do not mention anything about this story you say she's working on. You're putting yourself and everyone around you at risk, even if you're talking bullshit. You're not helping, even if you think you're smarter than everyone else. You're not. Not when it comes to this."

Pete felt his face redden. Sure, he'd made a mistake, but he would bet money on Kathy being in danger, and he wasn't going to disregard that instinct just because he'd fucked up the procedure.

"I know she's missing." Pete said, his voice shaking. "She's in trouble. Whether Chaz tells you or I tell you, it's true. Something is wrong and the longer you wait to start looking for her, the less likely it'll be that she comes out of this alive."

Broche stood up with a quickness that surprised Pete and darted around his desk until they were almost nose to nose. He could hear Broche's labored breathing, see the pores on his face, smell his cologne.

"Tell me one thing, right now," Broche said, pausing between every word. *For emphasis, or was he so angry he could barely speak,* Pete wondered? "How do you think your father would feel, seeing you like this?"

"What?"

"Reeking of alcohol, dressed like a bum," Broche said, his face contorted in a way Pete had never seen before. "It's not even this stupid girl. It's how you look, how you're acting. You're nothing like him. What happened to everything he taught you? Everything he spent his life on? He pulled you out of the gutter and you dive back in the first chance you get?"

Pete had no response. He backed away from Broche. His legs felt wobbly. He held onto the chair he'd been sitting in and looked at Broche, who was looking back, waiting for Pete to respond, to defend himself, but nothing came. Pete nodded at Broche and tried to straighten himself up.

"I'm trying to fix that."

Pete had ordered the vodka soda before he sat down at the bar. It was too early to be drinking, barely noon. Pete didn't care. He was past caring. His job was gone, Emily was gone and his past had just sucker-punched him. It wasn't his father tearing him down, but Broche was a close facsimile, and that hurt Pete in ways he was still processing. The bartender nodded as the glass tapped against the bar and Pete slapped a ten on the counter.

Foggy Notion, hole-in-the-wall that had once been a microbrewery but now sported a full bar, was a quick drive away from the police station and a few blocks from Biscayne. The décor was sparse, the clientele sketchy, and the music good. Pete wondered why he didn't frequent this place. Then he remembered: he and Emily used to. He didn't have to worry about running into her now.

He pulled his phone out and scrolled through his contacts.

He needed to talk to someone. Someone who wasn't tired of the random, midday phone call. Someone who wouldn't ask where he was and then ask how long he'd been drinking. He wanted to bask in being miserable with someone new. Not Emily. He'd feel bad calling Mike again. The yellow highlighted text found Javier's name and Pete clicked his phone to call.

The phone rang two times before Javier picked up.

"Hello?"

"Hey," Pete said, his mind finally catching up to his actions and realizing he was calling someone that — before yesterday — he hadn't spoken to in almost a decade. "It's, uh, it's Pete."

"Oh," Javier said, his voice sounding distant and confused on the other end of the line. "Hey, man. What's up? This is a surprise."

"Yeah, yeah," Pete said, taking a quick gulp from his drink, wincing as he noticed how strong it was. Not much soda water. Mostly vodka. He needed that. "Sorry, I . . . I just wanted to give you an update. Uh, you asked me to keep you updated."

There was a pause on the other line. Pete heard some rustling.

"Yeah, sure, thanks for calling," Javier said. "Sorry, I was doing some stuff outside. I'm at my place now. What's up? You mean an update about Kathy?"

"Well, sort of," Pete said. "I went to the police to file a report."

"Why?"

Pete ignored the question and pressed on. "It turns out Chaz never even called to say he thought she was missing," Pete said. "There was no record of a report." He polished off his drink and motioned to the bartender for another one. His need was quickly met.

"I don't think she's missing," Javier said. Pete thought he sounded slightly agitated. "But good for you to double-check."

"It's just weird Chaz would tell me he called the cops when he didn't, you know?" Pete said. "This whole thing is really strange."

"Yeah, I don't get it," Javier said, sounding concerned. "I mean, Kathy does this all the time. We'll talk, fight, then she'll go away for a while. I'd start worrying if it'd been a few weeks, but it just seems like she's off doing her thing. That's kind of how we operate."

"Yeah," Pete said. "Everyone's different. I just think I'm done with this whole thing. Whatever concerns Chaz had are in the police's hands, not mine."

"Yeah, definitely," Javier said. "It's not your problem. I mean, it's great you're concerned, man, it is. But Kathy's a big girl."

"Yeah," Pete said. He took another long swig from his glass. He felt the initial light-headedness that comes with drinking hard liquor too quickly. He didn't want the feeling to end.

"You there?"

Pete snapped out of his reverie.

"Yeah, yeah," Pete said. "I was just thinking about what a shitty few days it's been."

Javier didn't respond immediately.

"Sorry to hear that," he said. "But hey, at least we got back in touch after so long. It's good to talk to you, bro. Where the hell are you?"

Pete let out a dry laugh.

"In a bar."

"Shit, this early? It's barely lunchtime."

"Yeah," Pete said. "I dunno. I needed a drink."

"Wow," Javier said. "It has been a rough week, huh? I'd swing over and join you, but I've gotta head to work in a few minutes. Have a few for me, though."

"You got it."

"And thanks for keeping tabs on this," Javier said. Pete noted the sincerity in his voice. A tone he hadn't heard in a long time. "I realize Kathy's nuts, but she doesn't have many people looking out for her. I think she'd be touched in her own weird way if she knew you were."

"Well, that's good," Pete said, his hand slowly turning his glass.

They said their goodbyes and hung up. Pete thought he should feel better, but didn't. Without his job, he'd at least had this to keep him entertained and moving forward. With Kathy a police matter now, he had nothing. His eyes scanned the labels on the bottles watching him from across the bar. He nodded at them silently.

He had to deal with Chaz Bentley, he realized. Well, deal with him inasmuch as he had to tell him the matter was now in the hands of the authorities. Pete wasn't looking forward to the discussion, but if he was going to pull himself together in some way, he had to clear the deck of things that were not his concern. Like Kathy. Chaz. Whoever the Silent Death was or is. He laughed to himself. What had made him think he could even help find someone? Someone who probably wasn't even missing, he mused. He roughly rubbed his hand across his face. He felt like shit. He ordered another drink. The bar was now fully empty aside from Pete and the bartender. He looked out the dusty and greasy window and saw an empty street.

CHAPTER SIXTEEN

The sound of the flushing toilet echoed through Pete's tiny apartment as he slowly made his way to his couch. His eyes were half-closed as he collapsed on the sofa. It was close to four in the morning. He'd only gotten home about 20 minutes prior and had made a beeline to empty what little food he'd had in his system. He was such a seasoned drinker that throwing up was a rarity. But tonight — this morning, rather — had been one of those exceptions. He smelled of cigarettes and vodka. His clothes felt sticky and his breath stank of liquored bile. He didn't care. He noticed the cardboard box on his living room table, containing his father's files and who knew what else. He only felt the urge to rummage through them when he was like this—drunk, alone, feeling sorry for himself. He pulled out his phone and checked his outgoing calls. No, not this time. He hadn't made his usual mistake of calling Emily. He let out a quick sigh of and tossed the phone on the other end of the small couch.

"What would your father say if he saw you now?"

Broche's words rang in Pete's head. A constant drone merging with the throbbing hangover that was sure to consume him in a few hours. His self-pity had dissolved into a drunken anger with each new sip of alcohol, and by now, Pete was not only lucky to be home, but lucky he hadn't been kicked out of the last bar he'd visited, a tiny beer venue on the beach called Zeke's. Pete remembered a heated conversation—with the bartender? The driver of the cab the bartender had forced him to take? He wasn't sure. He didn't care. He kicked out angrily from the couch, aiming for the table, a gift from Emily while they were dating. Instead, his foot connected with his father's box, the missed connection causing him to slide off the couch and onto the floor, sending the box and its contents splayed across the budget brown carpet. Pete half-crawled to the area next to the table where most of the papers had accumulated. He felt pathetic. Here he was, close to dawn, crawling across his carpet after puking his guts out, picking up what little remained of his father's memory because he'd drunkenly kicked it over.

"Jesus, stop feeling sorry for yourself," he said aloud, grabbing piles of papers and stacking them on the table. "Get it together, man."

It was all stuff he'd seen before. Copies of police reports his father probably wasn't supposed to have, the incomplete Silent Death file and a few errant Post-it notes. But as he moved another stack of papers into the box, a manila envelope slipped loose from between two of the standard case files, landing awkwardly on the floor. Pete dropped the papers in his hands into the box and grabbed the envelope. In rough, block handwriting — not his father's, Pete noted — someone had written "FERNANDEZ MISC." on the outsic Pete carefully removed the tape lining the opening and undic the metal latch. Inside were a few more forms — police reports. Alongside them was a small, leather-bound beige book. Pete emptied the contents of the envelope on the couch and sat down next to the new discovery to investigate.

The police reports were a strange collection, Pete thought. None were filled out by his father, and they were all clearly copies of reports his father had pulled from other files. But that wasn't what caught Pete's eye. It was the names of the suspects. One, from about 10 years prior, was an arrest record for Charles "Chaz" Bentley — drunk and disorderly. Chaz had been arrested outside the Clevelander — a ritzy bar on Ocean Drive that Pete had trouble even picturing Chaz at. According to the report, Chaz had been kicked out of the bar after he threatened one of the bar's patrons, who was not identified. Chaz was described as a "noted newspaper writer for the *Miami Times*. Rumored to also be in great debt to certain criminal elements. No hard evidence to support this yet." Pete reread the information. His headache had kicked in, but he refused to make the same mistake he made the last time he perused his father's papers. Something was happening. There were strands of information dangling around him, Pete thought, and he just needed to look at them all before deciding which ones to pull on. He pushed the alcoholic drowsiness away. Curiosity was winning this fight.

The beige notebook was definitely his father's and seemed like something close to a diary. Dated entries — none longer than a few lines or pages, went as far back as a decade. Pete skimmed over the book's worn pages until his eyes fell on one date.

ptember 19, 1996. Just a few days after the incident with Pete and avier at the convenience store. Pete felt his shoulders sag, but he continued to read.

9/19/96

The boy continues to confuse me. I realize his mother's gone, but I've provided for everything else, and he's still proving to be a problem. This incident is the last straw. I have to watch everything he does. I make sure he goes into his class in the morning. I check with him during the day to make sure he's still at school. I pick him up after class. Bring him with me to work. It's an ordeal. He resents me for it. I can see it in his tone and how he acts. But someday he'll understand, I hope. Maybe when he figures out what to do with himself. Not a cop, though. Something a little more dignified. But what kind of world will this be? Not sure. I see a lot of terrible things every day. I pray he won't have to.

I've lost touch with his friend — Javier. The kid had no family to speak of, so he was taken into state custody. The store owner, Alfredo Florin, was intent on pressing charges. Pete — when he decides he is talking to me — tells me there's an uncle that might take him in. I should have. But that would never fly. Still, I can't help but feel like I've failed that young man. I pray God will forgive me. It's hard enough raising my own son. I hope he finds the right path. — PF

Pete continued to stare at the page long after he'd finished reading it. He felt his eyes welling up. Not from sadness. No, from some pride he'd denied himself for too long. He carefully put the journal down on the table, next to the box, for further reading.

He sat on the couch and looked toward his window. Dawn was near. Bits of light would be creeping into the house soon. He had nowhere to be tomorrow. He had nothing to do. Reading his father's written words — something unfamiliar yet comfortable — had left Pete with a strange, nostalgic feeling. What would his father think? He wasn't sure yet.

"There's still time," he said, under his breath, turning to the remaining papers on the couch. He'd finish these today. Now.

Another report seemed fairly nondescript, aside from the name. Jose Contreras. Owner of Casa Pepe's. It was dated about five years previous. Contreras was under investigation after a former employee complained about mistreatment at Casa Pepe's, claiming Contreras favored certain employees, and was verbally and physically abusive towards others. The report was long, from what Pete could tell, at least in comparison to some of the others in the box. This one was written by a name Pete didn't recognize — Bill Sheffield. He walked over to the tiny desk in his bedroom and rummaged for a notebook. He found one of his old reporter's notepads and grabbed a pen before returning to the couch. He began jotting down quick notes. Chaz. Clevelander. Contreras — abusive to certain employees? He kept reading — according to the final update on the file, no charges had been filed as there wasn't enough evidence to charge Contreras with a crime, but the ancillary text, summing up the employee's complaints, made for interesting reading nonetheless.

The disgruntled employee — also benefiting from the work release program Javier would eventually become a part of — claimed Contreras did little actual work, and instead spent most of his time meeting with out-of-town contacts in a back room of the restaurant. He mentioned seeing Contreras often leave with a new bag or suitcase, which led him to believe that an exchange of some kind was going on. Pete saw random notes scribbled on the photocopied police report. This handwriting he recognized — his father's. But why was his father collecting police reports about other cases? Cases that weren't even murders? Pete wasn't sure, until he reached the last page of the Contreras report, where he saw the restaurant owner's name circled, with a quick note written in the margin next to it. Pete felt his temperature drop, as if a cold breeze had made its way into his small, cramped apartment:

Silent Death?

CHAPTER SEVENTEEN

Pete awoke to a familiar sound — this time in stereo. His cat and his new roommate were crying at Pete's feet, each louder than the last. Pete let out a groan as he realized where he was. On the couch. In the clothes he'd worn for most of the day yesterday. He looked at his watch. It was close to noon. He'd slept away the morning. He bolted up and wandered to the kitchen, the two cats not far behind. He felt slow and ragged — fallout from the night's drinking. But his wheels were turning. Before he'd passed out on his couch in the minutes before dawn, the pieces had seemed to fit together. He kicked himself for not writing his conclusions down. His father thought Jose Contreras, the owner of Casa Pepe's, might be the Silent Death. Detective Pedro Fernandez had also thought Chaz Bentley of interest enough to pull an old police report involving Chaz's drunk and disorderly conduct for reference. Pete opened a few cans of food for the cats and set them on the floor, barely paying attention as the two tiny animals gorged themselves. His mind was elsewhere. For whatever reason, Chaz wanted Pete to look for Kathy — not the police. Chaz also got extremely agitated when Pete mentioned going to Casa Pepe's and interacting with Contreras. Why hadn't Chaz reported Kathy missing? What was it about Contreras that scared Chaz? And why did his father think Chaz was someone worth checking out in relation to the Silent Death? Pete had none of those answers. But he did have questions — some that even the good cops, like Carlos Broche, might not have considered yet. All this bounced around Pete's head as he tossed his shirt and then the rest of his clothes into the growing pile of laundry in his bedroom and headed for the shower. He had to talk to Broche again, even if the idea of interacting with the person that had dressed him down so severely less than a day ago seemed like anathema. But first, he was going to confront Chaz Bentley. Pete felt the hot water slap his face and body as he stepped into the shower, the bathroom slowly filling with steam. He felt awake. He had something to do.

The drive to Chaz's house had been smooth sailing until Pete reached the "city" of North Lauderdale — a tiny municipality in western Broward that was closer to a town. He hadn't bothered to check for directions online before he left his apartment, instead foolishly relying on his own memory — he had worked around the area as a reporting intern during college — to guide him to Chaz's apartment. Now he was lost. He called Chaz for the third time. No answer. Was he asleep? Not there? Pete turned down the volume of his car stereo, which was now on the second play-through of Neko Case's *Blacklisted* album. He needed to concentrate. He turned in to a strip mall — featuring a 7-Eleven, a Payless shoe store, and a small laundromat — and parked. He looked at the crumpled business card he'd had in his pocket. "Charles Bentley — Columnist." On the back, in Chaz's drunken scrawl from a few nights before, was his address and cell phone. Pete noticed another car entering the strip mall through his rearview. It was a black Nissan Sentra. It drove past where Pete was parked and out the other exit. *Odd*, Pete thought. *The exit led to a complex of apartments, nothing more. Maybe it was a shortcut?* Pete shrugged and stared at the card for another second before he heard his phone ring. He pulled it out of his pocket, expecting it to be Chaz. Instead, it was the last person he really wanted to talk to.

"Hello?"

"Pete, it's Carlos."

"Oh, hey."

"Where are you?"

"I'm in North Lauderdale. Trying to find Chaz's apartment," Pete said, turning the business card over in his hand.

"What?"

"I was going to tell him I'm done looking for Kathy," Pete said, defensively. "Like we talked about." The last thing Pete wanted was another verbal lashing from Broche. He was still recovering from the first.

"I need you to get over here," Broche said, his voice low and rushed. "Right now."

"Shit, what the hell is going on?" Pete said, annoyed at the idea of having to drive back to downtown Miami with his task undone. "I am literally right by his place, so it's going to take me a while to get back to Miami, I just need to find —"

"I'm at Chaz's," Broche said, choosing his words carefully. "You need to get here. Now."

The scene at Chaz's apartment building was subdued — at least compared to the crime scenes Pete had seen on television and the few he remembered as a kid, peering out from the back of his father's car as his dad went to work. Pete could easily tell which apartment was Chaz's by the bright yellow tape cordoning off the entrance and adjacent areas. He got out of his car quickly, having parked in the empty lot across the street, and walked over briskly. He saw Broche heading toward him, and they met a few feet from the tape. Pete didn't expect any good news.

"That was fast," Broche said, his hands in his pocket. Gone was the cheerful uncle that embraced him when he came into the police station. This was a seasoned homicide detective looking at, worst-case scenario, a possible suspect, at best, a nuisance. "Thanks for coming."

"What the hell is happening?" Pete said, short of breath for some reason.

"I'm going to ask you a few questions," Broche said. "Because, to be frank, this looks strange."

"What is going on?"

"Where were you last night?"

Pete was taken aback. He paused for a second.

"Is Chaz in there? Is he dead?"

Pete's genuine surprise seemed to soften Broche's features slightly. His mind was more at ease. But he pressed on.

"Where were you last night?"

Pete stuck his hands in his pocket and pulled out a crumpled piece of paper. He tossed it at Broche. The older detective grabbed it before it hit the ground. He unfolded the receipt and scanned the time stamp.

"Zeke's at 3 a.m.?" Broche said, his eyebrows raised slightly. "Still drunk?"

Pete didn't respond. He kept his hands in his pockets.

Broche slipped the receipt in his pocket.

"Chaz is dead," Broche said. "At some point last night someone came into his apartment and shot him."

Pete's brow furrowed. He couldn't process the information fast enough. He had just been on his way to talk to Chaz and now he was dead. Just a few days prior, he'd sat with him at the Abbey, having the conversation that started all of this. His job, memories of his father, and now someone was dead. Pete swallowed.

"How did he die?"

"I told you," Broche said, "He was shot."

"Two in the head?"

Broche's eyes met Pete's, confusion in them.

"How the hell did you know that?"

"It's the Silent Death, isn't it?"

Broche coughed and grabbed Pete by the elbow, walking with him away from the crime scene and further out of earshot.

"Shut the fuck up about that," Broche said, his voice low. "You have no idea who's listening here."

Pete lowered his voice.

"Well, is it?"

"I don't know," Broche said. "It has all the earmarks. Two shots to the head. No witnesses talking about gunshot noises, which points to a silencer being used. Our medical guys seem to think it happened in the evening, considering the scene, which is his M.O." Broche looked around, toward the yellow tape before continuing. "Look, we can't talk about this for long. But I wanted to call you — to warn you. If this is who it looks like, then you're in trouble, too. Whatever you've been sniffing around is not good. You need to step back. Take a vacation. Go away for a while. And definitely, definitely quit this shit. I can't think of a better reason to back off than this.

"This isn't about finding this girl anymore," Broche said, his words quick. He was pacing around Pete. He was nervous. "This is about staying alive. Whoever found Chaz knows what you've been doing, too."

"Do you think it's Contreras?"

"What?"

"I've read the reports," Pete said, no longer worried about upsetting Broche. He wanted to hear what the detective thought. He needed more insight than he could provide himself. "I know my dad thought Contreras was the guy. I think he might have been right."

"Why's that?" Broche said. "I'm not even going to ask how you got to those."

"Chaz was arrested a few years ago for harassing someone at a bar on South Beach," Pete said, surprised at his facility with the information he'd read the night before. "The Clevelander's a nice joint. Fancy. For people with money to burn. And from what I've read, Contreras has got some stuff going on outside of just running Casa Pepe's. Maybe the kind of stuff that puts schlubs like Chaz Bentley in his debt."

Broche cleared his throat and pursed his lips. He was thinking.

"Ok, hotshot, fair enough," he said, turning to the crime scene but still talking to Pete. "So why kill Chaz Bentley now?"

"Because he fucked up," Pete said. "He shared too much information with some has-been newspaper editor, who has nothing better to do than sniff around Contreras' operation."

Broche turned around, concern in his eyes.

"You reminded me of your father for a second," Broche said. He cleared his throat. "Sure, you may know what the score is, but whoever did this," he said, waving his arm toward the crime scene, "can do a lot worse to you."

Pete nodded.

Broche grabbed his arm. "No one is going to help you with this," Broche said. "No one is on the other side of this guy except me, and I can't do much. If you expect the Miami PD to do anything, you've already lost. This city doesn't speak his name."

"I know," Pete said, shaking off Broche's grip. "I've heard all the stories. We don't even know this is him, though."

"You just put the pieces together yourself," Broche said. "Now you're having doubts?"

"I guess once the rush of figuring it out faded away, I realized I could be dead any minute now."

CHAPTER EIGHTEEN

Pete pushed the security chime at the *Miami Times* employee entrance after realizing that his security pass had ceased to work, as Vance had said over the phone when he was suspending him. He waved and put on a smile as he saw Gustavo, the *Times'* elderly security guard, make his way to the door. He didn't wave back.

Gustavo pushed the intercom button, his eyes squinting at Pete. "Your pass not working?"

"Guess not," Pete said, waving it in front of the two-way glass for some reason. "Probably been in my car too long."

Gustavo nodded in disagreement, his movements slow and deliberate. "No," he said in his accented English. "Your pass was deactivated. I saw you last week. Worked fine."

Shit. He'd hoped for a few things to fall into place when — on his way home from the crime scene surrounding Chaz's apartment —

he'd decided to go back to the Times building. One was that his access card still worked. Another, in lieu of a working card, was that he'd be able to charm Gustavo, into letting him in. His plan was falling apart.

"It's weird," Pete said, talking louder than usual because of the glass between them. "I guess it just stopped working. Can you let me in?"

Gustavo nodded "No" again, pulling out a reporter's notebook from his back pocket. Inside the notebook was a folded piece of paper with printed text on it. Gustavo slowly unfolded it and turned it so Pete could see the text. It was a list of names, mostly people from his department. He figured the numbers were identification codes of some kind. His name was highlighted.

"You're not here anymore," Gustavo said. "Bosses say your pass not working. No pass, no entry."

Pete started to turn back, but stopped himself. He approached the glass window, hands up.

"Look, Gustavo," Pete said, making a point of using the guard's name, hoping the sense of familiarity would help his cause, "I just need to get a few things from my desk. I wouldn't bother you if it wasn't important. I just have a few pictures of my ex in there and . . . I know this sounds terrible, but it'd mean a lot to me to get them back."

Gustavo kept his eyes locked on Pete. He nodded, almost imperceptibly, before turning the door handle and opening the security entrance. Pete walked through and half-bowed, sheepishly.

"You hurry up," Gustavo said. Pete felt a pang of guilt for playing to the wizened security guard's kindness. "I get in major trouble if bosses know I did this."

"I know," Pete said, pushing the elevator button that would send him upstairs. "Thank you."

Gustavo returned to his post and Pete waited impatiently for the elevator, the beeping sound that signaled each floor the only noise in the poorly lit entrance.

The third floor was empty and dark when Pete got off the elevator. He'd chosen the floor — which housed mostly ad sales representatives and the business people who worked standard 9-to-5 schedules — because the last thing he needed was to run into a coworker, much less one who'd wonder why he was snooping around the *Times*. He made an immediate left and tried the first set of offices — ONLINE AD SALES. Locked. He walked down the hall and tried the next door — CLASSIFIED ADS. The door creaked open. Pete looked around quickly, noticed no one, and slipped into the office.

The room was relatively small, with a few cubicles stationed in the middle of the room and two locked offices on the west side. Pete decided against turning on the main light and slid into the nearest terminal. He scanned the computer — which was archaic and probably slow, much like his old work computer — and cautiously booted it up. While he waited for the machine to wheeze into existence, he pulled out a tiny black book from his front pocket. Kathy's address book. He flipped to the back of the book and folded it slightly to keep it from closing on itself. He waited for the usual login screen to appear on the computer monitor, prompting him to sign into the *Miami Times* internal editing server and employee network. But instead of using his own username and password, which, he guessed, had been deactivated along with his security pass, he carefully typed in the login and password from Kathy's book, hoping that he'd guessed correctly what the two words were. The slightly loud whirr coming from the old computer confirmed that Pete was right, and the login screen went blank and morphed into something else. The screen was still monochromatic, which reminded Pete of his computer classes in middle school. The *Times'* Usenet, or SCI as the tech support guys called it, was basically just a glorified file-sharing network, where a reporter or editor had his own private "basket" of files, either stories in progress, notes or miscellaneous text, and a number of public baskets. Depending on where a story was in the editing process, it could be in one of any number of baskets, from "Slot," meaning it was in the hands of the duty editor to "1A," meaning it was edited and ready to be placed on the front page. But Pete was very familiar with SCI and knew that the most interesting stories were the ones tucked away, either in reporters' private files or in the kind of baskets no one really bothered with, like "Enterprise," which was just a fancy way of saying it was a story you, as a reporter, had decided to research or begin working on without much editorial guidance. It was there that Pete started.

Since he was logged in as Kathy, he could not only access and view any folders that were public to all editors and reporters in the system, he also had access to areas that were restricted to news staffers and areas that were for Kathy and her administrator's eyes only. The Enterprise folder was barren, Pete discovered. Thinking about it for a moment, he figured not many reporters would want their work in a relatively public place before it was final. With a few clicks he was in a basket labeled "KBENTLEY." Kathy's private area. It was littered with files, about 30. Some were obvious, like "browardcourts09notes." But what would the title to her big, unfinished story be? Pete scanned the folder for the obvious choices. No "Silent Death." No "Miami Murderer." No "Contreras." After a few minutes he'd clicked on almost every file in the main KBENTLEY folder when he went back and found a subfolder, which he'd previously ignored as irrelevant. It was titled "Published Stories/Old Notes." He'd disregarded it because he knew this story hadn't been published — but it would be a good place to put a story you didn't want anyone to find very quickly, Pete thought.

He double-clicked on the sub-folder and found another handful of files. Most were, in fact, notes for stories Kathy had written. A recap of a double murder in Hialeah. A convenience store robbery in Opa-Locka. An interview with the outgoing police chief from three months' back. Pete was getting frustrated. That's when he heard the footsteps. He couldn't tell which direction they were coming from, but he'd definitely heard them. Whoever was outside wasn't walking in a straight line, but stopping and starting. Probably to avoid being discovered. Pete turned the monitor off with a quick push of a button and knelt down by his desk, which gave him a view of the office door, but also gave him cover.

Who would be wandering this floor so late in the day? Pete had no idea, but whoever it was didn't want to be found. He waited. A few minutes passed and the silence persisted. The hum of the computer was the only sound Pete could make out. He tried to keep his breathing low and calm. He let another minute pass before he got back on his chair and turned to face the computer, his ears still on full alert.

Pete tried to focus. He turned the monitor on and took a

moment to scan the dark office. Empty. The noises had been nothing, he thought. Probably a custodian or someone trying to catch up on work.

He went back to the subfolder and continued to scan the list of file names. All were fairly standard, and obviously were for stories that had already run — except one. Titled 'Groceries,' the file seemed innocent enough, but from what Pete could tell, it was also the file most recently edited by the user KBENTLEY. Pete double-clicked the file icon and waited for it to load.

After a few seconds — which implied the file was relatively large, especially for the slow computer to process — the file was open on the screen. This wasn't any grocery list, Pete thought to himself as he scanned the file. It was roughly organized, bits and pieces of commentary in red text, embedded into a loosely structured story. It was well-written, though, and would eventually become a great story. If it ever got published. This was what he was looking for. Pete glanced at the clock hanging over the main windows across the office. It was close to seven in the evening. He'd been in the Times building for close to an hour. The longer he stayed, the more he risked running into someone who knew he wasn't supposed to be around. He sent the file to print and began to turn away from the computer when he decided to take one extra precaution, one that might leave a bit of a trail, but would keep the information in his hands in case the paper itself was lost. He pulled out a tiny portable USB drive and plugged it into the computer. Once the computer recognized the hardware, he dragged the file onto the drive and disconnected it.

As he heard the first of about 40 pages begin to print across the room, Pete continued to skim the paragraphs of Kathy's story.

It was all in here — and more. While she agreed with his father's notes inasmuch as they both thought Contreras was involved, she didn't seem to see him as the Silent Death himself. Pete frowned. Not exactly what he was hoping for. The files painted the Silent Death as a unique commodity in the Miami underworld. A freelancer who, for the right price, took out other gang leaders and henchmen. He'd somehow managed to keep his identity secret, which in turn helped him stay alive and also be able to live some semblance of a normal life. According to Kathy's notes, the man who was the Silent Death also made a decent amount of money from a secondary business, laundering money for gangs and smaller drug dealing organizations in northern Florida, including Orlando and outlying areas like Titusville. The gangs would bring the money in and through outposts like Casa Pepe's, which was owned by Contreras. The money would come back out, written off, "clean" and ready to be used to further the respective drug operations. For a fee, of course. The laundering—though secondary according to Kathy, and spearheaded by Contreras — was run from the Keys, where the Casa Pedro owner had a number of real estate holdings, most notably a cluster of bungalows in Key West. Waterford Resorts, near the main strip on Duval Street. Pete pulled out the tiny black book he'd taken from Kathy's apartment and jotted down the name. If Key West was the heart of Contreras' operation, and Contreras was possibly the Silent Death, Pete couldn't think of a better place to start looking for Kathy.

The story went on, outlining the history of the Silent Death. A black-suited killer who wore a black mask and only appeared at night, the Silent Death was responsible for a string of murders dating as far back as seven years. His influence, in addition to aiding and colluding with gangs across the state, cast a shadow over the only force entrusted to bring him in, the Miami Police Department. Through a combination of payoffs and murders, the Silent Death had made himself immune to investigation and thus to arrest. Kathy noted in her text that over 60 percent of the force was actively taking money from either the Silent Death or Miami gangs who regularly employed him as a hitman. The last bit was italicized. She still needed more facts to support this line. Pete was impressed by Kathy's tenacity. She had a number of city officials on record, some retired and long gone from Miami, and it was obvious she'd done a fair amount of legwork, probably on her own time. But a key piece was missing. The first paragraph, which, as in any passable news story, was tasked with setting the stage for the entire piece, didn't have the key bit of info Pete was hoping for: the identity of the Silent Death. Instead, it was a list of names, some of whom Pete was unfamiliar with. Contreras was on the list, followed by a series of question marks. *She wasn't sure about him either,* Pete thought.

"Is he or isn't he?" Pete whispered under his breath. The signs pointed to it — the illicit meetings and funds, Chaz's murder, Contreras's antsy behavior when Pete arrived. He wasn't sure, though. Not yet. He didn't have time to sit and read the entire file here; and he didn't want to be discovered hacking into the *Times* system if he could avoid it. The computers would show that someone logged in as Kathy Bentley, but there was no way of tracing it back to him, unless they figured out the terminal and also decided to talk to Gustavo, Pete reasoned. He was covered, for the most part. He shut the computer off and walked over to the printer. He drummed his fingers on the machine as it spit out the last few pages. He grabbed a few extra blank pages and put them on top of the pile of papers. He found a manila folder, slid the pages in and gave the office another quick once-over before stepping out into the hallway. The printer's clicks and zips as it shut down echoed in the empty room.

Well, whatever problems Steve Vance had, they don't matter," Pete said into his phone as he fumbled around in his pockets, looking for the keys to his apartment. Emily was on the other line. They hadn't spoken since they had drinks at the Pub a few nights before. But a call from Emily was no longer routine to Pete. He had to remind himself of this each time they did talk.

"It doesn't matter?" she said, exasperation in her voice. "You've lost your job. What are you going to do once the suspension is up and all you have is severance?"

"Don't know yet," Pete said as he opened the door and walked into his dark apartment. Costello and Kathy's gray cat mewed in anticipation. "Stop your crying, you'll get fed."

"What?"

"Talking to the cats. I have no idea what I'm doing. I guess I'll start looking for work while I'm still getting paid. Maybe I should be a detective?"

Pete heard silence on the other end. "I'm kidding."

"I never know with you," Emily said. "What are you doing tonight? And since when do you have two cats?"

"No plans, why?" Pete said, ignoring her second question.

"Want to grab dinner?" she said. "Rick's stuck at work and we haven't really talked in a while."

"We hung out a few nights ago, what are you talking about?"

"Yeah," she said. "But you were wasted and Mike was there. You always act different in groups. So, yea or nay?"

"Yeah, sounds good," Pete said, dropping his keys back into his pocket. The two cats, who dealt with each other with general indifference, continued to follow him into his bedroom. "I'll be there in a couple hours. I just want to relax a bit and maybe take a nap."

"OK, just don't come here already wasted," she warned. Pete bit his tongue.

"I'm not going to be wasted," Pete said. The cats both looked toward the front door at the same time. They must have heard something, Pete thought. "I'll see you at nine-thirty. It's almost eight now."

"Ok, cool, see you then."

Pete tossed his phone on his desk along with the printouts from Kathy's file and sat down on the edge of his bed. He placed the portable USB drive in his nightstand. He slid his hand through his dark hair and scanned the mess that was his room. Huge pile of laundry. A stack of unread novels on the nightstand. The lights from his stereo blinking. Things needed to be organized, he thought, and not just material ones. He was still processing what just happened. Chaz was dead. Whatever was left of his career was probably equally dead. But Kathy was still missing. And now, because of Pete's growing certainty that the so-called Silent Death was involved, he knew the Miami Police would be of little help when it came to finding her.

Pete felt a strange mix of fear and relief. He had no choice, he reasoned. If he didn't look for her, no one would. Right?

He noticed the cats were no longer in his room. That was odd, he thought. They usually pestered him incessantly until they were fed. He heard a soft thud at the door. He got up and walked back to his living room. What now? A delivery? He looked out the front door's eye hole and saw nothing. He started to turn around when his door swung open.

Pete felt outside his body for a moment, as he watched the dark figure enter his apartment. He was wearing a black trenchcoat, fedora, and dark glasses. He seemed stocky and he had a gun in his right hand. He was looking straight at Pete as he closed the door. Pete backed into his apartment. His mind raced. He felt a surreal calm spread over his body. This was probably it, he thought. The years of backyard brawls and high school fist fights would be of little service when facing off against an assassin, Pete thought. He took the few moments left and scanned the figure. He was bigger than Pete had imagined him. His face was hard to make out, shadows masking his features. He was breathing heavily. There was a slight sheen of sweat on his face. Pete wondered where he'd put his father's gun.

He felt the growl of the killer's voice before he spoke. His gravelly speech sent a shiver through Pete.

"You've made a mistake," the Silent Death said, raising his gun hand, but not yet pointing it directly at Pete. He thought he sensed a slight Spanish accent when the Death spoke, but that revealed little.

"Who are you?"

"Don't you know?"

"I think you should leave," Pete said, almost laughing after he spoke. Yeah, he's going to just turn and leave based on my suggestion. He needed to do something drastic.

"I don't think so," the killer said, finally raising the gun to Pete's head. They were a few feet apart. Pete felt a cold sweat overcome him. He tried to look away, but couldn't. "You have something I want. Information."

The noises at the *Miami Times*. There had been someone there, after all.

"I've got no idea what you're talking about," Pete said, barely able to get the words out before he felt the handle of the gun smash him across the face, sending him down to the ground. He propped himself up, trying to recover, his hands sliding over his mouth full blood.

"Don't play stupid," the Death said. The gravel tone of his voice had faded, replaced by a more normal-sounding, vaguely familiar one. "Give me the files and I'll make this as painless as possible."

"Well, you sure know how to sell a man on something," Pete said, getting up slowly, his left hand still on his face, rubbing where he'd been hit, his other hand raised defensively. "The files are in my room. You can have them. I haven't even read them yet." He wondered how far the lie would get him.

The Death cocked his head and motioned toward Pete's room with the gun.

"Go get them," he said. The gravel voice was back. He seemed antsy, Pete thought, almost nervous.

Pete backed into his room and walked over to his desk, which was out of the Death's line of sight. He scanned his desk for anything that could help. That's when he saw the box of his father's files. The gun. He crouched down and rummaged through the box, finding the police issue Glock near the bottom. He slid it behind his back, resting it on the waistband of his jeans. Pete whispered a silent prayer, even though he never prayed.

He walked back into the living room and held out the large stack of papers, out of reach.

The Silent Death looked at Pete for a second. He hesitated before stepping toward him. Pete felt the gun sliding, the sweat trickling down his back making it hard to keep it in place.

"Who else knows about these files?" the Death asked.

"No one," Pete responded truthfully. "Where's Kathy?"

The Death hesitated before responding, raising his arm so the gun was pointed directly at Pete's head. He paused, as if wondering if he should even elaborate on the point.

"She's dead," he said. Pete could sense a slight uptick in his tone, as if he were enjoying the revelation. His heart sank. "Her stupid father is dead, too. You're next. Then my deck is clear for a little while."

"All this pro bono work must be driving you nuts," Pete said, stalling. "Did you think you'd be able to ride this train forever? I mean, sooner or later, someone else is going to find her computer files — you realize this, don't you?"

"Oh, I'm not worried about that," the Death said, a sneer working its way across what little Pete could see of his face. "In fact, you're my only immediate concern."

He noticed the slight twitch of the Death's hand, as if in slow motion. Pete had little time to think. Again, he felt himself detached from his body, as if he were watching a movie absentmindedly while doing something else. He saw himself lunge at the killer, knocking his hand up. He heard the silencer's pop, and he felt himself fall atop the Death. They rolled around his apartment floor. He felt his hand gripping the killer's gun hand, pulling and pushing it as far away as possible, keenly aware that even a grazing shot would guarantee tonight would be his last on earth.

The Death groaned as he hit the ground, cursing to himself, shoving Pete off him. Pete tried to hold on, but a swift knee in the groin, followed by an elbow to the face sent him reeling, his back slamming into the wall opposite the apartment's main windows. The Death got up slowly, his hat on the floor. That's when Pete recognized him. The curly black hair. The sweaty, greasy face. The long scar running down the left side of it. Contreras. Contreras was the Silent Death. His father had been right. Kathy had been right.

He couldn't die here.

He didn't think before he pulled the gun from his back, pointing it squarely at Contreras, who was in turn pointing his gun at Pete. His eyes widened slightly at the sight of Pete's gun. He was surprised, but also impressed.

"Huh, nice one, kid," Contreras said, wiping sweat from his forehead with his free hand. "You're not as much of a pussy as I thought you were."

"Get the fuck out of here," Pete said, his eyes locked on Contreras.

Contreras smiled. "Well, look at the brave little shit," he said, his grip tightening around his weapon. He stepped closer. Pete felt his hand shaking, the gun getting heavier. "You think this is a game? You can just pick up and start sniffing around where you don't belong? I own this city, *papo*. You're just a fly on the wall. A fly I'm killing with a brick instead of a swatter."

Pete swallowed and kept his gun pointed at Contreras. *Keep him talking. Let him blow out some hot air. Anything to delay more bullets being fired.* Contreras took another step closer to Pete. He was less than a foot away.

"You're just avoiding the inevitable," Contreras said. "So, you did it. The son of the dead detective turns out to be a decent detective himself. Who cares? You get to go to the grave knowing who I am. But your dad's still dead, you're still a loser, and the girl you were supposed to find is still gone. Sounds like a Pete Fernandez special, huh?"

Pete lunged at Contreras, fueled more by rage than any kind of logic. It was a dangerous miscalculation. Contreras saw it coming — hell, he'd probably planned it that way — and stepped slightly to the side, allowing Pete's momentum to take him right into Contreras's waiting knee, which slammed into Pete's gut and sent him to the ground. His hand hit the cheap brown carpet and he heard the gun rattle out of reach.

He felt Contreras grab him by the shirt and lift him up. He smelled Contreras' breath — a mix of Cuban food and cheap whiskey. He was getting dizzy. He couldn't remember the last time he'd been in a fist-fight, and he was certain he hadn't won. It took him a second to feel his body being thrown toward his couch, another moment before he registered his head slamming into the wall as he slid down to the ground in a heap.

"Who else knows about these files?" Contreras asked as he walked toward Pete, hovering over him.

"I have no idea, I told you." Pete felt the fist slam into his midsection before he could finish his sentence. He felt his body curl into a fetal position as Contreras' knee crashed into his jaw, sending him back to the floor, face first. He tried to scrunch his body into a tighter ball, protecting himself from more blows. None came. He felt blood drip out of his mouth. He couldn't breathe.

"I'm going to enjoy destroying you." Pete felt Contreras' spittle hit the back of his neck as he closed his eyes, trying to shut out the pain. What a failure. What a disaster he had made of his life. This was how it was going to end? Curled up in a ball, crying and about to die at the hands of some kind of boogeyman serial assassin? His mind wandered. Back to his old house. Coming home from middle school with a fat lip. He'd swung at a bully who'd beaten up his friend Steve Carvajal. The bully relished destroying Pete in front of his friends and classmates. His teachers. He was humiliated. His father had been silent as he picked Pete up from school, the suspension immediate and unforgiving, as Pete had swung first. Pete remembered his father's car quietly pulling into the carport of their house. How his father slowly shut the engine off and turned to face Pete, his eyes sharp and unblinking. Pete expected a verbal lashing, a physical one, too, but later. His father's eyes softened slightly. "You made a mistake," he said. "You started this fight. That makes you the bully." He raised his hand slightly, feeling Pete begin to protest. "No. Next time, you don't start the fight." He let the words hang over them as they sat silently in the car. Pete seething. Even his father was against him. He felt him getting out of the car. Pete looked over to see his father leaning over the open driver's side door, his eyes still on Pete. "But next time, you finish it."

Another swift kick hit Pete in the back and he screamed in pain, sending the memory back to where it came from.

Pete felt himself being picked up. He let his body go limp. His ribs ached. Broken? He wasn't sure. His breathing was slow and forced. He felt himself being propped up in front of Contreras. He could feel him close, all cheap cologne and heavy breathing. Pete coughed and felt blood speckle out of his mouth. He was dizzy. He just wanted to close his eyes. He felt Contreras grabbing him by his hair and slapping his face.

"Wake up, wake up," Contreras said, annoyed his victim was passing out so quickly. "You don't get to miss the final moment, oh no, I've been waiting for this. Ever since you came into my restaurant, acting like some kind of TV cop."

Pete felt his body slam into the wall. His entire back ached. His vision was fuzzy. He wasn't sure if it was because he was dizzy or because his eyes were bruised shut. He couldn't even speak. The hands holding him up were gone, and he dropped to the ground. His limbs splayed out like a corpse. His head throbbed. He wondered about the cats. He still felt Contreras hovering over him.

Then he opened his eyes. He saw the gun pointed at his face. It was over. He could see Contreras' grin. Wide and evil. He was going to win. Kathy was dead. Chaz was dead. His father was dead.

"Fuck this," Pete said almost inaudibly. It was loud enough to give Contreras pause, and that moment was long enough to allow Pete to kick out with what little force he had left, connecting with Contreras' left shin. Pete grimaced as he heard the crack of bone, then the shrill scream as Contreras fell backwards. It took Pete's remaining energy to get on his feet. He leaned over Contreras, who was flailing on the ground, his hands clutching his leg, and took a quick swing at his face, connecting with a fist that probably did little but add to the killer's shock. With that came a wave of dizziness that Pete understood to mean he wouldn't be awake much longer. He slowly half-walked, half-crawled toward the apartment door, and eventually made his way outside to the hall. He closed it behind him, giving Contreras a quick glance. The black-draped killer was already getting to his feet, cursing Pete's name. Pete had maybe a minute of lead time, if that. He flung himself at his neighbor's door, across the hall, using what little energy he had left to bang on it. He heard someone coming. He felt his weight shifting as the door opened. His neighbor, a cute, thin brunette named Melissa, who Pete had probably drunkenly hit on a number of times, stood over him in shock, screaming. He mumbled something. *"Lock the door. Call the police."* She dragged him in and closed the door behind them. Pete thought he saw Contreras getting out of what was left of his apartment.

Melissa sank down and patted Pete's face, trying to keep him awake. She fumbled with her portable house phone, dialing the police as she held his hand.

"Jesus, what happened?" she said, terror in her voice. "What the fuck happened to you?"

Pete blacked out.

CHAPTER NINETEEN

Pete leaned back in his chair and turned his face to look out his office window. The Manhattan skyline was darkened by rain. It'd been a cold and wet winter, and it was only going to get worse. He checked his holster and absentmindedly caressed the revolver he carried for protection. He had a license, but still didn't feel very comfortable carrying a firearm. But Kathy wouldn't let him do most of his jobs if he didn't. The radio was playing a Beatles song. "It's All Too Much." He wondered where the music was coming from, as he didn't remember buying a radio for his office. The phone rang.

"Fernandez."

"It's me."

"Hey, darling," he said. It was Kathy. He should have known better. She always called around lunchtime to see how his day was going. "Where are you?"

"I'm nearby," she said; she sounded harried. *Another busy day of shopping*, Pete mused to himself. "I can't talk much, but I wanted to let you know. Come get me when you're done."

"I'll pick you up in a few hours, honey," Pete said. He fiddled with one of his Fernandez Detective Agency business cards. The sun had popped out from behind the clouds. It was summer suddenly.

He was sitting in the backyard of his father's house. The lawn furniture was gone. It was hot — Miami hot — but he was wearing a black suit. They'd buried his father earlier in the day. Emily was standing over him. He was on the ground.

"I know you're in love with me," she said.

"Well, that's good, I think," Pete said. He looked up at her. She didn't smile. She seemed disappointed. He frowned. She was wearing a black dress now. The same one she wore to his dad's funeral. The funeral they'd just returned from.

"This isn't working. You're drunk."

Pete realized he had a drink in his hand. He wasn't sure what. It was clear and had a lime in it. It was in a red plastic cup. He took a sip. It tasted sour. He couldn't drink anymore. It burned his throat. He looked up at Emily.

"I'm not," Pete said. "I'm sober. This drink tastes wrong."

"I don't ever want to see you again," she said. "Can't you respect that?"

"I didn't ask you here," Pete said. "My father just died."

"I know you want to bump into me," she said, smiling without emotion. "It's not happening again. Please understand this."

"Understand what?"

His stomach clenched and he was overcome by wracking sobs.

He bent over and saw his tears flowing into the ground. He felt Emily was gone. He looked across the yard and saw Kathy a few feet away, buried halfway into the ground. She seemed unconcerned. Her pink dress was sullied by the dirt and grass. She was smoking a cigarette and sipping from a champagne flute.

"You said you'd pick me up," she said. Her eyes were dazed. She seemed drugged.

"You're halfway in the ground now," Pete said. "I can get you out."

"No you can't," she laughed — a long, mournful laugh. She was shaking with laughter. "Maybe my mother can help you."

She kept laughing. Pete felt uncomfortable.

He got up and wiped the dirt off his pants and jacket. He felt a hand on his arm. His father tugged at him. They were in the police station. Pete looked around. Javier was sitting down near an interview room, a sad, sullen look on his face. He didn't meet Pete's eyes. They were adults, though. Broche came out of the interview and walked over to Pete and his father. He turned to Pete.

"This is a rerun," he said.

"I'm tired of reruns," Pete sighed. He looked at his father. He was old. The way he looked the day he died. Old and worn out. Defeated and sad. His suit was big on him, like a kid wearing his big brother's clothing.

"Change the channel," his father said, before a fit of coughs overtook him. He let go of Pete's arm and fell to the ground. No one rushed to help him. Pete tried, but was held back. It was Emily. She was holding his arms.

"Just let me help him," Pete said, his eyes watering. "He's dying."

"He died a long time ago," Emily said.

"I know," Pete said, falling to his knees. Emily let him fall. As his knees hit the ground, blackness spread over the area near his legs and around the floor. Soon it was everywhere. He knelt in a black room. Only Emily remained. She was dressed casually, with no makeup. Pete stood up to face her. She moved to touch his face, but pulled back.

"This is wrong," she said.

"What is?"

"Everything. I can't fix you."

"I know."

"But you want me to," she said. She pulled out a cigar and cut off the tip. She lit it. "Didn't your father smoke these?" she asked as she took a few puffs.

"I think so."

Emily stopped smoking the cigar and began to chew on it, her mouth becoming dirty and brown. Her eyes were dark and red. She was wearing a T-shirt and shorts. His Pixies shirt. The way she looked the first time they'd slept together. It was torn under the left sleeve.

"You don't have to do anything. You're good at that."

"What should I do?"

She spit a piece of the cigar out on the floor and turned to him.

"Stop being so fucking literal."

CHAPTER TWENTY

"Is he waking up?"

"His eyes are moving, so yes."

"Mike — now is not the time for stupid jokes."

Pete squinted at the bright fluorescent lights. He felt a dull pounding in his head and a general ache. He opened his mouth, but couldn't form any words. Before he could try again, he felt a hand on his arm. He turned slowly. It was Emily. She looked like she'd been crying. Mike was behind her. Pete was in a hospital room. He looked himself over. He wasn't visiting. He was in the bed. Why? Had there been an accident? Then he remembered. Contreras. The Silent Death. Stumbling into Melissa's apartment. He must have passed out. She called the ambulance. But what happened to Contreras? He felt like shit. He wasn't dead.

"The cats . . .?" Pete almost coughed.

"What?" Mike asked.

"Are the cats OK?"

"The cats are fine," Broche said, as he walked up to the bed. "You, on the other hand, are not in good shape." Pete noticed that even Broche's usual expression had softened. How bad did he look?

"Where am I?"

"You're at Baptist Hospital," Broche continued. "You're lucky. Emily called you a few times after you missed your dinner date, then headed to your place. Your neighbor said you stormed into her apartment and that someone was after you. She said she was already going to knock on your door because of all the screaming. Emily got there a little while after that."

"I thought you'd just gotten drunk, passed out on your couch, and forgot to call," Emily said. "Not this. Jesus. What the fuck happened?"

Pete tried to sit up, but felt a wave of dizziness overtake him; he let his head plop back down on the pillow. Broche put his hand on Pete's shoulder.

"Let him rest," Broche said. He turned to Pete. 'You have a concussion, a few broken ribs and some heavy bruising. That black eye is not going to heal very quickly. But aside from that, you should make a full recovery."

"Well, that's good. Thank you, Dr. Broche," Pete said, his voice a low rasp. The longer he was awake, the more new jabs of pain he discovered in his body. "I'm not a fan of hospitals."

"Who did this to you? Do you remember?" Mike asked, his usual self-control lost to the situation. "This is fucked up. Was it a robbery?"

"I guess so," Pete said. He didn't want to elaborate too much with Broche in the room. He didn't know what was found at the scene and what Broche knew, but he was not in the mood to hear it from him. Not yet. "I don't remember that much."

Broche frowned. He'd known Pete long enough to know when he was being evasive.

"Guys, I need to talk to Pete," Broche said, turning to Emily and Mike. "Can you give us a few minutes?"

Emily nodded and Mike followed her out of the room. They seemed relieved that their friend had awoken, so a break was in order. Broche waited until the door closed behind them before walking a few steps closer to Pete's bed.

"Talk to me."

"I don't remember," Pete said.

"Don't lie to me."

"I'm not lying," Pete said, his mind at half-speed, trying to figure out how to sidestep the detective. "I just remember getting home from meeting with Chaz; then I woke up here, all fucked up."

Broche pulled up a chair next to Pete's bed and leaned in close to him. He had a forced smile on his face.

"I'm going to tell you one more time not to lie to me," Broche said, his tone slow and deliberate. "It was clear this wasn't a robbery. Your apartment was wrecked, but nothing of value — as far as we can tell — was taken. So, quit the 'I don't remember' story. OK?"

"OK," Pete said, resigned.

Pete exhaled slowly. He didn't know what to say. He let Broche continue.

"I did a little digging on Chaz," Broche said. "He was a deadbeat gambler who racked up thousands of dollars in debt to some bad people. Some of those bad people include Jose Contreras. I can't verify it, but my snitches tell me most of Chaz's debts point to Contreras."

Pete nodded at Broche.

"From what I can tell, Chaz was working on something for Contreras," Broche said. "But that's all I know."

Pete rubbed his eyes. His head was still throbbing, and the tiny nuggets of info Broche had provided were not helping.

"So, Chaz was looking for his daughter," Pete said, "while also working for Contreras?"

"Seems like it."

"Contreras is the Silent Death," Pete said, closing his eyes and leaning his head back. "He attacked me. He'd been following me, I think. I had this feeling, like something weird was going on, and then he sprung on me when I got home. I don't even know how I got out of it."

Broche paused. Pete could feel his eyes on him, even with his own eyes closed.

"So much for not remembering."

"So sue me, man," Pete said. "I'm not sure what the hell is going on anymore. A couple days ago, I'm just another cog in the newspaper machine. Next thing I know, Chaz is asking me to find Kathy. Now Chaz is dead, I'm in the hospital, and I'm pretty sure Kathy's dead, too."

"She's dead?"

"According to Contreras she is," Pete said, resignation in his voice. He ran his hands over his face, feeling for cuts and bumps. "But I'm not sure."

Pete opened his eyes and turned to Broche.

"What can you do?" he asked. "How can you help? Can we send

someone looking for Kathy? Anything? I mean, I've just given you the identity of this legendary killer. The least you can do is make sure I don't end up dead when I leave here, right?"

Broche made a clucking sound with his tongue and let Pete's question linger for a second.

"I can't do anything," he said. "Nothing beyond what I've already done. This is why I warned you. The Silent Death, or whoever he is, isn't just another thug or a serial killer. He's connected. The department isn't exactly clean, either. Your father . . . he was the last person really still digging around to find out who was doing this."

"You're fucking kidding me, right?" Pete said, too angry to face Broche. "So what now? I go home and wait to die?"

"No, nothing like that. You just need to lay low. Go to your dad's house. Maybe take a vacation. Just get away for a few weeks."

"Run away."

"Well, however you want to phrase it," Broche said.

Pete sat up, wincing and gasping at the shock of pain rushing to his brain. Broche got up and put a hand on Pete's bed.

"You need to rest," Broche said.

"I need to run, apparently," Pete said, shaking off Broche, his voice sharp and sarcastic. He was taking out his anger — over the fight, over his life, over everything that had gone wrong in the last week or so — on Broche.

Broche sat back down and rubbed his legs.

"You did what your father had been trying to do for years," he said. "You figured out who this guy is. The only difference is you have no power to do anything about it. Even if your father had figured it out, what would he have done? Arrested him, and watched as a judge — paid off by whomever — let him off the hook. It's just the lay of the land here, kid. There is nothing to do but step back and try to stay alive."

"What about Kathy, then?"

"You said yourself she was dead."

Pete paused for a moment.

"Contreras said she was dead."

"Right."

"But if they wanted her dead, they would have just killed her, no?" Pete said, his eyes clear and locked on Broche, the pain in his head ignored. "Why kidnap her and delay the inevitable? Why take her somewhere and kill her, when the Silent Death's M.O. has always been about killing people quickly, efficiently and with little fuss?"

"No reason," Broche said, thinking aloud. "Unless she has something he wants."

She was on the brink of figuring out who he was, Pete thought. She had enough information to piece it together. But it wasn't just that she knew. The information existed outside of her head. It was in the *Miami Times* system and, Pete remembered, on a portable drive in his apartment.

"Kathy was working on a story uncovering his identity," Pete said. "She was close. But she was also smart — she didn't just keep this info with her. It's in the newspaper's system. The story's not done, but it's close to enough to being done that, even if she was killed, her editors would find it and run with it. It may not definitively confirm who the Silent Death is, but it would create enough problems for the people that it points to."

Broche let out a long sigh.

"I'm just going to assume you're never going to listen to me from now on, OK?" Broche said, looking at Pete, waiting for an answer, then proceeding. "So, I'm not going to ask about how you got that info. Even though, knowing the *Times*, you don't have access to that building anymore. If what you say is true — and I don't doubt it is — then she's alive until she tells them how to get to those files and destroy them. That would be a reason not to kill her off the bat. A bit of a stretch, though."

Pete felt the pieces coming together slowly, and it painted a grisly picture. Kathy inching toward the revelation of the Silent Death's identity. Her father, riddled with debt, pressured into trying to find the story files. Chaz reaching out to Pete. He'd wanted Pete to find the files. He'd enlisted Pete to do his dirty work. And once Contreras figured it out, he killed Chaz. Pete felt a wave of nausea. He was more involved than he'd ever imagined.

"What?"

Pete turned. "What? Did you say something?"

"No," Broche said. "But you suddenly went blank on me."

Pete ignored him.

"So Contreras enlists Kathy's father to look for her? That's strange."

"No, I'd imagine Contreras found her pretty easily on his own," Broche said. "But if you're right, and she didn't have the info they wanted, or wasn't giving it up, that made them enlist her father."

"Who was deeply in debt to Contreras, and not particularly close to his own daughter."

"Exactly."

"Real class act, that Chaz Bentley," Pete said. He felt like an idiot.

Why had he allowed himself to get into this mess? And what could he do to get out of it with no help from the police beyond his dead father's old partner?

"How do you know Chaz was in Contreras' debt? I mean, beyond your snitches?"

"A lot of it is guesswork at this point," Broche said. "He wrote the man some hefty checks over the last few years, according to his bank records. And he wasn't exactly living in the lap of luxury, you know? Even though he made a decent salary."

"But why would he ask me to look for his daughter if he knew she was in trouble?" Pete asked. He felt weaker the longer he stayed awake. It was slowly dawning on him how badly he'd been beaten. Even though he knew where the evidence pointed, Pete was having trouble with the thought that a father would so easily accept that his daughter was in danger and, in turn, work for her kidnapper.

"From what little we could discover," Broche said. "He wasn't remarkably close to his daughter. They barely spoke. Contreras probably figured his best chance at getting whatever info was in her story was by forcing her father — who owed him tons of money and worked at the same paper — to find the information."

"Ah," Pete said. "But there's the rub. Chaz is a columnist. He's never in the newsroom. Works from home mostly. And the home system isn't synched to the network beyond your own personal basket and your editor."

"Tell me in English," Broche said.

"Chaz couldn't check Kathy's information or articles," Pete said. "He'd need to come into the newsroom, log in to her computer with her password and find it. Something that would certainly raise suspicion."

"So . . .?"

"So he goes to the biggest idiot he can find," Pete said, a tinge of sarcasm in his voice. "The drunk from Sports. Kind of smart, but not too smart. Gullible enough he'd believe Chaz was just a concerned parent, but smart enough to be able to crack into Kathy's system and alert him to anything that might put her in danger. He just wasn't expecting me to actually start sniffing around Contreras."

"You're being too hard on yourself," Broche said. Pete appreciated the gesture, but questioned how genuine it was.

"No, I'm not."

Pete looked at his hands and over his body. He was hurt. Not irreparably so, but still more damaged than he'd ever been before in his life. For what?

His brief flirtation with stepping back seemed wrong. He needed to see this to the end. Bruises and concussion aside, he needed to find out what the hell was going on. No one else would.

"Let this serve as a warning," Broche said. "You can't meddle in business like this. You're not even a detective — you're just a guy who's lost direction. You've done a lot of good here, but it's not your place. You're looking for some kind of weird validation. You're like family, Pete. Don't fall apart over this."

Pete dropped back down into his bed, signaling the conversation was over.

"I'm proud of you," Broche said. "Your father would have been, too. What you did was stupid, but brave. But you've done enough. You need to stay alive. I want you to get some rest and let this drop."

Pete nodded. He moved to grab the cup of water resting on the nightstand. Broche passed it to him. Pete sat up slowly, feeling the same wave of dizziness, but deciding it was best to ride it out. The cold water felt good.

"And don't think for a second I don't know you're holding out on me," Broche said, his tone tougher. "I'll be back when you're up and around to pick your brain further. For now, get some sleep."

"Will do," Pete said, not bothering to argue.

Broche clasped Pete's hand in a firm shake and gave him a knowing nod.

"Alright, feel better," he said, before turning and leaving. Pete could see Emily waiting on the other side of the door. She took the opening as a sign to come in. She slid into the chair Broche had vacated. Her eyes were clearer, but she seemed tired. Pete realized he had no idea what time it was.

"How long was I out?"

"A couple hours," Emily said. "Not very long. It's early in the morning now, around five. How are you feeling?"

"Shitty."

"Are you going to tell me what happened?"

"I'm still figuring it out," Pete said. "Some guy came in and beat the shit out of me. That's the short version."

"Well, that's somewhat obvious," she said, frustration in her voice. "What did he want, though?"

"I don't want to talk about it."

He felt suddenly tired. Pete realized he'd said the wrong thing immediately. Even in the frayed state of their relationship, any withholding of information between them was something taken very seriously. When they were together, it was all in or nothing. Now, Pete didn't understand the rules.

165

"I just, I need to process it, that's all," he said, backtracking.

She put a hand up. "Don't worry about it."

He didn't believe she didn't care, but he let it go. He'd mend the fence another time. He did feel relief at having her next to him. She was in a loose-fitting Style Council T-shirt he'd bought her in college and worn-out blue jeans. She didn't have any makeup on, either. She looked tired. Pete thought she looked nice, regardless. He reached out his hand and she took it. They were never much for physical affection, at least not since the breakup, but he was happy for this. She wove her hand into his. They both sat silently for a few minutes.

In less than a week, he'd lost his job, been pounded mercilessly, and had pissed off or offended every friend he had. He almost laughed to himself. He turned to Emily to share the thought and noticed she was wiping her eyes quickly.

"What's the matter?"

"Nothing, I'm fine," she said, pulling her hand away from his to blow her nose softly.

"I'm going to get better, don't worry," Pete said. "Just a few bumps and bruises."

Pete was surprised to hear her laugh through the tears and stuffed nose.

"Jesus," she said. "It's not you. I know you'll be OK. You're stupid and reckless, but always seem to be OK."

"Um, thanks?"

"I mean, I'm worried," she backtracked. "Whatever you're into is stupid and dangerous. But I'm used to you doing stupid shit. You have this weird ability to pretend you're listening to someone, and I just know that you're going to do whatever the fuck you want."

She was right, Pete thought. The ease with which she could get into his head bothered him. He used to love it.

"Rick and I had a stupid fight," Emily said. "It's not a big deal. I just feel really isolated down there. Everything is here. My family, my friends. I'm not sure moving there was such a good idea."

"What does he think?"

"He loves it. He works from home, he can take his boat out, his favorite bar is down the street," Emily said. "It's just boring as hell. Maybe that's what getting older is all about."

"It sounds more than just a stupid fight," Pete said. "But what do I know?"

She didn't respond. The conversation was over. Pete had dealt with this maneuver before. But he was too tired to press the issue.

"Where's Mike?"

"He went to get some food," Emily said. "You know how he is in these situations. He gets really antsy and protective. He tries to do things when all you can really do is wait around."

She slid her hand back into his and smiled at him. A sweet but forced smile. Her mind was elsewhere. Pete wasn't sure where.

"I'm going to be fine," Pete said, his voice drowsy.

She tightened her grip on his hand briefly.

"I know."

"Thanks for coming here."

She let out a dismissive *tsk*. "Of course. Where else would I be?"

Pete smiled and felt his eyes close. In a few moments he was asleep. He didn't dream.

I need to go to the Keys."

Pete's statement hung in the air of the hospital room. It was early the next day. Pete had slept through most of the previous 24 hours. The only other sound was the television remote control as Mike clicked through the four channels on the room's TV. He took a few seconds to respond as he watched a scene unfold on a random episode of Judge Judy.

"Sure," he said, not bothering to look at Pete, who'd just awoken. "Once you get out of here, we'll hit it up. We both need a vacation. We can go to that bar you like. The Green Parrot?"

"No, now," Pete said, swinging his legs over the side of his bed, ignoring the throbbing in his head that increased the more he moved. "We need to find Kathy, or she's dead."

Mike put the remote on the nightstand and finally looked at Pete, as if confirming he was actually there, and saying what he'd just said.

"What's in the Keys?"

"Contreras has a place there," Pete said. Maribel's information and Kathy's notes both pointed him there.

"Who?"

"The guy who attacked me."

"Are you insane?" he said. "Did you forget the part where you got your ass beat and almost murdered because of this bullshit?"

Pete grabbed his shirt and jeans from a nearby table and began to get dressed, tossing his hospital gown on the bed.

"I have to do this," Pete said, sliding his feet into his worn pair of Chuck Taylors. "As crazy as it sounds, I need to see this to the end. No one else is going to find her."

Mike stood up, his hand hovering over the button that would

summon a nurse. "No, you don't," he said. "The end could have been a few nights ago, if that guy really wanted to put a bullet in your head."

Pete, now fully dressed, checked his pockets. He was relieved to find his car keys and wallet in their right place. It was all about the little victories lately, he thought to himself. He turned to Mike.

"The nurse won't get here in time to stop me from walking out," Pete said, leaning on the bed to keep himself from getting too dizzy. "Someone is going to get killed if I don't do something. I know it."

"Fuckin' A, man," Mike said. "I am tired of this conversation. You've lost your job over this. Are you ready to die, too?"

Pete shrugged.

Mike waited for more of a response but got nothing. Pete saw him push the nurse alert button.

"I'm not going to be able stop you, but don't expect me to make it easy," Mike said.

"Great, good," Pete said. He backed up, his face to Mike, his back to the nightstand where he'd noticed Mike had left not only his wallet, but his car keys as well. "I understand what you're saying. This is dumb. I feel like shit, too."

Pete leaned on the nightstand slowly, allowing the keys to slide into his hands.

"Just lie down," Mike said, concern spreading over his face. "You shouldn't be moving around."

"You're right," Pete said, lying on the bed, careful to keep the keys hidden, hoping Mike wasn't awake himself enough to notice they were gone. "Can you get me some water? Might want to tell the nurse the alarm was an accident, too."

Mike nodded and headed out. Emily stood in the doorway, two Styrofoam cups of coffee in her hand. Pete had to stop himself from cursing aloud. She had heard everything. And she had a look on her face that told Pete she had seen what he did with the keys.

Mike closed the door behind him. Emily calmly placed the two coffee cups on the nightstand and returned to her place between Pete and the door.

"You're leaving," she said, not as a question.

"I have to," Pete said.

"That's debatable." She sounded tired, Pete thought. "But I'm not surprised. What's in the Keys?"

"Contreras has a place there," Pete said. "I think that's where he went to hide out. I think that's where he has Kathy."

"So, you're going to find Contreras? Is that the guy that beat you up?" Emily asked, her eyes drilling into Pete's. "Then what? Make a citizen's arrest?"

"I'm not sure yet."

"Sounds like a winner, I'll say," she said.

"If I don't find her, Kathy's as good as dead," Pete said.

"I think that could be said of any moment during the last few days," she said. "She's missing. No one has seen or spoken to her in days. She probably is dead, Pete. Bad people don't drag out stuff like this. They get what they want or people get hurt."

"Are you going to let me go or not?"

Emily walked over to Pete. He could see the concern in her eyes. He stood up. He could smell the Chanel.

He took Emily into his arms instinctively, kissing her on the forehead.

"I'll be fine," he said, his voice a low whisper. He pushed her chin up.

"I can't process this," Emily said, looking away, but pulling him in closer, her head on his chest. "I don't know what to feel or think about you anymore. I feel like I drove you to this. Which is stupid, but shit, everything is stupid lately."

"It'll be fine," he said, stroking her hair. She pulled back from his touch and looked up at him. He continued. "I'm going to find Kathy and we'll go from there. I'll see you tomorrow."

Emily put her hand on Pete's face for a second and looked into his eyes. He was still holding her close. He had dreamt of this moment. A chance to connect with her again. If he'd had a few drinks in his system, he'd probably lean down and try to kiss her. But it wasn't the time for that.

She kissed him on the cheek, a friendly, almost sisterly gesture. Then she pulled back.

"Be careful," she said.

Pete walked past her. She coughed as the morning news sputtered from the television set. Pete closed the door.

CHAPTER TWENTY-ONE

After a quick stop at the remains of his apartment — to canvass the destruction and to pick up his father's gun — Pete began his trek south. Mike's car, a black Ford Focus, seemed to be driving nicely, and Pete silently hoped it wasn't in dire need of a tune-up or an oil change. The last thing he needed was to be stranded on the Seven-Mile Bridge for hours. Pete hated driving. Hated it even more without his own music to play. He contented himself by listening to a few Pearl Jam CDs Mike had lying around the backseat.

The drive went quickly, and before too long a few hours had passed and Pete had managed to find a few other discs in Mike's glove compartment. The Kinks' "David Watts" faded into New Order's "Ceremony," and Pete began to feel himself getting sleepy. He was worn out, bruised and exhausted, despite being asleep for almost an entire day. Then his phone rang. Mike. Pete braced himself for the lecture he was going to get.

"Hey," Pete said.

Mike ignored the greeting and started talking.

"It took me a little while to figure out what you did," Mike said. "If it wasn't my car, I'd find it almost comical."

"I'm sorry," Pete said.

"Emily was pretty pissed, so you know," Mike said.

"She wasn't happy, that's for sure," Pete said. "She thinks this whole thing is stupid."

"It is," Mike said.

"She seems upset about more than just this," Pete said.

"Yeah," Mike said. "I think she's having trouble with Rick. But she doesn't talk about it, so who knows." He trailed off for a second, and then changed topics. "So, say you do find this Contreras dude. What then? You call the cops?"

"Well, the cops aren't even looking for him," Pete said, stifling another yawn and straightening himself in his seat. His left leg was falling asleep. He was surprised and confused by Mike's reaction to having his car stolen. He chalked it up to Mike's Zen resignation during stressful times. "I have to hope he can somehow lead us to Kathy. She's the one in immediate danger."

"That's a stretch," Mike said. "You're hoping that by finding the person that did the crime, he'll lead you to the girl?"

"Well, when you put it that way . . ." Pete stammered.

"I'm serious," Mike said, his voice growing slightly more agitated.

"Look, I'm sorry, but—"

"Shut up," Mike said. "I'm tired of the constant apologies. You did what you did because you wanted to do it. If you didn't want to do it, you'd still be in the hospital, man. Don't bullshit me anymore."

Pete remained silent. He hadn't thought his plan out in detail. His gut told him to follow the lead to the Keys, and then take it from there. But explaining that out loud to Mike made it sound more like a whim and less like a plan. He didn't feel like arguing, either.

"I'm going to find Contreras and Kathy, and we'll see what happens next," Pete said finally.

Mike hung up. It took Pete a few seconds to realize the line was not dead because of a bad connection but because his friend had gotten fed up with his antics. They rarely argued, and when they did have disagreements, it never happened this way.

The skies had darkened and a light rain was falling, slowing his progress slightly. Pete let those thoughts hang in the air as he turned the car off at the exit. Key West was a series of hotels, seafood restaurants and bars, sprinkled over a chunk of lovely Florida landscape. Even in the rain, the area looked peaceful and welcoming. Pete wished he was visiting under better, more relaxed circumstances. It was dusk. The combination of the rain and disappearing sun gave the island a desolate, eerie vibe. Most people were coming home from the beach or resting up before going out for dinner or drinks. It almost felt like he was sneaking in between shifts. Pete drove to the center of the nightlife district, looking for a parking space.

Pete fumbled through his pockets for the scrap of paper with the name of the bar Maribel had mentioned. He found it. Willie T's.

He snagged a parking space on the corner of Fleming and Duval and walked toward the bar. Despite the early hour, it wasn't hard to pinpoint Willie T's — the crowd and noise beckoned like a lighthouse on a dark night.

Walking in, Pete quickly determined that Willie T's was a run-of-the-mill beach bum dive. It was wallpapered with dollar bills and photos, and crowded with tan tourists and regulars sipping Corona and Presidente beers. He thought he heard Bob Seger's "Night Moves" on the jukebox, but wasn't certain. Pete grabbed a stool near the end of the bar and ordered an Amstel Light. He couldn't afford to get wasted tonight. A light buzz maybe. The bartender, a rough-looking older man with salt-and-pepper hair and a closely cropped moustache, looked like he'd been born behind a bar.

"Welcome to Willie T's, bud. I'm Ash. I run the place," he said, his hand outstretched. Pete shook it. He'd briefly worked with a guy named Ash while reporting on a sports story in New Jersey. That Ash was younger and tougher-looking than this guy. "Never seen you around here before," Ash said. "You visiting? Looks like you've had a rough go of it."

"Just stopping in," Pete said, trying to act casual. "I'm actually looking for a friend of mine."

Ash's eyes narrowed slightly as he put a beer in front of Pete.

"OK, well, here's hopin' you find them. Not much of a friend if he's making himself hard to find and all," Ash said, slapping the bar gingerly. "Lemme know when you need another."

"Maybe you've seen him around? Jose Contreras?" Pete said. "Comes down here from time to time. He owns a place around here, I just don't know the address."

Ash snorted and walked over to another cluster of customers at the opposite side of the bar.

Pete felt his face reddening. He downed his beer quickly. He felt a rush to his head. He motioned for Ash. The place was crowded.

Some people were seated at the tables enjoying dinner while a large group converged at the bar, some already knocking back shots and ordering their second or third pitchers of beer. Pete's eyes drifted over to the jukebox, where a waitress, who was — like a lot of people at the bar — way too tan and looked older than she probably was, stood, chewing gum and talking to a shorter man. Pete focused on the man. He couldn't get a good look at him in the dim bar, and the constant movements of the crowd made getting a clear line of sight difficult. But Pete didn't need much time to figure out who it was. The stocky build and glaring scar down the left side of his face gave it away: Contreras.

Pete fought the urge to get up and bolt to the car. He turned around and saw Ash looking at the bar, as if he expected something to be there.

"You really ain't much of an investigator, kid," Ash said, as he put another Amstel in front of Pete and walked off.

Pete sighed to himself and slapped three twenties onto the bar, near his drink. After making his rounds, Ash returned to Pete's spot. He nonchalantly picked up the cash as if Pete were closing out a massive tab. He leaned in slightly. Pete could smell the tobacco on his breath. He tried not to cough.

"Your buddy's been comin' down here for years," Ash said, his voice low. "He's a friend of mine. He's got a place near the Comfort Inn, couple miles from here. Complex called Waterford."

Ash grabbed a napkin and pulled a pen from behind his ear. He jotted down the address.

"How do you know him?" Pete asked. He looked back quickly. Contreras was gone; the waitress he'd been chatting with was now talking to a table of frat guys intent on getting obliterated before dinner. He felt a wave of relief.

"He comes in here a lot," Ash said, lighting himself a cigarette. "I visit him sometimes. He has business interests here. He's a good guy. Comes down here for fun or if things get too sticky up north."

Pete nodded and stuck his hand out to Ash, who didn't shake it.

"Just get going," Ash said. "I don't want any problems here. I know Contreras ain't a friend of yours, but I also know he's not an innocent, either. I mean, look at you. I'll take a few extra bills for doing some of your legwork."

CHAPTER
TWENTY-TWO

H e was lost.

Pete cursed under his breath. Ash's notes said Contreras' bungalow was off Center Street, but finding the street was another matter. Pete drove around the block in silence. The radio was off. Pete ran his fingers over the napkin as he looked out his window. He noticed a smallish street and turned.

Pete found himself in a cul-de-sac, surrounded by four tiny, standalone apartments, each with variations of the same lawn furniture set. The Waterford sign confirmed he was in the right spot. Pete noticed the lights were off in all but one. He gripped the wheel tightly for a second and let out a long breath. He opened the glove compartment and rummaged around before pulling out his father's gun and looking it over. He kept the safety on.

Pete got out of the car. He began to walk the short distance between the car and the bungalow's front door. The ground was wet from the rain, and the parking lot lights had yet to pop on. The air smelled smoky, Pete thought. He pulled the gun from behind his back and held it close to his left leg.

He wondered what Mike or Emily would say if they saw him now, toting a gun into an apartment with who knows what waiting for him.

He walked up to the door. Though the lights were on, Pete didn't notice any movement or noise coming from inside the bungalow. Feeling awkward with the gun in his hand, he slid it back behind him and reached out to knock. Before Pete could make contact with the door, it wheezed open, slightly ajar. Pete pulled out his gun again and waited.

After a few moments, he pushed the door slightly. There were no signs of life or movement coming from inside.

"Fuck it," Pete said. He pushed the door fully open and walked in. The bungalow was tiny. There was a lightly furnished living room and a door to another, secondary room that was closed. The living room had a small sofa and two chairs that looked, to Pete, like they once belonged to a dining set. Tied to one of the chairs with rope was a man. He was dead. Pete covered his mouth. There was a gaping, bloody hole where part of his face used to be. Pete fought the urge to vomit. He felt his own hands shaking.

Pete stepped gingerly toward the body. He had no sense of when the man had been murdered, but the kill had been messy. There was blood all over the floor and couch. From what little Pete knew about forensics, he could tell the murder weapon hadn't been a run-of-the-mill handgun. Probably a shotgun. He looked up at the ceiling and noticed a hole —the result of another, errant shot. Pete looked at the man's hair and what little remained of his face. He didn't want to be right.

It was Javier. He was certain. He recognized the watch, too. The clincher.

He tried to look at the mangled face of his former friend from different angles, not to nauseate himself further, but to somehow prove himself wrong. But he couldn't. It was him.

Then he heard the scream.

Kathy Bentley was dazed and unresponsive as Pete scrambled to remove the rope tying her to the tiny twin bed in the bungalow's second room. She was splattered with blood, probably Javier's, Pete thought as he raised her off the bed and into a sitting position. She was conscious, but barely. He had to hold her up.

"Kathy," Pete said, shaking her slightly. "We have to get you out of here. Can you try to stand up for me?"

Kathy didn't respond. Her eyes were at half-mast, her hair matted with dirt and sweat.

Pete's mind was whirring. It looked like Kathy had been in the room for a few days — there were small, empty cereal boxes, a few gallons of water, and a rifle resting near the westernmost wall, out of Kathy's reach. A drawer set had been toppled over and emptied, along with a shoddy black nightstand. The floor was littered with papers and clothes. Contreras hadn't been concerned with keeping the place tidy while he held Kathy.

"We have to get the fuck out of here," Pete said, as much to himself as to Kathy. "If Contreras just did this, my guess is he left for only a short time. No way he'd leave it like this. Can you walk?"

"The couch . . ." Kathy mumbled.

Pete looked at her in surprise.

It was the first thing she'd said since screaming.

"We're leaving now," Pete said. "I'm taking you home."

"Baginthecouchgetit," she slurred.

Pete tried to carry her out of the room. He managed to drag her into the living room and tried, unsuccessfully, to prevent her from seeing Javier's mutilated body. Pete heard her sob softly. He glanced back at his former friend as they inched toward the door, and felt a crushing sense of failure. As much as this disaster was about finding Kathy, it was also about reconnecting in some way to the friend he'd left waiting in the police station for the father that never came to pick him up.

"Please," Kathy said, more clearly this time.

"We're almost out the door," he said, trying to distract her.

"No, we have to get the bag in the couch," she said, her voice hoarse but forceful. She was waking up. "That's the money."

"Money?" Pete asked.

"Cut open the cushion on the left," she said, ignoring Pete's question. "There should be a gym bag in there."

"We don't have time for this," Pete said, growing anxious. He'd been in the bungalow for almost 20 minutes.

"Fuck, fine," Kathy said, pulling away from Pete. She moved back to the couch and unzipped the cushion, snaking her arm inside. After a few seconds of searching, she came back with a medium-sized blue gym bag. Pete loomed over her as she unzipped it to reveal stacks of hundreds tied in various bundles. He'd never seen so much money in one place. She looked up at him, as if to say "See?"

"We have to get the fuck out of here," he said, his eyes still on the cash. He expected Contreras — in full Silent Death garb — to stroll into the tiny apartment at any time.

"Yes," Kathy said, swinging the bag over her shoulder. She seemed much more alert than when Pete first discovered her. "They're coming back. They should have been back by now."

"They?" Pete asked, nerves clear in his voice.

"You have no idea what's going on, do you? This is where everything starts," Kathy said, motioning around the living room as she opened the front door. "Javier figured it out and came here, and he got killed for it. I knew they were stashing money in the couch between deals because he wouldn't stop talking about it. I thought I was going to be shot next. I'm not sure why they kept me alive this long."

They walked outside the bungalow and began the short walk to Mike's car, Kathy in front. She paused for a second and turned to Pete, who was trailing a half step behind.

"And thank you," Kathy said. "I don't know how the hell you, of all people, found me, but thanks."

Her second thank you was drowned out by the sound of a large black truck pulling into the small parking lot. Pete could make out Conteras' silhouette. He slid his father's gun from his waistband and gripped it tightly as they ran for Mike's car.

Pete slammed the driver's side door shut as the Focus' tires squealed violently in reverse while Kathy slid into the passenger seat. He backed up the car carelessly and slammed his foot on the accelerator, trying to gain a few seconds on the truck, which could easily overtake the slow-moving sedan.

"They're not going to be behind us for long," Kathy said, turning around to look out the car's back window.

"No shit," Pete responded, as he turned the car onto Duval Street. He had to reach the expressway, fast. "We have to get to a busier area, or we're fucked."

"Or we're dead," Kathy said.

Pete gripped the steering wheel and changed lanes abruptly, hoping to gain a few seconds on the truck. From what Pete could tell by checking the rearview, the diversion did little. The fastest way off the island was by taking Duval Street, the main drag of Key West, littered with bars, restaurants and late-night revelers. Pete focused on the road, trying his best to dart through traffic without being too obvious, as the area was not bereft of police cars. The thought of getting pulled over sounded almost appealing. Pete had counted at least three fender benders in the last few minutes due to Contreras' driving. And, despite Pete's best efforts, the truck was still only a car's length behind them.

"Where are we headed?" Kathy asked.

"Back to Miami," Pete said, looking at her briefly. "Where else would we go?"

Kathy seemed confused.

"Well, wonderful. Are we expecting to lose them in some way?" Kathy said, exasperated. "Because driving down the busiest street toward the busiest one-lane highway in the state isn't the best way to do that, FYI."

Pete never got the chance to respond.

The car lurched, sending them hurtling forward. Pete felt himself slam into the dashboard. The car was spinning, Pete realized. He heard the back window shatter and turned to see Kathy crumpled next to him, her body curved in a weird position, her back against the windshield. Pete groaned. His face was plastered on the steering wheel, his eyes felt sluggish and heavy. There was glass all over the backseat. Pete felt a shooting pain in his left arm. He was dazed. Kathy wasn't moving. The truck had crashed into them from behind.

Pete opened the driver's side door and toppled out, rolling on the concrete. Cars were now weaving around them. The black truck was still crunched against Mike's car, which was dented badly, but might still be able to run. He wasn't sure where Contreras was. He got to his feet and felt wobbly. He noticed some movement from the truck. Nothing from Mike's car. He'd been wearing a seatbelt, but Kathy might have been seriously injured, Pete thought. He saw his father's gun near the gas pedal and snatched it up.

"Told you not to fuck with me, son," It was Contreras. "How many times did you think you'd be able to get away? Once was pure luck. This time it'll be different."

Pete's vision focused and cut through the smoke surrounding the crash. He saw Contreras walking toward him. He wasn't in Silent Death garb, Pete noticed. The gash down his left cheek seemed sharper in contrast to the dirt on his face from the crash. He seemed relaxed, as if high-traffic car chases were commonplace. They probably were, Pete thought. For him. "That stupid slut wasn't happy to just get away. She had to take something that belongs to me."

Pete felt blood dripping from a cut on his forehead. He raised his gun to Contreras. He put his hands up, but let out a laugh.

"Wow, this old trick?" Contreras said, still walking to Pete, albeit more slowly. Pete took the gun's safety off. Contreras laughed again.

"Sure you know how to use that thing?"

"Fuck you," Pete said. He was tired. He just wanted a warm bed and a few days to sort out what was going on. He turned to the car and saw Kathy was moving. He wondered if the car could run, or if they would have to explain everything to the cops. He couldn't hear the sirens anymore. There was a crowd forming, however. A few bar patrons had gathered outside of Willie T's after the crash. The newly present gun had sent most running.

"Kid has teeth all of a sudden?" Contreras said, as he inched closer. He slid his hand into his vest and pulled out his own gun, bigger than Pete's. Pete wagered he knew how to use it better, too. "That makes two of us."

Pete thought for a second. He'd had a gun pointed at him twice in his life. He could try and play hero and end up dead in the next four minutes, or he could put his gun down and probably live for a few more hours.

"Put the gun down, you little shit," Contreras said, getting agitated. "How hard did you get hit in the head?"

Then the sirens came back. This time, much louder.

Pete didn't recall much of what happened next. He remembered crouching down to slide his gun over to Contreras, who was patiently pointing his weapon at Pete. That's when he heard the screeching. He felt something push him forward and heard another crash followed by a man's scream. Pete remembered grabbing his gun for some reason. He looked up and saw Contreras, his face contorted. Not in anger, but pain. Was he looking at me? Pete thought. Mike's car was suddenly closer, and Contreras was pinned between his truck and Mike's black Focus. Pete glanced back and saw Kathy behind the wheel. He couldn't hear much. His ears were ringing. Contreras managed to move away from the two cars and collapse on the street awkwardly. Was he dead? Pete wasn't sure. He couldn't tell if the sirens were getting farther away or if he just couldn't hear them.

He sat on the street, his hand still on his father's gun when he felt someone jostle him. He looked up to see Kathy's face. She was screaming something at him. Pete didn't understand. He nodded. Kathy took the gun. Kathy tried to pick him up and drag him to the car. As he was partially sliding on the glass-covered Key West street, Pete turned and saw Contreras, crumpled on the ground, as if he were just pausing for a few winks like a drunk local.

"He's dead," Pete said, pointing at Contreras's immobile form.

He felt Kathy heaving him into the passenger side.

She put her hand on his forehead.

Pete expected it to be cold, but it wasn't. She took it off for a second and looked at it. It was red — blood? His blood, Pete realized.

"We have to get out of here," she yelled as she ran around to the driver's side seat. Then they were gone.

CHAPTER TWENTY-THREE

Pete couldn't go home. Even if Contreras was dead, his apartment wasn't safe. He guided Kathy to the route toward Mike's apartment in Fort Lauderdale. This way, he could return the car he'd stolen and damaged, rest for a moment, and determine what to do next. He'd found Kathy. He hadn't thought the next step through. There wasn't much talking on the way back. Kathy focused on the road; Pete stared out his window and ran the events of the last few hours through his mind. Had they killed someone? What evidence was left behind? Were the cops looking for them? Javier was dead. Kathy was begrudgingly grateful but grating on Pete's nerves. His shoulder and head ached, a dull, throbbing pain that was getting gradually worse. Pete's dizziness had lessened, but he still felt off. The rain had subsided, but the air felt heavy and wet.

Pete looked back and his eyes landed on the bag of money. Wind snuck into the car through the shattered rear window.

"Thanks," Pete said, breaking the silence.

"For what?" Kathy said, her tone flat, eyes on the road.

"For pulling me out of there," Pete said. "He was going to kill me."

"You're welcome."

Pete looked at Kathy. She was shaking slightly. Pete looked away. He let the silence linger.

"I killed someone."

"I know, I—"

"I killed someone today," Kathy repeated, still staring at the road, accelerating slightly. "And I don't feel a thing. That scares me. I've been tied up for almost a week, dirty, eating cornflakes and shitting and pissing in a bucket, threatened and prodded. I don't know who I am anymore. I don't even know if this is real — you, this car, the people."

"What do you mean?"

"I wasn't thinking clearly," Kathy said. "I just knew we had to get out of there. Away from that man. Away from everything."

An awkward silence followed. For a few minutes, Pete kept himself occupied by staring out toward the repetitive scenery that would take up most of the four-hour drive. The partially opened window allowed for a slight breeze, which he let slap his face.

"I know they killed my father, too," Kathy said. "Contreras told me. I'm not surprised. He was a washed-up deadbeat and a piece of shit. But he's still my father, you know?"

Pete looked over at her quickly and could see the tears streaming down her face, her eyes barely open. She tried to stifle the sobs, but she couldn't. Pete wasn't sure what to do.

"I can't believe they killed Javier," she said, mid-sob. "They killed him. For what? I don't even know what he was doing there. But now he's dead and I'm barely alive. I have nowhere to go. What am I going to do? Go to the *Times* and write this story? I'll be dead before it goes to press. I'm dead already."

Pete gripped the passenger side door handle, half-expecting Kathy to veer off the road, but she maintained control.

"I'll never forget it," Kathy said. "The way Contreras trotted him out. He dragged me from that tiny room and tossed me on the couch and showed me Javier. Said he'd come to save me. Yeah, right. Who knows why the fuck he was there? Then I knew it was over. He tossed me back into the room and a few minutes later, I heard the shot. No way anyone survives that."

"One shot?" Pete asked.

"Yeah, one," Kathy said. "Why?"

"Just curious," Pete said. Kathy wiped the tears from her eyes roughly, more angry than sad now. The radio remained off. The rain returned, a soft sprinkle falling as the black car sped into the darkness.

Mike lived in a small one-bedroom apartment off Las Olas, the main thruway in downtown Fort Lauderdale. The complex, named Sole and decorated with tropical pictures and imagery, was faux-luxurious, but comfortable enough. They parked across the street, Pete not sure how to actually get into the apartment complex's parking garage. They got out hastily and walked to the main entrance, where Pete tapped Mike's apartment number from memory. They waited for a response.

"Hello?"

"Mike," Pete said. "It's me. I've got your car. I'm back."

Static filled the seconds before they heard the ringing sound that meant Mike had cleared them to enter. Kathy swung the door open and walked in, not waiting for Pete to lead the way. They met at the elevator, where Pete tapped the button for the fifth floor. They rode up in silence.

They reached the door and Pete knocked tentatively. A few seconds passed and he looked at Kathy. She seemed exhausted. Her hair was caked with dirt, her face streaked with tears and her clothes torn and sullied. She caught him looking and turned her face away.

The door opened and Mike stood in the doorway in a pair of khaki boxers and a black T-shirt with some kind of animal on it. He didn't step aside to let them in.

"Nice of you to visit," he said.

"I brought the car back," Pete said, almost phrased like a question.

Mike ignored him and looked at Kathy. "Hello."

"I'm Kathy," she said, waving her hand in mock greeting. "Your friend here decided to save my life."

Mike nodded and stepped back, signaling that it was OK to enter. Pete walked in first and gave him a hug. Mike slapped him on the back and laughed quickly. Pete knew Mike wouldn't stay mad forever. But he was mad now.

"Your car's parked across the street," Pete said, stifling a yawn. Now that the insanity seemed over, his body was shutting down. "I didn't know how to get into the garage."

Mike shrugged and closed the door behind Kathy.

"No big deal," he said. "I have work in the morning anyway."

Kathy dropped the bag on the floor by the front door. It hit the ground with a thud. Mike looked at it curiously.

"What's that?" he asked.

"A bag full of money," Kathy said dryly.

Mike's eyebrows went up, but he didn't comment further.

The apartment was small. It wasn't much of a toss for Pete to get the keys on the kitchen counter.

"I'm done," Mike said. It was close to two in the morning. "I need to get some sleep."

"Thanks for letting me stay," Kathy said.

"Don't mention it," Mike said. "There are some towels, shorts and T-shirts in the bathroom if you want to shower and change into something clean. You guys OK sharing the couch?"

"I don't care," Kathy said looking at Pete. "I'll sleep on the floor if you feel weird."

"I'm fine with the couch," Pete said, sitting down and turning on the television. He flipped through some channels until he got to the local news. A repeat of the 11 o'clock edition. "I'm sure we'll all sleep pretty well tonight."

"Your last night of freedom," Mike said jokingly, raising his arms to the air. Pete heard the bedroom door close behind his friend.

Kathy plopped down on the couch next to Pete, absentmindedly rapping her fingertips on the arm of the three-seater. Pete turned up the volume. The newscaster, a bubbly blonde twenty-something subbing for the more recognizable local news celebrity, delivered the report quickly and with little flair, but Pete and Kathy watched in rapt attention.

"Some odd news coming from Key West this evening, as Duval

Street partygoers got a first-hand look at a heated car chase," she said, stumbling over her words slightly. "Police are still looking for one of the vehicles involved in the chase, along with at least two suspects. Onlookers say the chase ended with a crash on the eastbound lane of Duval Street in front of local watering hole Willie T's. That's when, according to witnesses, guns were drawn and one man was injured, the apparent victim of a hit-and-run. Police are asking that anyone with any information related to this please contact Crimestoppers at . . . "

Pete flicked off the television, but continued to stare at the blank screen.

After a minute, Kathy slowly took the remote control from Pete's hand and set it on the table. Pete leaned back on the couch. He wasn't sure what had him more worried—the fact that he was probably a wanted man and Kathy potentially a murderer, or that Contreras might still be alive. He wanted to scream. Instead, Pete looked up at Mike's ceiling.

"They're not going to find us," Kathy said matter-of-factly as she got up from the couch and headed toward the bathroom. "There's no way to place us there."

"That's not true at all," Pete said, still staring at the ceiling. "We were in a standoff with Contreras. I had been in the bar across the street a few hours before, looking for Conteras's place. And they'll eventually find Javier tied to a chair with his face blown off. Of course they'll be . . ."

Pete stopped talking when he heard Kathy's whimpering sob. He looked over and saw her, standing just outside the bathroom and watching Pete with bloodshot eyes. He felt like a complete asshole.

"Shit," Pete said. "I'm sorry. I wasn't even thinking."

She nodded, Pete wasn't sure why, then turned on her heels to enter the bathroom. He could hear more muffled sobbing from inside.

A half hour passed, and Kathy came back out of the bathroom, this time wearing a Miami Heat basketball T-shirt and a pair of shorts. She was showered and scrubbed, but still looked worn out and defeated.

"Tired?"

"Not really," she said, sitting next to him on the couch. "Can I use your phone?"

"Sure," Pete said, handing her his cell phone. "What for?"

"I'm just going to call Amy to let her know I'm OK," she said as she dialed quickly. Pete tried his best not to listen to the conversation as he got up from the couch. It was brief, from what little he could hear, and emotional. The crying and updating slowly changed to sarcasm and some laughing. Pete felt relieved. He wondered what Amy thought of him now. Maybe he wasn't such a fuck-up.

He popped open a beer. Mike thankfully had a 24-pack of Heineken resting in his fridge. After a few gulps, the bottle was mostly empty.

"Any more in there?"

Pete walked over with two beers, a new one for him and another for Kathy. He sat down next to her.

"There's a case in the fridge," Pete said. "So we should be good, at least when it comes to getting drunk enough to pass out."

"You worry too much," she said before taking a long pull from her beer. "Think we can put some music on?"

Pete looked around. Mike was a relatively deep sleeper. He walked over to the entertainment center and scanned Mike's CD collection before choosing a few discs and plopping them into the CD-changer. The opening chords of the Velvets' "Here She Comes Again" played from the stereo at a reasonable volume. Pete returned to the couch.

"Lou Reed? Seriously?"

"What's wrong with Lou Reed?"

"Well, nothing, I guess," Kathy said. "It just didn't strike as the right song for now."

"What would you suggest?"

"Oh, I don't know," she said. "Something more upbeat?"

"I don't think Mike has any Lady Gaga," Pete said, enjoying the banter.

"Wow, someone's sensitive," Kathy said. "Did I offend your macho music sensibilities?"

"Not at all," Pete said. "I just can't fully respect someone who doesn't like the Velvet Underground."

Kathy let out an exasperated sigh. "I did not say that, and you know it."

Pete laughed. It was nice to drink and unwind a bit, even if everything else was falling apart. Kathy joined him in laughing. He got up and brought another round, unprompted. She took the new beer gladly. The Velvets bled into the Supremes "Love Is Like an Itching in My Heart."

"This is much better," Kathy said, closing her eyes as she took a long drag from her beer. "Motown makes anything better."

Pete caught himself looking at her before she could notice.

"I tried to mix it up," he said quickly.

"Well, good on you."

There was an extended silence as Pete and Kathy listened to the music. The night air flowed into the room through an open window. The song's thumping bass and Diana Ross' plaintive vocals danced around the room as Pete and Kathy soaked up more alcohol. Pete got up and turned down the main room lights so they were in a dimmer, more intimate atmosphere. He wasn't sure what he was doing, he thought. Kathy didn't comment.

After a while, Pete realized he was on his fifth beer. His head was spinning slightly. He hadn't eaten anything all day, and Kathy probably hadn't eaten properly in days. Their eyes met for a few seconds before she broke off the stare and looked around the room.

They'd lost track of the music and were sitting closer together. Pete felt himself loosening up. His tired muscles relaxing. He would sleep well tonight. He turned to Kathy and she turned to him.

"We need to go to the cops tomorrow," he said.

"Did you just determine that now?"

"We don't have much choice," Pete said. "That money, however much there is in the bag, is dirty money."

"I didn't realize drinking made you more of a moral person," Kathy said, her voice sharper. She readjusted her seat and ended up sliding closer to Pete. She turned her face to match the angle of his. He could smell the soap she'd washed herself with. "It's usually the opposite."

"I know someone," Pete said, trying to maintain his composure. He broke their connection by leaning over and taking another sip of beer. "With the police. He can help us if we explain the situation to him."

"Sure," Kathy said. "Whatever works."

Pete was surprised at the sudden lack of resistance. Then he remembered they were both drunk and tired. He was having trouble keeping his eyes open. The stereo had run out of tracks to play or had jammed up. He didn't feel inclined to put on more music. It was close to four in the morning. Pete stared at the wall opposite the couch.

"I just feel empty," Kathy said.

"Yeah."

"Do you know what I mean, or are you just saying that?"

"I know exactly what you mean," Pete said, looking at her. "I feel like everything has come apart. All the good things people did for me, I managed to erase. And there's nothing left, nothing I did that was good."

He felt Kathy's head resting on his shoulder.

"That's terribly sad," she sighed.

He wove his arm under Kathy's and around her waist, bringing her closer to him. With his free arm, he finished his sixth beer with one long sip. He felt her breath on his neck as put the beer on the floor by the couch. He turned to catch her looking at him. She didn't turn away. He was tired. He didn't care. He leaned in and kissed her lips. She responded at first, then pulled back and slid over to the opposite end of the couch.

"I'm sorry, but no," she said raising her hands. "That's not what I should be doing now."

Pete nodded. He felt embarrassed, but not totally guilty. Drinking was good at eliminating feelings of shame — for a while, at least. He took another sip, finishing the beer, before talking.

"It's fine," he said. "We're drunk."

"No, it's not fine," she said, looking at him. "My boyfriend is dead. My father is dead. And I'm kissing some random person — who, yes, did very brave things today — but nonetheless. . . . No. I'm sorry. I wasn't thinking clearly."

"Don't worry about it," Pete said. He really didn't care. His head was buzzing and he'd already forgotten the kiss itself. But he did feel a lingering wave of discomfort.

She coughed awkwardly and sipped her beer.

"You're pissed now, aren't you?" she said, putting the bottle on the table in front of the couch.

"Why would I be pissed?" Pete said, almost annoyed. "Leave it to me to hit on the girl who's been tortured for days. I'm an asshole. I'm sorry. I thought I was better at life than I guess I am."

Kathy laughed for a few seconds.

"Dude, it's fine," she said. "This was not the first, nor will it be the last time I awkwardly make out with someone after one-too-many drinks. It happens."

Pete leaned back on the couch and felt his eyelids drooping.

"Yeah."

"Any other decent music in this place?"

Pete smiled. He got up and started toward the bathroom.

"Pick something out," he said. "I'm going to get ready for bed."

He flipped on the bathroom light and smiled at Kathy as the door closed slowly. He could feel his head begin to hurt. He sat down on the cold bathroom tile and rubbed his eyes slowly. The cool floor felt good against his body. He wanted to stay there forever.

CHAPTER TWENTY-FOUR

Pete awoke to pots clanging. He turned and saw Kathy, on the other side of the sofa-bed, curled up with the covers bunched up around her. Pete looked up to see Mike preparing himself some breakfast — probably his usual eggs and toast. The room was slowly filling with light. It was early. Pete looked himself over. He felt slightly rested, but still groggy and out of sorts.

He sat up and scratched his head. It was probably a little after seven. They'd have to either hitch a ride with Mike to the TriRail station or get a cab to see Broche downtown. Pete was leaning toward the cab. Lugging around a bag stuffed with money on public transport was not ideal.

"Yo," Mike said as Pete stood up and started to stretch.

"Good morning," Pete said.

"Get any sleep?"

"A little," Pete said. He wasn't sure what Mike was implying. He remembered the awkward kiss and then changing and passing out. He felt guilty again. He tried to ignore it, and instead shrugged at Mike. He was surprised he wasn't hung over.

"I'm gonna take a shower," Pete said. He stepped into Mike's tiny bathroom after collecting his clothes from the day before from around Mike's floor. He could tell his friend was upset. He hadn't considered how Mike felt about last night's events. His best friend had run off with his car, nearly gotten himself killed, and come back with a strange woman. Instead of silently going to sleep and being thankful, they'd probably been noisy and had drunk most of Mike's beer. Classy. He hadn't thought about Mike. The beer was cold and the release of conversation and music was needed, but with the clarity of morning came a sense of shame for Pete. He decided to apologize.

The shower was quick and hot. Pete thought about the news report he'd watched the night before. They didn't report any casualties. That meant Contreras could still be alive. He knew where Pete lived. A cold chill ran up his spine, despite the scalding shower.

Pete got out abruptly and toweled himself off. He changed into yesterday's clothes quickly and opened the door. Kathy was on the other side. She seemed surprised.

"Oh," she said. "I thought you'd run out to get coffee or something."

"No," Pete said. He wasn't sure how to act around Kathy. She had seemed understanding about their awkward kiss, but that didn't mean anything. People get retroactively weird about stuff like that, Pete thought. He stepped to the side and let her into the bathroom. "All yours."

"Thanks," she said as she slinked in and closed the door behind her.

Mike was in his room, already dressed for work and leaning over his computer. He was shutting down. Pete rapped on the door. Mike looked at him.

"Think we can hitch a ride to the TriRail? We're gonna try to clear the air with Broche," Pete said.

Mike closed his laptop and turned to Pete.

"I'm late already, so, no." Mike said, not meeting Pete's eyes. "What are you going to tell Broche?"

"The truth."

"The truth?" Mike said, spitting out the words. "That'll go over great."

"Mike," Pete said, raising his arms in surrender. "What do you suggest we do, then?"

"It's not about 'we'—it never was," Mike said, moving past Pete and into the living room. "This is all about you, man. You're just dragging us along with you because we're stupid enough to still be your friends. You stole my fucking car, got into God knows what, and then come back here — you were on the fucking news, bro. All over it. You should be in jail now. Instead, you come here to hide out and think you can have a casual chat with the police about how you left the scene of the crime and basically ran some dude over. Great thinking, man. Grade-A planning on your part. You're really on a fucking roll. You know — I've tried to be patient with you. You're like my brother, but you keep fucking up and doing the exact opposite of what makes sense. You have no job, you can't go back to your apartment. You've lost your mind. I don't even know what to tell you anymore, and that makes me really sad."

Pete followed him to the door.

"You don't mean that," he said.

"Like hell I don't," Mike said, turning to face Pete. "Explain how any of this is not your fault. Please. Enlighten me."

Pete's shoulders sagged. He could hear Kathy exiting the bathroom and hovering behind them.

"I'm sorry."

Mike ignored the apology and opened the door. He turned around briefly.

"Keep me out of this," Mike said, his tone low and calm but pulsing with anger. "Do whatever you need to do, but do not — I repeat — do not talk about me to the police. I don't want to see either of you here when I come back."

"You're right," Pete said. "Look, I'm sorry. I don't know what else I can say or do."

Mike didn't respond. He turned around and closed the door as he walked out.

"He'll calm down," Kathy said. "Just let him blow off some steam."

"No," Pete said, heading toward the window opposite the front door in the living room. "I have to talk to him."

Pete opened the window and saw Mike—across the street, his Focus parked near the curb where Kathy and Pete had left it the night before—getting into his car. Pete waved and yelled Mike's name, but got no reaction. He heard Mike start the car engine and his heart sank. He began to step back from the window, but lingered for a second, hoping Mike would have a sudden change of heart. Maybe he forgot something, Pete thought.

Pete winced at the intense flash and grabbed his ears.

CHAPTER TWENTY-FIVE

Pete knew he was screaming. He felt his throat burning and vibrating as his fists banged on the window and the wall. He felt his body begin to shake as he fell to his knees. He saw Kathy run up to the window and cover her mouth in shock. Pete felt himself lean over, his palms on the carpet of Mike's apartment, trying to stop himself from collapsing fully. He tried to get up. Maybe Mike was alive, he thought. Maybe he survived. Maybe it was someone else inside that car. His peripheral vision picked up Kathy darting away from the window. He saw smoke rising in the early morning air. He couldn't bring himself to look out again. No. If he didn't, Mike would be OK. This was a nightmare, he thought. He was still in bed, curled up, warm. Things were not allowed to get this bad.

He was still on the floor. Shaking all over. He felt his eyes begin to water. He got back to his knees. He heard a siren in the distance.

He was still facing the window when he felt movement behind him. He turned around slowly to find Kathy, clutching the bag full of money with one arm, a gun in her other hand — pointed at Pete. Not his father's gun, Pete thought. Another one.

"The hell?" Pete said. "Where the fuck did you get that?"

"It was in the bag with the money," Kathy said, holding the gun calmly.

"But . . ." Pete was having trouble thinking. There was too much going on.

"But what? You don't know me, Pete. Don't act like you do," she said, motioning to him with the gun. "Get in Mike's room. I don't have time for this. That explosion probably alerted every cop in Fort Lauderdale."

Pete did as he was told, his eyes locked on Kathy. She was in Mike's doorway.

"Did you have something to do with this?" Pete said.

"Come on, Pete," she said. "What do you think?" She swung the bag over her shoulder and moved in closer to him.

"These guys are after me . . . They want to kill me and they're not going to stop because you're looking out for me . . ." Kathy said. "I have to go. I hope you can understand that, OK?"

She backed out of Mike's room, closing the door behind her. He heard noise on the other end. She was propping something to block the door, Pete thought. After a few minutes he tried the door, but couldn't open it. He walked over to Mike's bedroom window, which overlooked the street. The flames were reaching higher into the air. A crowd had formed around what used to be Mike's car — what used to be Mike, Pete thought.

SILENT CITY

He lay down on Mike's bed and curled up into himself tightly. Then, finally, he began to cry, his body racked with a violent bout of sobbing. He couldn't hear himself. He could only hear the explosion. Of Mike's car. Of Mike. Of everything that used to make sense.

CHAPTER
TWENTY-SIX

The interrogation room in the Fort Lauderdale police station was unfamiliar to Pete. But he knew what it was used for. The air smelled of cigarettes, sweat, and coffee.

But he wasn't looking around now. His head was buried in his arms, and they rested on the wobbly wooden table near the back of the room, opposite the main door. He'd been in the room for going on five hours, and had met with a handful of different detectives. The barrage of questions had Pete's ears ringing. He could smell the cheese fries devoured by the last cop, a bovine detective named Solares. From what Pete could tell, based on the questions he'd been asked, the police had not found Contreras. Meaning he was still alive. Meaning Pete — and everyone around him — was still at risk. They did, however, want to know how his best friend came to explode earlier in the day, and just what Pete was doing in his friend's apartment, barricaded in the main bedroom.

The Fort Lauderdale cops didn't care about what happened in the Keys — they wanted to clear the murder case that happened within their jurisdiction. But all they had was smoke and rubble and an unemployed newspaper editor who had little to say.

He told them everything, though. About Kathy, Chaz, Contreras, and his own ill-advised trip south after being pounded to a pulp. They jotted down notes studiously, nodding their heads at Pete to keep talking. But he didn't know what, if anything, they'd do with the information. He also didn't know how far north Contreras' powers reached, and if this department was as soiled and corrupt as the Miami-Dade PD. Solares had seemed almost sad for Pete, wondering aloud why a guy with no detective experience, no license and no connection to Kathy Bentley would take it upon himself to be her last hope and savior.

"I had nothing else," Pete remembered blurting out. "And now I'm fucked. I'm totally fucked. I have nowhere to go, nothing to do, and no one who'll talk to me."

Pete would never forget the sad eyes that met those words, and he felt shame. Shame for pulling his friends into a mess of his own creation, shame for losing his job, shame for ruining everything around him and still wanting more. Mike was dead, and it was his fault. Had Pete not taken Mike's keys, had he not driven south on a wild hunt for Kathy Bentley, Mike would be alive. Pete wouldn't be in this room, and things would be better—not great, but not this bad.

He took a deep breath, soaking up the terrible stench of the interview room as the main door creaked open. He didn't bother to look up. He heard heavy, tentative footsteps approach, followed by the squeak of the chair across from Pete being pulled back. The soft thud of a heavyset figure taking the seat.

"They're gonna let you out in a bit."

Not even Broche's voice could make Pete look up. But gradually, he lifted his head and gave the room a once-over. He probably looked like shit, he thought. His eyes red from crying, his clothes rumpled, his face and arms bruised and cut from two skirmishes with Contreras. Pete didn't care. He deserved worse. He didn't deserve to live.

"They gonna charge me with anything?"

"The Keys police may cite you for leaving the scene of a crime," Broche said, scratching his chin. "But Fort Lauderdale doesn't care about that. As far as they're concerned, you were cooperative and you can go."

Pete nodded. He had nothing to add.

"I don't really think you'll get even that, though," Broche said. "Proving, once again, what a lucky fool you are."

"I'm not lucky."

Broche slid a cigarette into his mouth and met Pete's eyes with a cold stare that Pete had never encountered from the detective before.

"Oh, you're lucky," he said. "Lucky to be alive. Your friend? Not so lucky. And that's on you now. You — you get to go home, or somewhere similar, to rest, look for a job. You get to start over, if you want. Or, if you don't, you can keep drinking yourself stupid, keep getting in trouble, keep embarrassing me and the memory of your father. But you can keep doing something. You're alive."

He was right, Pete realized. And that made it all the worse.

"You want to talk to me?" Broche said.

"What is there to say?" Pete mumbled. "Mike's dead. I went down to the Keys to find Kathy, and I did. Contreras spotted me. Followed me, caught me in his place cutting Kathy loose, and he chased me down. I thought he was dead."

"Dead? When?"

"Kathy backed Mike's car into him," Pete said, taking no pleasure in ratting on Kathy, despite her untimely exit. "She saved me from getting shot. Then we went to Mike's — to return the car. I didn't even think that he'd follow us. Or would know where we'd be going. That's what I don't get."

"What's that?"

"He knew what I was doing — twice — before I did it," Pete said, his voice clearer now. He was thinking out loud. "He knew I was going to the Keys. He knew where I'd be sniffing around. Then he knew I'd be heading to Mike's."

Broche cleared his throat and placed his palms on the table.

"Kid, you're not dealing with some equal here," he said. "This is not some random thug. This guy knows his shit. You ruffled his feathers. You've pissed him off and lived longer than most people. Did you really think he was just going to forget you existed after he put you in the hospital? I told you to get out of this, to lay low. Then I hear you're leaving Baptist without the doctor's sign-off to go do who-knows-what. Jose Contreras is not to be fucked with. You'd be lucky if that girl had killed him, because it would have bought you some time."

"What do I do now?"

"What do you mean?"

Pete cleared his throat. His eyes met Broche's for the first time.

"How do I stay alive?"

"This is not going to blow over for a while." Broche counted off on his fingers as he leaned back slightly on his chair, "I'd move if you could. Stay at your dad's for a bit. Look for work. Quit doing stupid shit, and let all this go the fuck away. Keep me posted on what's going on and I'll keep my ears to the ground for you — if we hear about Contreras or any of his people, I will let you know. I'm going to do my best to keep you safe."

"Yeah?"

Broche nodded. "Someone's got to, right?"

Pete winced as he walked out of the station. He rubbed his neck, his entire body sore from the last week. He turned around and saw Emily opening the station's front door, a few steps behind him.

"You're lucky," she said, walking past him toward her car. He followed without saying anything. "That's all I'm going to say about this." She was upset. Her face was red. Though Mike had always been more like Pete's brother than Emily's, they had become friends nonetheless, and the idea that he was gone hit them both hard.

Pete nodded as he opened the passenger side door to Emily's Jeep. They got in. She gripped the wheel and looked ahead. Pete remained quiet. She turned and scanned him.

"You look like shit," she said.

Pete sighed and tussled his hair. He'd spent two more hours in the interrogation room and a holding cell before all the paperwork was cleared and he was given the OK to leave. All he wanted to do was to curl up in a dark hole and disappear — forever, if that was an option.

Still, Contreras was out there. Kathy was out there — with a bag full of money, no less. Javier was dead. Mike was dead. Too much had been lost to leave this be, he thought. And though he'd told Broche he would take his advice, he wasn't sure cowering in the shadows was the best plan. In fact, it was the opposite of Pete's plan. He didn't even stop to think about how awkward he should feel, sitting in a car with his ex-fiancée, hours after his best friend exploded in front of him. He didn't care about that anymore.

"I feel like shit, too," he said, looking out his window.

"I'm not going to lecture you, if that's what you're worried about," she said, still looking at him. "I don't care anymore, Pete. And that's the saddest part. Mike's dead. I don't know what to make of all this anymore."

Pete looked at Emily and nodded, then straightened up in his seat. She was crying, but looking away from him. He could see her lips quivering.

"I know exactly what to make of this," Pete said, his voice cold. "It all fell together. I know what to do about it now."

"What?" she said. "Do about it? Are you fucking kidding me? You do nothing. You say nothing. You should have left this alone from the beginning. And you didn't."

She almost yelled the last sentence. He couldn't meet her eyes. He looked out his window.

"Don't lecture me," Pete said, his voice low, almost a whisper.

"What did you say?"

"I said, 'Don't lecture me,'" Pete repeated. They were looking at each other now. "Don't lecture me, because I know exactly what I've done. I know exactly what I've lost. And while I guess on some level,

I should be thankful you're here—it doesn't give you the right to pass judgment on me like you're some kind of saint."

Pete watched Emily's face contort, as if in slow motion, anger taking over and eliminating the tears she'd cried for Mike.

"What the fuck are you talking about?" Emily said.

"This isn't about Mike," Pete said, his teeth gritted. He was tired. He figured he'd regret this later, but whatever dullness his drinking had created, whatever filters had been in place when it came to Emily were suddenly gone, and Pete felt a door opening he'd never wanted to touch. "This isn't about me. This is about us."

Emily recoiled, leaning against the driver's side door.

"Whoa, what?" she said. "Seriously? I thought we were past that, Pete. It's been almost a year. You're going to bust out the 'us' topic now? Mike's not even in the ground."

"Stop bringing him up," Pete said firmly. "Just stop it. I'm sick of this. I'm sick of pretending we're buddies and I'm some kind of clown college fuck-up. I'm not perfect, and neither are you."

"What is that supposed to mean? Where is any of this coming from?"

"I'm just tired," Pete said, his body suddenly feeling heavy. "And you didn't have to be here. You didn't have to pick me up. You just did it to be right — to be the adult. To grab poor Pete by the arm and try to get him on the right path. Well, fine. Thank you, angelic, sweet Emily. Thank you, Carlos Broche. Thank you, one and all. Thank you for saving me once again from myself."

"Oh, and it's so easy to be your friend," Emily snapped back, her eyes red and voice raw. "It's a walk in the park watching you slowly drink away everything I liked about you, and go from someone I was in love with to a creep. Yeah, I really love being your pal. I love acting important in front of you. Go fuck yourself."

Pete let out an exasperated sigh and continued. "I just find it amazing that you — after all we've been through and after how you left me literally holding the bag — can still act like some kind of moral authority," Pete said. "It's mind-boggling. I do not understand you, and I never will, and that's part of the allure and part of the problem. I try and keep you in my life as desperately as I can, thinking that some kind of miracle might push us back into place, but that's never going to happen. I know that. Deep inside, I know you'll never want me the way I want you, or the way you used to want me. But you still dangle the carrot, and you still talk to me like I'm your stupid boyfriend. Well, I'm not. I'm barely even your friend."

Emily cleared her throat slowly. "I don't know what you want me to say," she said.

"I don't want you to say anything," Pete said quickly. "I just want to go home and do what I need to do."

Emily started the car and kept her eyes looking forward. "Mike was your best friend," she said, her voice calm — a forced serenity. "He cared about you. Please, for him, for me — just let this drop."

"I can't. For Mike," Pete said, "I have to see this to the end, for him."

"Then get out of the car," Emily snapped.

CHAPTER
TWENTY-SEVEN

Pete sat in his car in the parking lot of the Caballero Funeral Home. It was near Pete's family home, in Westchester, off Bird Road and Galloway, where he'd grown up. They'd held his father's service here, too, Pete recalled. The area had made a bit of resurgence in his day-to-day of late, Pete thought sadly. A few days had passed since Mike's car had exploded in downtown Fort Lauderdale. A little over a week since his life went from an intriguing adventure to a miserable failure.

He'd barely been home, instead taking Broche's advice and staying at his father's old house, which still hadn't been sold although it was two years since his father's death. He'd moved very little in—a bag of clothes, toiletries, and his father's files. Pete unfastened his seatbelt and looked at the small crowd milling outside the funeral home. He recognized a few faces.

It was odd living in the house, but also comforting. He hadn't heard from Emily, aside from a curt voicemail explaining that she never wanted to speak to him or see him again. Pete understood. He'd put his closest friends in danger, then he'd inadvertently caused his friend's death, all in one fell swoop. To Pete's surprise, Broche had been unnervingly kind over the past few days. In what he'd dubbed a favor to Pete's father, not to him, Broche had pulled a handful of strings and had called in a dozen favors to minimize Pete's police entanglements. The Keys police dropped any charges and, aside from a dozen hours spent in the Fort Lauderdale police department, Pete had been very lucky. Mike's death was still under investigation, but from what little Broche had told Pete, there were few leads and even fewer people actually looking at the leads. Pete closed his eyes. The idea that his friend would just die, with no retribution, made him angrier than he could really understand. Broche's words haunted Pete: "I can't think of any punishment that will make you feel worse."

He was probably right.

He almost didn't hear the tap on the passenger-side window. He looked over to see Amy, dressed casually for a funeral, Pete thought, and pointing to the door, motioning for him to let her in. He leaned over and clicked the door open. She slid into the passenger seat and nodded.

"Attending the funeral remotely, I see?" she said. She put her purse on her lap and closed the door, and looked out the window quickly before turning back to Pete. "Good turnout for your friend."

Pete said nothing. The last time he'd seen Amy it hadn't been the most pleasant exchange.

She raised a hand quickly. "Don't worry," Amy said. "This isn't going to be a message about how you should live your life. I just wanted to pop in and thank you for what you did for Kathy. I realize it wasn't easy, and she'd probably be dead if you hadn't stumbled down there."

"Has anyone heard from her?" he asked. "Is she alive?"

"I haven't heard from her since she called," Amy said. "But I imagine she's fine."

She didn't elaborate. Pete figured she was lying, but had little incentive to press the issue. He was no longer concerned with Kathy. He'd found her and she was alive.

"I'd hope so, what with the bag of cash she made off with."

"Oh come on, don't start pouting," Amy said, dismissively. "You're acting like she stole it from your bank account. That was drug money."

"How'd you know it was drug money?"

"What?"

"The news never reported anything about the bag," Pete said carefully. "They definitely didn't say anything about Contreras's drug ties. So, how'd you figure that?"

Amy's face went blank; she'd been caught. Pete could see the wheels turning in her head in an effort to explain the gaffe away. She tilted her head slightly.

"You got me there," Amy said. "I've talked to Kathy a few times. She's fine, if you're worried. And she does feel bad about how she left, especially after what you did for her."

"She has a funny way of showing gratitude," Pete said.

"You're all the buzz at work," Amy said, changing the subject. "Well, you and Kathy are. She's been fired — hasn't shown up and people know she's alive. But your exploits have made for a lot of water cooler conversation."

"My dream fulfilled," Pete said. "I don't mean to be rude, but — what do you want? I appreciate the visit and all, and I am genuinely glad Kathy's living it up on the Contreras dime, but —"

Amy cut him off. "I figured you'd be here," she said. "And I wanted to pick your brain. With Kathy gone, we're scrambling a bit for a new investigative reporter —"

Now it was Pete's turn to interrupt. "You'd think they'd take me back?"

Amy stifled a laugh. "No, no, that's not what I meant, sorry," she said. "Let me finish. Now, Kathy's gone, but I still have her notes about this entire 'Silent Death' thing — and I think it's time we ran with it. But as an editor, I can't just print suppositions and innuendo. Her notes are good, but I imagine you have some insight that I can add to her evidence and hopefully hammer something out in the next week or so. Blow the lid off this entire thing and give you and her some peace."

Pete scratched his head. Amy, for all her years of experience and police know-how, obviously wasn't fully versed in how totally corrupt the Miami PD was, especially in relation to the Silent Death. He didn't feel inclined to tell her, either. But the idea of a story hitting the *Miami Times* and forcing not only the Miami police but the powers above it to act sounded good. And if it meant Pete wouldn't have to worry every time he woke up in the morning or every second he spent outside his house, then it'd be worth it.

"From what I read in my dad's files, and skimmed over in Kathy's notes," Pete said, "it all points to Contreras. The ties to Chaz, the drug money coming from upstate, and the front that is Casa Pepe's. I'm not sure who else it could be."

"OK. Well, first off, I'm going to ignore that little tidbit that involves you somehow getting into Kathy's notes," Amy said. "Do you have access to your dad's files? Aren't those police property?"

Pete shrugged. "I suppose. I found them in my dad's stuff. He must have kept them."

"That's amazing," Amy said, her eyes widening. "Those would be hugely helpful. Do you think I'd be able to see them? Or even copy them?"

Pete thought for a second before responding.

"I'll do anything at this point," he said. "So, yes. If it means getting Contreras off the streets and bringing in the person that did this to Mike—and to me—then I'm all for it."

"That's the thing, though," Amy said. "I'm not totally sold on Contreras."

"Why's that?"

"It just seems too easy," Amy said, turning to look at the people entering the funeral home. "Maybe that's just the editor in me. When a story's too good, you have to question the basics, sometimes even the reporter. 'Did they flourish this quote a tad?' 'Did they double-check these facts?' Does your father say definitively that it's Contreras?"

"No," Pete said. "If he had been sure, he would have arrested him."

"How do you know that?"

Pete gave her a confused look. "What do you mean?"

"The Miami police aren't exactly squeaky-clean," she said. "And no offense to your father, who for all I know was a fine officer of the law, but he wasn't exactly paired with the most respected partner."

"Carlos Broche?"

"That's the one."

"What about him?"

"Chalk this one up to my gut, too," Amy said. "But I never got much help from him when I was the cops reporter. About the same when I was editing the other cops folk. Never heard a good word about him."

"But never a bad one, either, right?" Pete said.

"True, but after a few decades of reading and working with cops," Amy said, "you start to get a sense for them. Anyway, I don't know much about him, and my point is, even if your dad had the goods on Contreras, it would have been nearly impossible for him to have arrested him, with the department the way it is."

"His notes aren't definitive," Pete said. Maybe Amy knew more than she initially let on. "But I need to look at them again." His mind flashed back to his few moments with the files, drunk and high off the adrenaline around the search for Kathy, unaware of the tragedy to come.

He closed his eyes for a second.

Amy reached for the door and clicked it open, turning to Pete.

"If you do, let me know," Amy said. "I'd love to look them over and see what they can do to help."

She passed him her card and nodded.

"It's a good thing," Amy said. "We can make a difference for once. The paper can actually do some good for a change. Imagine what it would mean for this city to finally have this guy behind bars, huh?"

"Yeah, what a wonderful world," Pete said sarcastically. "I'll let you know. It's not like I'm swimming in appointments and meetings, anyway."

Amy gave him a pitying smile and left, closing the door quietly as she walked to her car, avoiding the ceremony. The dashboard display told him it was getting late.

Pete reached for his car door but hesitated. He leaned back. He was parked in the far west corner of the lot. He could see the front door, but doubted anyone was looking far enough to notice him. He reached into his shirt pocket and pulled out an envelope addressed to him. It was from the *Miami Times*. A severance check. His suspension was not even over, but the paper had decided they didn't want him back. Two months' pay was what they deemed worthy. For the first time in his life, Pete was unemployed and with no prospects. He was alone, his two closest friends gone—one literally, another by choice. He couldn't even go back to his apartment for fear a gangland killer would be waiting for him.

"Fuck me," Pete whispered to himself as he stepped out of his car. He could feel the eyes on him the second he reached the funeral home entrance. He walked past a cluster of strangers and stepped into the lobby. He saw Mike's parents, Steve and Mary, huddled near the door of the chapel housing Mike's dead body, whispering to each other and looking at Pete. He swallowed hard and walked over to them. They stopped talking suddenly and made eye contact as he approached.

He'd met them a number of times over the decade he'd known Mike, but had never interacted with them beyond casual pleasantries. What did they know about Pete's involvement in their son's death?

"Hello," Pete said, never sure what to say in these situations. "I'm sorry I'm so late. I just wanted to let you know how sorry I am about what happened."

Pete noticed a flare of anger on Steve's face, which quickly softened into sadness. Pete was surprised when he felt Steve enveloping him in a strong hug.

"Pete," he said. "Oh, Pete. We're glad you made it. We were wondering where you were."

Pete felt another hand rubbing his back. Mike's mother. They had no idea. He felt a sense of great relief, combined with shame.

Pete pulled away from the hug.

"I know," he said, facing Mike's parents.

"It's just hard to accept this happened."

"It was a terrible mistake," Steve said, his deep baritone wavering slightly. "That boy never did anything to deserve that kind of death."

"We couldn't even have an open casket," Mary, sputtered, choking back tears as her husband pulled her into his large arms. She looked off toward the ceiling. "Oh Lord, how does this happen?"

"I'm sorry," Pete said, holding Mary's hands. "There wasn't a better person — a better friend." Pete stopped talking, feeling himself begin to choke up. He didn't want to cry anymore. "Spent" was the best way he could describe his life the last few days. Mike's parents nodded furiously, hugging him and thanking him. His sense of shame quickly overwhelmed any relief he'd first felt.

He was a liar.

They stepped back into the chapel just as Pete felt a tap on his shoulder. He turned to find Broche there, an unlit cigarette in his mouth. He looked tired. The last few days had been exhausting for everyone, not just for Pete.

"Walk with me," Broche said, heading toward the front of the funeral home. Pete followed. He saw Emily pop out of the chapel entrance. She looked at him for a split second, then turned away and went back in.

Broche wove past the small group milling outside the funeral home and walked to the sidewalk before lighting up. Pete stuck his hands in his pockets.

"Kathy's still AWOL," Broche said. "I'm hearing rumblings from my informants that she had more money than she let on in that bag. She may be gone for good. We still have nothing on the explosion, though. No evidence — fingerprints, tire treads, witnesses, nada. This whole thing is a mess, you realize this?"

Pete nodded. He was in no position to argue with the man that had basically saved what little life he had left. But he also wasn't inclined to share the information he'd just gleaned from Amy, either. He waited for Broche to continue.

"I need you to promise me you're not going to get crazy with all the free time you have," Broche said, taking a drag from his cigarette and looking at Pete. "Your friend is dead. From what I can tell, your other friend doesn't think speaking to you is on her to-do list."

Pete paused for a second. He looked at Broche. His father had been a year younger than the 60-year-old detective, on the verge of cashing in his pension. Pete wondered if his father would have closed the case by now, if his health hadn't forced him into early retirement and then killed him. Pete knew he wasn't going to give up using what little resources he had to avenge Mike, but he wasn't sure he could tell Broche that anymore. He'd expended what little goodwill he had left with the man.

"Yeah, I'm done with this whole thing," Pete said. "What about Contreras? Any sign of him?"

"*Nada*," Broche said. "We have enough on Contreras to nab him on laundering money. Seems like he had a nice operation going from his restaurant. A big bookie, that guy. A waitress from Casa Pepe's gave us a statement after we barged in with the info about Javier being killed. Says she spoke to a private detective not long before. Wonder who that might have been?"

Pete didn't bother to deny the truth. He knew Broche was baiting him. He deserved it.

"What are you gonna do now?" Broche said. "Don't let all this be a waste. Let it be a lesson."

"I don't know yet," Pete said, looking out onto the busy Bird Road traffic. "I just feel like sitting in the dark."

He didn't mention to Broche that he had, in fact, been sitting alone. But with a light on. Taking notes. Thinking over everything that had happened. He couldn't stop. Mike's death compelled him. His desire for vengeance replaced the strange curiosity that had entertained him before things derailed. His best friend was dead, this was true, but someone he could find had strapped the bomb to Mike's car, and he wasn't inclined to let that slide.

"Take a few days for yourself," Broche said, putting a hand on Pete's shoulder. "Then start looking for work. The rest will fall into place over time."

Pete nodded and shook Broche's hand. He couldn't bear to enter the chapel and see Mike's casket, so he decided to head for his car. He was only slightly surprised to find Emily leaning on it, waiting for him.

"Hey," Pete said, pulling his car keys out of his pocket absentmindedly. "How are you?"

"I'm fine," Emily said. Her arms were crossed. She looked at the funeral home entrance and then back at Pete. He waited a second before realizing she wasn't going to say anything else.

"Look," Pete started before Emily raised a hand to silence him.

"I don't want to hear it," she said, her voice clear and strong. "I just wanted you to know — in person and not from a voicemail — that I can't have you in my life anymore."

Pete bristled a bit. He'd beaten himself up enough. He was a little tired of getting beaten up by everyone around him, deserved or not.

"You came here to repeat your message to me?" Pete said, his voice low. "Should I help you load up your car with your bags, just like old times? Because, really, this 'leave me alone forever' routine is getting old."

"I just felt like I needed to say it to you directly," Emily said, slightly surprised that Pete was being argumentative. "And I came here to make sure you were done with all this."

"Done with all what, Emily?" Pete said. "I've got nothing. No job, no friends, no home. If this isn't 'done,' then what the fuck is? If you're asking me if I'm sitting in the dark drinking myself to death, then the answer might be yes. If you're asking me to stop trying to figure out what happened to Mike, or to stop trying to bring the people that did this in for some kind of punishment, then no. Mike's killer is out there."

"He wouldn't be dead if you hadn't dragged us into this," she said. Pete noticed her face contort slightly. She hadn't meant to be so harsh.

"You're right," Pete said, taking a step toward his car. "And I have to live with that."

Emily looked down at her feet. "I don't want to hate you," she said. "But I don't want to talk to you, either."

Pete felt his hands gripping his keys. It hurt.

"Look at me," he said. She did. "What more can I say? How else can I apologize? Don't you think I'm torn up inside about this?"

"Maybe," she said. "But you haven't learned anything. If you die doing this, you make Mike's death worthless, too."

"It's not about learning anything or any value," Pete said. "It's about finding the people that did all this. Killed Mike. Took Kathy. Everything. Then I can go do something else."

Emily frowned. She stared past Pete, past the funeral home. Her eyes looked tired.

"What can you do?" she said, some contempt in her voice.

"I'm not sure," Pete said. Emily stepped back. He opened the door and got in. He turned to her, the driver's side window sliding down. "You have every right to hate me."

With that, he closed the door and started his Celica's creaky engine. Pete felt a slight rap on the driver's side window.

Pete waited for more. But it wasn't forthcoming. He nodded. She backed away from the car as he pulled out of the parking space and turned to leave. He watched her as he drove by, standing alone in the dark parking lot, her pale skin in stark contrast to the darkness around her.

CHAPTER
TWENTY-EIGHT

It had started to pour halfway from the funeral home to his father's house. It took Pete an extra moment to notice her, huddled by his front door with a hoodie over her head, as he walked over from the carport. He recognized the lanky figure as Kathy. She was soaked. He scampered over and stood in front of her, letting the rain pelt them both, for a moment before she spoke.

"I had nowhere else to go," she sputtered, rain on her face and in her mouth.

Pete said nothing, but motioned for her to follow him. He got the key in the door and opened it quickly. He flicked on the parlor light and she doffed her hoodie without asking, letting it drop. Pete looked at the clothes on the floor, then at her.

"Sorry," she said.

"It's fine," Pete said, turning and entering the living room. "Do you need a towel?"

"Sure."

Pete darted to the bathroom and returned, handing Kathy a large gray towel. She began feverishly drying her face and hair.

"Aren't you going to ask me why I'm here?" she said, her voice muffled slightly by the towel.

"I'm not. But I guess you're going to tell me," Pete said, walking into his father's kitchen and rummaging through the cabinets. He found what he was looking for — a bottle of Johnny Walker Black and two glasses — and set them on the counter, the bottle and glasses clinking as they made contact. He pulled an ice tray from the freezer and dropped a few cubes in each glass. "Though, I imagine this isn't a social call."

Pete returned to the living room and placed the two glasses — now relatively full and on the rocks — on the dining table, which was close to the front door. Pete felt strange drinking liquor in his father's house, but he didn't really care at this point. Everything made him feel strange these days.

Kathy sat down next to Pete, picked up the other glass, and took a long sip.

"You're right," she said. "I had to do some digging to find you. You weren't at your apartment."

"That'd be stupid."

"Probably, yeah," she said.

The house was silent for a few seconds as Pete took a sip of his drink. He let the glass touch the table before he spoke again. "What do you want? The last time I saw you, you were pointing a gun at me."

"I know," Kathy said, slinking back into her chair. "I'm sorry for that. I just — I was just losing it. I'd been trapped for days; your friend's car — which we'd been driving in for hours — had just blown up. It was too much. I saw the money as my out, and I didn't really feel like spending hours talking to the cops about everything that had happened."

Pete put his elbows on the table and rubbed his eyes. He was tired. He had no sense of what to do next, and finding Kathy on his doorstep was the last thing he wanted.

"Why are you here?"

"He's alive."

"Who's alive?"

"Contreras," Kathy said. "He's alive, and he's been following me — sending me messages. Not written notes and shit, but little things. Newspaper clippings in my car while I'm at the store. Following me in another car. I just know he's around. It's driving me nuts."

Pete moved his hands away from his face and gave Kathy a surprised stare.

"Are you telling me that Contreras has been following you and you led him here, to me?" Pete said. "This is just a sick joke, right?"

Kathy took another long swig from her glass. She was thinking.

"I don't think he's been following me the whole time, I don't know," she said. "I just know we need to do something. I can't live like this. I made a mistake. I want my life back."

Pete got up without warning and walked toward the back of the house. He returned a few minutes later, a large box in his hand. He dropped it loudly on the table. He tossed a tiny, portable USB drive next to it.

"Let's get our lives back."

"Oh my God, Nigel!"

"What?" Pete said. He was sitting by his laptop at the dining room table, reading over the text file containing Kathy's notes on the Silent Death when he heard her screech. She'd taken a break to use the bathroom. He walked briskly over to where the squeal had come from to find her petting her cat — the cat Pete had basically adopted since discovering him a few weeks back while searching her apartment.

"Nigel?"

Kathy ignored Pete's snark and continued to snuggle with the cat, who was more than happy to take the overflow of petting. Pete wasn't exactly the most loving cat owner. Costello meowed plaintively and began rubbing his side on Pete's left leg.

"Too many cats in here," Pete said.

Kathy turned to Pete.

"Thank you," she said. "Seriously. I thought he'd just run away or gotten stolen. You watched him for me. That's wonderful."

She stood up, Nigel in her arms, and walked back toward the dining room area. She plopped the cat in her lap as she went back to flipping through the stack of manila folders that were around her area. Pete's father had been an extremely organized detective, which meant that sorting through his notes on the case would take some time.

The bottle of Johnny Walker stood at half-mast, but Pete felt alert. The decision came to him quickly, especially after talking to Amy outside Caballero. The only way out — and the only skills he could rely on — were the newspaper. As much as he loathed putting any faith in the *Miami Times*, he knew that going to the police was fruitless. Only a story that received the proper attention would force those above the local police to take action and, in the process, save both Pete and Kathy from living the rest of their lives in fear.

They'd set up a mini war room on the dining room table, Pete using his laptop to read Kathy's saved notes more closely and Kathy, with a printout of her notes in hand, focused on scanning Pete's father's box of reports and notations. They'd been at it for a few hours, and the clock was now at three in the morning. They were far from being done.

"So, why isn't it Contreras?" Pete said, his eyes still on the laptop, his hand scrolling down the page with the mouse.

Kathy looked up from the files.

"What do you mean?"

"Well, everything points to him," Pete said. "The drug front, the record, the relationship with your father, the place in the Keys. What made you hesitate on publishing this earlier?"

"That's all good evidence," Kathy said, looking back at the file she had in her hand for a moment. "Trust me, because I worked really hard to get it. But it's circumstantial. That's the problem with Contreras as a suspect. There's just enough evidence to make you think it's him — we saw Javier's body, he took credit for my father's murder, you tussled with him in your apartment. But he has no connections to the 'official' Silent Death murders. And it's not like the Silent Death hasn't killed. From what your father thinks, there are at least a dozen, if not more. All with two silencer bullets in the head. All with reports of witnesses saying they saw a man in a dark overcoat and hat in the area, or near the victim. There's something funny there. I feel like we're missing something."

It felt like they were close, but even with the stacks of evidence surrounding them, he wasn't sure there was anything in the files to guarantee a story worth printing. Plus, Kathy and Pete were not exactly lauded *Miami Times* alums.

"How many people do you think are definitely his kills?" Pete asked.

Kathy put the file down and thought for a second, then looked at her pad.

"Like I said, at least a dozen. Most of them other criminals in the Miami underworld — Alfredo Rangel, Jose Aparicio, Andres Fuentes, Rodrigo Perez. Not nice guys, by any means. And all — according to my sources — people who had fucked up in some way. Either with their gangland bosses or they somehow offended another, opposing leader. The Silent Death didn't work for anyone, but he did work for everyone, y'know?"

Pete thought for a second. "Were there any exceptions?"

"What do you mean?" she said.

"Well, people that aren't clearly criminals," Pete said. "Some kind of inkling as to who this person was, you know? If I was this guy, and I didn't want anyone to really find out who I was, I'd clear the decks beforehand."

Kathy bit her pen and looked at Pete. "You're pretty good at this," she said. "Why'd you stop? Weren't you a sports reporter before?"

Pete nodded. "Yeah," he said. "I did some investigative stuff in Jersey. It was fun. It felt good to crack a story."

"Why'd you quit?"

"My dad died," Pete said, a little too quickly. "I came back here, got tangled up making sure his affairs were in order, and ended up staying."

"Hm."

"What?"

"Well, don't take this the wrong way," she said, shuffling the papers in front of her. "But do you really think your dad would let you get by, using him as an excuse? You're smart. You could do better than hiding and drinking, you know?"

Pete turned back to the screen and clicked the mouse, reverting his attention to the laptop. "Maybe."

They each went back to their respective tasks — Pete scanning Kathy's notes and jotting down any detail of interest, and Kathy doing the same with the box of files.

"Here's something," Kathy said, breaking the silence. She had a police report in her hand, pulled out of one of the older files in the box. "This report's about 10 years old. Same M.O. as the Silent Death, but before any actual criminals were killed by him, as far as we know. Your dad circled the guy's name. Scribbled something next to it — 'Check to confirm' it looks like?"

Pete grabbed the paper from Kathy's hand and scanned it. His eyes widened slightly. The man's name — Alfredo Florin — lingered with Pete.

"What is it?"

"I'm not sure," Pete said. "The name's familiar, but I can't place it."

Pete's cell phone rang, vibrating loudly on the dining room table.

"Who the hell is calling you at four in the morning?"

Pete grabbed it. From his experience, no call at this hour could be positive. He braced himself.

He listened intently to the voice on the other end; nodded.

"OK, I'll be there," he responded, then pushed a button to end the call. He stood up and put his phone in his pocket, a glazed look on his face.

"What? What is it?" Kathy said, still seated.

"Amy's dead," Pete said, clearing his throat. "Broche needs me at the scene. It's the Silent Death, and he left me a message."

CHAPTER TWENTY-NINE

Pete pulled his Marlins cap down on his head as the lingering rain soaked him further. He shivered slightly as he waited outside the yellow police tape surrounding Amy's North Miami Beach condo. From his vantage point, he could see the white tarp that covered Amy's body, which had been splayed out in the small parking lot that was adjacent to the building. Pete felt a headache forming. Not from the drinks earlier, but from the aching realization that he might have been one of the last people to see Amy alive. Four uniformed officers stood around the scene, trying to preserve as much evidence as possible. Rain was the enemy of homicide police. It washed away vital clues and made a difficult job even harder. Pete felt for them. He remembered many a night when his father would come home soaked to the bone, frustrated at all the information that he'd lost due to an unexpected rainstorm.

"Any one of those clues could be the one that sends the killer to jail," he'd said. "And they're gone. I'm starting at a disadvantage. I have to make up the difference."

Broche's approach brought Pete back to the present. He too, was soaked, his khaki trench coat splattered with raindrops. He moved past the police tape and walked over to Pete.

"No umbrella?"

"Came over right after you called."

"This is becoming a bad routine," Broche said, trying to lighten the mood, even a bit.

Pete didn't laugh.

"What happened?"

"Two shots to the head," Broche said, in a tone that implied it wasn't the first time he'd had to utter the lines. "Right outside her apartment. She was getting out of her car. Couple hours ago."

After the funeral, Pete thought. Someone knew she'd been there. Someone must have also seen her talking to him. He wiped rain off his face.

"It's definitely him?"

"Gotta be," Broche said. "Old lady down the street says she saw a guy — dressed in all black, even a black umbrella — walk up to her. Two shots, she drops. Then he dropped this next to her, made a point of tucking it under her body since it was raining."

Broche handed Pete an envelope. In very plain, almost blocky handwriting was Pete's name. He hesitated before taking it.

"Don't worry," Broche said. "It's been dusted. No prints on it. Same for the paper inside. You think we're amateurs?"

"No," Pete said. "Not exactly."

Broche stiffened a bit at Pete's comment. "What's that supposed to mean?"

"Nothing," he said, taking the envelope and opening it.

Pedro,

I think it's about time we ended this little back and forth. You have something I want — namely, the notes you stole from your former workplace and the notes your father stole from his former workplace. An interesting parallel, no?

Anyway, why don't you be a sport and bring them — and any copies you've sneakily made — to Casa Pepe's tonight. I imagine there are a few police officers who don't take advice from me. I'd suggest they not come along or wait around. It's either you alone, with the materials I've requested or there will be problems. You'll know what I mean when you get here.

I realize walking into a situation like this alone doesn't exactly warm your heart. Fair enough. But let's look at the downside, too: If you don't, I'll continue to make what's left of your pathetic life a living hell, and the next person you find dead will be much closer to you than some ragged old editor with a bad dye job. Do as I say and you have my word you'll be left alone as long as you respond in kind.

See you tonight.

There was no signature on the letter, and Pete hadn't expected one. The Silent Death moniker wasn't one of the killer's own creation, but something the press had dubbed him early on in his "career."

"It'd be stupid of you to go," Broche said.

"Oh, I'm not going," Pete responded, handing the letter back to Broche.

"You're not?"

"What is this, a comic book?" Pete said. "Will he reveal his master plan to me while I'm tied to a giant pan, sliding into a giant oven?"

Had the circumstances been different, he would have laughed at his own attempt at humor, but this wasn't funny. Nothing was funny anymore. Three people he knew were dead. All because of a killer Pete had never wanted anything to do with. All because he thought it'd be a good idea to help find a woman he'd barely spoken to.

Broche raised his hand, as if to hold Pete back.

"You need to do something, though," he said. "Your best bet is to give this guy what he wants and step away."

"Really? Really, Carlos?" Pete said, getting in Broche's space. "Because 'stepping away' hasn't done me a whole hell of a lot of good up to now, man. Maybe I should consider some new fucking options?"

"You need to watch your mouth," Broche said, his voice lowered. "You have no idea the things I had to do and the strings I had to pull to keep you out of trouble."

Pete shrugged his shoulders. "It doesn't matter, anyway."

"What do you mean?" Broche asked.

"Kathy's putting together a story," Pete said. "We figured out who the Silent Death is. It's over. She got in touch with an editor once you called me about Amy — Steve Vance of all people. Said everything was forgiven if she'd give the *Times* the story. She's over at the *Times* building now, putting the story together. It'll be on the stands with the early edition, tonight. We're taking control of this. I'm getting my life back."

Broche babbled something and then regained his composure for a second.

"Who is it? Who's the Death? You need to share it with the police."

Pete cupped his hands around his mouth and moved closer to the cluster of uniformed cops on the other side of the yellow police tapes. He channeled his old rock singing voice, from when he used to play bad punk covers in college.

"The *Miami Times* is going to reveal the identity of the Silent Death tonight," Pete yelled, feeling Broche tugging at him. "Be sure to pick up the paper!"

Pete felt his body being yanked backwards and slammed into a nearby police car. He was jarred by the motion, but not hurt. He felt Broche grab him by his shirt and pull him closer.

"Are you fucking nuts?" Broche said, his breath hot and bitter on Pete's face. "You can't just decide to announce shit like that. What if you're wrong? You've just signed your death warrant."

Pete pushed Broche away.

"Leave me alone on this one," Pete said, backing away "I know what I'm doing." He turned around and headed for his car, ignoring Broche. Ignoring the new rain. Ignoring everything but the clock ticking in his head.

CHAPTER THIRTY

Pete rang the doorbell after a few moments of hesitation. The drive down to Homestead — to Emily's house — had taken almost an hour. An hour he could have probably used doing something else — something more productive in the short term. But he didn't care. If the last few days had taught him anything, it was that you have little idea of when you're going to see someone for the last time. He didn't want to have his last conversation with Emily be an argument. Like things had ended with Mike.

The door opened to reveal Rick, Emily's husband, a tall, burly man with a clean-cut hairstyle and a strong build. He seemed surprised to see Pete, who, in his untucked shirt, faded jeans and ratty sneakers didn't look his best.

"Pete," Rick said, still holding the door half-closed. "Uh, Emily didn't mention you were coming over. It's not even seven in the morning."

Pete smiled.

"Ah, well, I was in the neighborhood," Pete said, his hands in his pockets, looking anywhere but at Rick. He was a good man, Pete thought. But he would never like him. He couldn't. That would require him to admit Emily had made the right choice by leaving Pete. "Is Emily around? I needed to talk to her about something."

Rick stepped back and opened the door.

"Sure, sure, come in," he said. "Wait here. I'll go get her. I think she's in the garden."

Pete took a seat on the couch in the living room. He didn't know what to expect from Emily — anger, dismissal, love. She was unpredictable and emotional, not to mention extremely sharp. It's what drew Pete to her in the first place. It's what kept him dancing around the edges of her world, pretending to want to be friends with someone who'd stomped his heart out.

Emily walked into the living room, through the glass patio door. She was in a dirty pair of jeans and a red Fugazi T-shirt, stained by the dirt and grass.

"Pete?"

He stood up awkwardly from the couch. She walked over to the living room. Pete noticed that Rick stayed outside. He was giving them their privacy.

"Hey," Pete said. He'd felt like coming here was such a good idea when he hopped into his car. Now he wasn't so sure.

"This is kind of a surprise," Emily said. She sat down in the chair across from the couch. "What's up? Are you OK?"

Pete sat down. "Well, I felt like we left on bad terms the last time we talked."

"That's one way to put it."

"I'm here because I want you to know that I think all of this is going to be resolved soon, one way or the other."

"What do you mean?" Emily said, her eyebrows furrowing. "You're acting extra weird."

"Kathy and I figured out who the Silent Death is," Pete said. "We pooled our research and we think we've cracked the case."

Emily nodded, motioning for Pete to keep talking.

"And I think we've figured out a way to nail him," Pete said. "But I'm not totally sure. Not 100 percent, at least."

"Why are you here, Pete?"

"I'm here to say goodbye," Pete said.

Emily took a quick breath. "Goodbye? What are you talking about?"

Pete cracked his knuckles quickly and looked around the house. It was nice. He'd never really spent time here. He wondered if they would have gotten a house like this, had things not fallen apart. He'd never know, he told himself.

"You've got a life here," he said. "A job, friends, a husband. I feel like even if none of this had happened, we'd still be in this weird limbo state. Me wondering about what was, you thinking about what could have been if I hadn't screwed up."

"That's not true at all," Emily said, defensively. "I don't see what the point of this is. 'Goodbye' as in I don't want to talk to you ever again, or 'goodbye' as in, I may be dead tomorrow? You're being really creepy and ominous, and I don't know what to say."

"I don't know either," Pete said. "This all sounded much better in my head."

He stood up.

"That's it?" Emily said, also standing up. "You come in here, disrupt my day, freak out my husband, and for what? To just act all mysterious and vague? What the hell is going on?"

Pete hugged her, pulling her in quickly, but holding on to her as if his life depended on it. After a few seconds she started to hug him back. And he was grateful for that. Almost happy. To know that even with everything else between them being weird and disconnected, they could still share something.

"I love you, Em," Pete said, pulling back, his hands on her arms. "Just know that. Even when I hated you, I cared about you. It's terrible. I don't know what to do about it. And I know I'm a fuck-up. Try to forgive me."

Pete could tell she was trying her best not to cry — from a combination of sadness and confusion. He let go of her and stepped back. She just looked at him. He turned around and walked out the door. Despite the cloudy weather, he put on his sunglasses to hide his eyes.

CHAPTER THIRTY-ONE

The sun had begun to set by the time Pete pulled into the *Miami Times* visitor parking lot. He positioned his car to the north side of the building, giving him a direct view of the building's main entrance. He remembered how empty the lot would get on Saturdays and Sundays — when it was only the newspaper personnel working through the night. All the businessmen and ad people were off enjoying their weekends. He took a sip of his coffee and scanned the lot quickly. He was exhausted, but alert. He hadn't seen any movement in the lot since he'd parked, which led him to believe he'd arrived at the right time. He'd driven by both secured entrances and found guards at their stations. Pretty good for early on a Sunday evening, he thought.

Pete felt a strange calm overtake him. He wondered if this was what athletes felt before a big game, or when they were at the foul line, taking a crucial shot — deciding the game. He'd never know. He opened the car's glove compartment and pulled out his father's gun. He checked it. Loaded. He saw a figure head toward the side entrance — to the elevator that would take someone down to the printing presses at the bottom of the *Miami Times* building — and he knew it was time. He got out of the car slowly and slid the gun behind his back. He prayed he wouldn't have to use it.

It was close to six in the evening and the presses weren't even warm. From what Pete could tell, it was too early. The area — large metallic printing presses surrounded by stacks of newspapers and blank rolls of newsprint paper — was imposing to someone like Pete, who had never really spent much time in the area when he worked at the *Times*. He could only imagine what it looked like to a total outsider. The shadowy figure was a few yards ahead of Pete, walking very slowly. *Probably out of his element*, Pete thought. The plating area — where the files were transferred digitally from the editorial floors to the press editors, who then guided the ink to page, loomed above the machines, like some kind of futuristic surveillance station. There were two metallic staircases, one on each side, leading up to the plating area.

The shadowy figure had come into better focus, but Pete still couldn't get a good read on him. He wasn't sure if he'd played his gamble correctly. He kept his distance and watched from behind one of the presses as the figure made his way up the creaking metal stairs on the west side of the pressroom. Pete slowly pulled the gun from behind his back. He wondered if he should say a prayer of some kind.

He looked up and saw the door of the plating room close. Now was his chance.

He made his way to the metal stairs quickly and silently, looking up to the plating area, which faced a wall of windows. The figure was hovering over the main computer terminal, which was opposite the windows; it faced a bay of cubicles and paste-up areas, where last-minute changes to the paper could be made. Pete inched up the ladder, trying to avoid creaks from the rusted metal.

He realized, a few steps short of the top, that he wouldn't have much of a chance to peer into the plating room without giving himself away. He couldn't risk losing the element of surprise. Pete knew he wasn't a fighter; his encounters with Contreras earlier had shown him that. No, this would have to be quick and painless, he thought, or he'd be a dead man.

With that in mind, he leapt over the final two steps and into the main plating area, gun drawn. Before he could speak, he realized who the figure was. Carlos Broche turned, surprised, and stepped backwards, his hands raised in response to the gun Pete was pointing at him.

"Pete? What?" Broche said. "What the fuck are you doing here?"

"You tell me," Pete said, his breathing heavy from the run up the stairs. "Tell me why you're here. Give me a reason why you'd come here that makes me believe you. Please."

Broche coughed and continued to back up. He was stalling.

"I came to talk some sense into you," Broche said. "This whole thing is crazy. You can't just run a story about someone if you don't know it's true."

"Don't you get it?" Pete said. "There is no story. The empty pressroom should have been clue enough for you. But I figured that information was too inside-baseball. That's why I yelled at the cops. That's why I told you. I figured someone would get word to the Death. Someone would show up here and try to stop this imaginary story from happening. I wasn't sure it'd be you, but here you are, proving me right. You're not here to talk me out of anything. You're here to protect your boss from being outed."

"My boss? The fuck you talking about?"

"You put on a good show," Pete said, the gun still pointed at Broche. He took a few tentative steps in the detective's direction. " 'I'm just looking out for you, Pete,' 'Try to stay out of trouble, Pete,' 'You wouldn't believe the strings I pulled, Pete.' Bullshit. You're as corrupt as the rest of the Miami PD. I just didn't let myself see it."

"You've lost it, man," Broche said putting his hands by his side.

"Hands up, asshole," Pete said. "Do not even think about going for your gun."

"You've got this all wrong," Broche said. "All wrong. You're going to be in deep shit. Just put the gun down. You have some serious issues to deal with, you know that?"

"It took me a while to figure it out," Pete said, his eyes and the gun still locked on Broche. "But it dawned on me after Mike's car blew up. In the interrogation room. The Silent Death was always a step ahead of me. He knew I was going to the Keys. The only people that knew that were Mike, Emily — and you."

Broche shook his head, but didn't speak.

"You kept pushing me to stop, telling me I was on the wrong track, this and that," Pete said, feeling his anger boil to the top. "But I was on the right track. You told them I had Mike's car, so they knew

I'd head back there after I got Kathy. You led them right to me. How did you even know?"

"No, no, it's not like that," Broche said, shaking his head. "You've got it wrong. I didn't know they were going to kill him . . . your friend. It wasn't like that. I was trying to help."

"How was it, then? Why did you come here?"

"You have to understand," Broche said, his voice cracking. He had backed up a few paces and was now up against a wall. "I'm old. I'm about to retire. My pension is shit. I started doing jobs for him — everyone did now and then. After your father died, there was no reason not to. It was my turn to get paid. But when you got tangled in this, I had to get you out. I couldn't have your life on my conscience. I talked to him. He said he just wanted to put a scare in you, get you off the trail so everything could go back to how it was."

"You son of a bitch," Pete said. He had his father's gun pointed at Broche's face.

"You have to believe me," Broche said. "I was just trying to do what was best — for you, for your father. You have no idea what you're up against. I was trying to help you. I know how to handle situations like this; I was looking out for — "

Pete struck Broche with the butt of the gun across the face with a ferocity he didn't realize he had in him. The detective reeled back, his head slamming into the wall, blood dripping down his nose and out of his mouth. For a split second Pete felt a pang of guilt for hitting the older man.

"Answer my question," Pete said between gritted teeth. "Why are you here?"

"He sent me . . . he told me to stop you," Broche gurgled, blood dripping down his face. "Stop the story . . ."

"Who?" Pete yelled. Broche was losing consciousness. "Who sent you here?"

"I did."

Pete turned around quickly to face the gravel-tinged voice. He was met by a tall man in a dark overcoat, hat, and mask. He had a gun pointed at Pete. Jose Contreras stood behind the masked man, weapon in hand.

CHAPTER THIRTY-TWO

"**Y**ou've become surprisingly problematic," the Silent Death said, his voice coarse but almost friendly in tone. He didn't move. The gun remained pointed at Pete. Contreras winked awkwardly. Pete's head was spinning. "Put your gun down and step away from Mr. Broche."

Pete almost hesitated, still thrown off by how casual the man in black sounded. Broche was unconscious, crumpled on the ground near the far wall. Pete got on one knee and laid down his father's gun. Both the Silent Death and Contreras watched Pete, the Death following Pete's descent with his gun. Pete noticed Contreras wince as he took a step closer to the Death. At least they'd hurt him in the Keys, he thought. Pete got back to his feet, raising his hands slightly to show they were free.

"Good, now we can talk," the Death said. "I hope you realize how annoying you've been these last few days. Really."

That voice, Pete thought. In a way, his ploy had both succeeded and failed — it had brought the Silent Death to him, but it wasn't who he or Kathy had expected. Contreras was here, but he wasn't the Death. Broche was here, but he wasn't the Death either. Pete took a deep breath and tried to clear his thoughts. Had they missed something while going over the files? Then it hit him — the name of the Silent Death's first victim: Alfredo Florin. He remembered why he even knew it. And why someone else would've wanted him dead years ago.

"Wow," Pete said.

"What?" the Death responded, hesitating for the first time since he appeared in the plating area, turning his masked face in confusion. " 'Wow' what?"

"I'm just impressed," Pete said, staring at the Silent Death, watching his movements. Remembering. "I would have never guessed. But that's the plan, isn't it, Javier?"

The Silent Death took a step back, still pointing the gun at Pete. His hand wavered.

"You're a fool," the Death said. "And a nuisance. You couldn't leave well enough alone. I didn't even want you involved, but that old drunk couldn't do the work himself, so he had to lure a young drunk into it."

The pieces suddenly started to fit together in Pete's head. The nice watch on the hands that didn't look like they'd ever done a day of hard labor. The cushy job at Casa Pepe's. Maribel the waitress. The two shots that Pete saw in the Keys versus the one Kathy heard. The body in the bungalow couldn't have been Javier, Pete realized. And who else would keep Kathy alive for days in the hopes of getting her notes and letting her go but the man dating her? Even as a merciless killer, Javier still apparently had a heart.

The reality stung Pete. The realization that the friend he'd felt such guilt over abandoning years before had turned into a monster would haunt him the rest of his life. Which, he realized, could come to an end sooner rather than later.

"Why, though?" Pete said, hoping to stall, his eyes looking around the plating room in the hopes of discovering some kind of miracle escape. He heard Broche groaning to himself. He was coming to. He had to slow things down. He had to think of a way out. "What happened, man?"

"Oh Jesus, really? That's your tack? The 'Hey, bro, what happened? Let's reconnect' bullshit?" the Death said. Tossing his hat and mask aside, he was fully revealed as Javier Reyes. Dark bags under his eyes, a few days of stubble on his chin, but still the same friend Pete remembered from high school. He had to keep looking at him to try and convince himself it was true. "I took your father's advice, Pete. He told me — after that nutjob pulled a gun on us — that I had to be smarter. That I couldn't get myself caught up in that kind of thing anymore. Well, look at me now. I am smart. I fooled everyone for years. I never got caught. Your stupid old man couldn't even figure it out."

Contreras walked over to Pete and grabbed him by the arm before turning to Javier. "We have to get this over with," Contreras said. "This is taking too long."

Javier nodded. His face was flushed. He was angry, Pete realized. He'd lost his cool. Perhaps there was still a chance.

"Do you really think killing us will prevent people from knowing who you are?" Pete said, his voice calm and measured. "It's gonna come out. If a washed-up nobody like me can put the pieces together, someone else will, too."

Javier stepped closer to Pete, the gun now at his side, his face inches away from Pete's own. He could feel the hate coming from Javier. The bruised ego. Someone had figured out his game. Someone had made him work and step outside of his role. The plan had not been flawless.

"It doesn't matter," Javier said. "Javier Reyes is dead. That body in the bungalow might as well have been me. This —" he said, looking down at his black trench coat and gun, "This is me now. I've carved my own place in this city. People respect me. I make the rules here. People live or die because I say so. I refuse to let you ruin it."

"Do you realize how spoiled you sound?" Pete said. He could feel the shocked look Contreras was giving him. "I mean, really, what do you think the life expectancy for megalomaniacal killers is? You've gotta be near the high end, sure. But all good things and all that jazz, right?"

Pete didn't see the right hook coming, but he almost welcomed it. Anything but more prattling from Javier. Javier's fist connected with Pete's face roughly, knocking him back into Contreras and a row of desks at the far end of the plating room. Contreras groaned as he slammed into two chairs. Pete rolled with the punch and landed to Javier's left. He sprung himself at Javier, tackling him and pushing them both toward the door that led down the westernmost flight of metallic stairs. He gripped Javier's hands — one with a gun, one not —and slammed them both against the main door. The gun fell out of Javier's hand and rattled away. Pete struggled, his grip on Javier's arms loosening as his old friend tried desperately to get out from under him. Javier's knee swung upwards, connecting with Pete's midsection. He rolled off Javier, gripping his left side. More broken bones, he thought. Not ideal timing. Javier got to his feet and hovered over Pete. He could hear Javier's winded breathing. He rolled away from him and got up slowly.

"This has been fun, kid," Contreras said, pointing his own gun at Pete now. He'd recovered from his spill and now stood between Pete and Broche, who was still out. "But it's over now."

Contreras raised the gun. Pete closed his eyes. He'd done the best he could, he thought. If this was how he was going to go out, so be it. He heard the gunshot and searched his mind and body but found no pain. His eyes opened quickly enough to see Contreras fall to his knees, a chunk of his head no longer there, blood dripping down his face and body. He looked like half his face had folded over the other. Broche stood — more like wobbled — behind him and nodded. Behind him, Pete heard Javier race toward Broche. Pete stepped back. Javier quickly overpowered the older man, knocking him against the far wall and taking his gun. Pete started to get up to help Broche — his side still shooting pain —when the sound exploded around the small room.

Another shot. This time it was Broche who fell, his head snapping back. Javier stepped away from the kill, his eyes on the old detective as he fell, smearing blood on the far wall as his body slid down. He was dead. Pete didn't hesitate and dove for Javier's legs, knocking him forward to the ground. The fall gave Pete enough time to reach for his father's gun. He stood over Javier, gun drawn, and pointed as the killer rolled his body around to face Pete, a twisted grin on his face, Broche's police-issue Glock in his hand. The weapon he'd used to kill his father's partner.

"Pathetic, isn't it?" Javier said, the blood splattered on his face making for a weird, clownlike appearance. "That this is how it all goes down, huh? Just the two of us. Just like old times, my friend."

Javier got up. Pete backed off, his gun still trained on him. Javier was holding Broche's gun at his side, the grin still plastered on his face.

"We're not friends," Pete said. "We haven't been friends for a long time."

"Now, don't say that. You were the one all excited to take a trip down memory lane with me. You seemed almost ecstatic when I saw you at Casa Pepe's, sniffing around and stirring shit up."

Pete said nothing. He felt his hand sweating. The grip on his father's gun tightening. Javier took a step closer, his face smeared with Broche's blood, his eyes wide.

"We know where this is gonna go," Javier said, pointing his gun at Pete. "So let's not drag it out, shall we?"

"We're tied, it seems," Pete said, his voice cracking. He felt a drop of sweat slide down his face. "Except you're in a bit of a time crunch."

Javier raised an eyebrow.

"Any minute now, the press people are going to come into this room and find blood and bodies everywhere," Pete said. "Do you think you'll just be able to walk out of here without any explanation?"

"Oh, shut the fuck up," Javier spit and stretched out his gun arm. Pete's eyes zoomed in on the gun. He tried to dodge, but it would be impossible. A split second before he heard the gunshot and felt the searing agony, he heard the pressroom alarm — the signal that the giant newsprint machines were being warmed up and preparing to print all the papers that would be distributed across South Florida. The momentary distraction made Javier hesitate. Made his shot veer slightly off. The bullet tore into Pete's shoulder, sending him backwards, slamming into the main door and knocking it open. He reached for the wound. His father's gun landed on the floor beside him. Blood. His blood. Everywhere. Blood all in his mouth. He couldn't breathe.

"Fuck!" Javier screamed. Pete could hear people downstairs, alerted by the gunfire, no doubt. He could feel air from the press room — the fans — filtering in from the open door. He reached out his good hand and grasped his gun. It was his gun now. He saw Javier head toward the door. Weak, shivering, and not sure how close he was to dying, Pete slammed his good arm into Javier's legs, sending him tripping forward. Javier managed to grab the metal railings in time, preventing his fall. He turned to face Pete, looking down on him, that smile still plastered on his face.

The bullet hit Javier in the neck, causing a small fountain of blood to spray out, spreading down his neck and further bloodying his face. The force of the shot sent Javier back into the railing, propping him up awkwardly as he gurgled his last breaths, his face no longer smiling. Pete thought he heard him try to form words, but the look on his face was enough for Pete. Confusion. Anger. Surprise. All replacing the cocky laugh that Pete had once admired.

Pete's gun hand fell to the floor. He saw Javier's body sag at an odd angle. He tried to keep his eyes open. He heard voices. People rushing up the stairs. A scream. Emily? He wasn't sure. Pete groaned and tried to focus his vision on the room around him. Then everything went dark.

EPILOGUE

He drained the last sip from his beer and placed the glass back on its coaster. The bartender, a youngish-looking girl with too much makeup on, was quick to reappear in front of him.

"Want another?" she said, putting on her best bartender smile.

"No, I'm good," Pete said. She gave him a nod, but Pete also noticed how her eyes lingered over him. How often did she get a guy with his arm in a sling, cuts all over his face and a black eye in her bar ordering drinks? Not very often, he hoped. For her sake.

Big City Tavern was your typical yuppie after-work watering hole, if a bit too bright and not nearly as welcoming as it should be. Pete remembered sitting in a nearby booth with Mike many times over, talking until the wee hours about who knows what. He turned the beer glass around slowly, his fingers tracing over the Stella logo. The place was a few blocks from Mike's place — well, where he used to live. When he used to live, Pete corrected himself.

He yawned. He winced as the yawn ran through him, hurting his broken ribs. His body was a mess. By some strange twist of fate, the shot that Pete's shoulder took didn't do any major damage. It did cause a lot of bleeding, though. Had the paramedics on the scene not acted swiftly, the loss of blood would have meant the end of the line for Pete. He was surprised he was alive. Arm in a sling, bandages over his broken nose and a purple — almost dark blue — black eye that got him more attention than he ever wanted. Sprinkle that over the broken ribs and concussion he hadn't really allowed himself to recover from and you had what was left of Pete Fernandez, former sports copy editor of the *Miami Times*.

He didn't feel like drinking. The numbness that spread over his arm when he got shot lingered — but not in a physical or literal sense. He felt dulled, without sensation. He wasn't sure if he'd ever get back to the man he was before — the twenty-something fiancé working his dream job and traveling the nation. He was OK with that now. He just needed to figure out what he was going to be instead.

Emily dropped her bag next to Pete's barstool and leaned in to give him a kiss on the cheek. She mussed his hair as she slid into the chair next to him.

"You still look like shit," she said, smiling. She seemed happy to see him. She looked at his empty glass. "Are you already trashed?"

"I looked worse last week," Pete said, smiling warily. "Twice as bad the week before that. And no, that was my first beer."

Emily nodded.

"Well, you do look better," she said.

"It's nice to not be in the hospital for a change."

"Or the police station."

"Or that, yeah."

Pete closed out his tab and they moved to a small booth near the bar. They sat across from each other. Emily was in a yellow summer dress and a black sweater-jacket. She looked more dressed up than usual. Then again, he hadn't really seen her outside of the confines of his hospital room in almost a month.

The waiter came by and Emily ordered a glass of Chardonnay. Pete ordered another Stella.

"Where's Kathy?" Emily said as she fiddled with her napkin. "Is she coming?"

Pete shrugged. After Javier's death — the real one — Kathy had managed to finagle her way back into the paper. She wrote the definitive story about the Silent Death, both as a killer and as a person, from the perspective of someone who not only knew about the murders themselves, but also had shared a bed with the killer himself. It was riveting reading. She'd kept in touch with Pete, interviewing him a few times for the story and eventual book. But her visits had dwindled over the last few weeks. Pete was fine with that. He wasn't quite as fine with the idea that she might've gotten away with a big bag of drug money.

There was a saying about romances or friendships born during times of war, but the exact phrasing was not coming to mind. He scanned the appetizer menu as he spoke. "I don't think so."

Emily made a low, humming sound and nodded. Their drinks arrived.

"Do the cops still want to talk to you?" she asked, sipping her wine. "Or are they too embarrassed their entire department was on the take?"

"Yeah. I dunno," Pete said. "I remember a few different guys coming by my hospital room. It was fine. I'm just glad I'm not being charged with anything. I mean, I killed someone."

"You were defending yourself."

"I know, but still."

She reached out for his hand.

"You were defending yourself," she said. "You saved yourself and the price was the death of someone who'd killed so many people. We probably have no idea how many."

Pete took a long sip of his beer and looked around the bar. He wanted to change the subject.

"We all used to come here a lot," he said, nostalgia in his voice. "Seems like it was a long time ago."

Emily looked around as well, but without the same wonderment as Pete.

"This place kind of blows," she said, turning back to Pete. "But you liked it, so we came here a lot."

Pete nodded.

"Yeah," he said. "I'm still surprised you and Mike listen — listened — to me as much as you did."

"I'd like to think it's more me looking out for you than listening to you."

"Fair enough," Pete said.

"What now?" Emily asked. Her eyes locked on his. Over the last few weeks, as Pete improved — physically from the injuries he suffered and mentally from the entire affair — Emily had dedicated herself to his recovery, spending entire days keeping him company in his hospital room. Now that he was out and left to his own devices, she still managed to pop up to "hang out" or check in with him more often. Pete was OK with that.

"I think I might try this detective thing," Pete said. "I got the paperwork last week. Filled it out and sent it for approval this morning. We'll see. I don't exactly have a sterling record. But everything after this has got to be easy, right?"

"So, you're going to open up an agency?"

"I'm not sure, yet," Pete said. "I doubt I'll be swimming in clients off the bat. But it probably beats working at the *Times*."

Emily smiled, resting her face on her palm. She felt relaxed. Mike's loss still stung both of them, but for the first time in what seemed like an eternity, it didn't feel like death or tragedy was around the corner.

"It's a start," she said, tracing lines on the table with her index finger. "I've got office space downtown, too, if you need a work line or a desk so it feels like you're actually going to work, instead of checking e-mail in your boxers."

"But I like checking e-mail in my boxers," he joked.

"I bet," she said. "Think about it. I could use someone to help me split the rent."

"It'll be a while before I can pay rent on anything that isn't my apartment," Pete said, lifting his beer up to his mouth and stopping. He looked at the half-empty glass and placed it back on the table. The bar's jukebox kicked in suddenly and loudly. The bartender scurried to the controls and lowered the sound. The Stones. "If You Really Want to Be My Friend." Pete nodded at Emily. She shrugged.

"What, is this another one of your songs?"

Pete laughed.

"I guess so," he said. "I'm a sucker for Stones album tracks. You know that."

Emily pushed her glass away and looked at Pete.

"How are you feeling, aside from the physical?" she asked.

She was talking about the fact that he'd killed Javier. She always came back to it, even if she knew Pete hated discussing it. That he'd led Mike to his eventual death. That he'd failed to save Broche or Amy. All the guilt and pain that surrounded his life for the last few months. He looked into his glass at the golden liquid.

"I feel fine."

"No you don't," she said.

"I don't want to talk about it," Pete said. "Javier's dead. The problem is solved."

"Is it?" she asked. She instantly regretted it. It had come across as mean, when she was genuinely curious.

To her relief, Pete seemed to take it the way she intended. He leaned back into the booth and rubbed at the stubble forming on his chin.

"I have no idea," he said. "I don't think I'll ever know."

He moved his glass a few inches away and folded his arms. He looked out at the central part of the bar, and then spoke.

"It all seems like a weird dream," he said. "At first, when I was lying in that hospital room, full of tubes and feeling almost dead — even before then, seeing Mike's car explode or watching you as I drove off — I wanted it to be a dream. I wanted to wake up in my father's house, in my old room, covered in sweat, but relieved that all these things had just been an exercise in my subconscious. Not my life. But it is. And I'm fine with that. Not because I don't have a choice, but because for the first time in a long time, it's my life because I chose to make it mine. I'm a fuck-up, but the mistakes are mine. I'm not fumbling through it all and hoping someone else can pick me up and point me in the right direction. I'm allowed to start again."

Emily straightened in her seat and nodded, smiling.

"What?"

"Nothing," she said, nodding, impressed. "I just didn't think you had that in you. You know, that level of self-awareness and reflection."

Pete rubbed his eyes and stretched his good arm.

"Me neither," he said. "So, I guess there's that."

Pete's eyes wandered to the jukebox as Emily finished her glass of wine. They'd be leaving soon. It wasn't going to be a late night.

The Stones faded, and he heard the jukebox lurch to a stop. No money, no songs. Pete watched as the bright, red numbers on the digital jukebox's display blinked in the dark, empty bar.

An excerpt from Alex Segura's new Pete Fernandez novel

DOWN THE DARKEST STREET

Available from Polis Books

CHAPTER ONE

PETE FERNANDEZ DIDN'T see the kick coming. The boot crashed into his jaw, sending him farther into the dank alley. The two men paused to see if Pete had any plans to fight back. He didn't. He felt blood trickle down his face.

Pete tried to stand up. His feet gave way. He slipped and landed on his ass, slamming into the metal garbage cans that lined the alley. He wasn't sure where the pain was coming from anymore. The Miami air felt thick and heavy around him. His breathing was fast. Short, quick gasps.

Bile rose in Pete's throat. He could taste some of the Jim Beam shots he'd downed over the course of the evening. He tried to wipe some of the sweat—and whatever else—from his face, but stopped when he caught a glimpse of his hand, shaking and bloody, gravel and dirt embedded in his left palm.

One of the guys laughed as the other walked up and grabbed Pete, lifting him up by his shirt. The guy reeked of cheap beer and cheaper aftershave. He spit a wad of mucus at Pete's face, most of it splattering on his left cheek. The guy let Pete drop and turned toward his friend.

Pete watched the duo lumber away, their curses muffling the sound of their footsteps. He wiped the gunk off his face and let out a jagged breath.

It had been another Miami scorcher. One of those days where you don't want to consider leaving the house, or wearing pants. Where you get sunburned taking out the garbage. Where your shirt sticks to your slick body before you even get to your car. Pete's phone had said ninety degrees that morning but it felt closer to a hundred. The evening had only brought a small respite—dimmed lights in a sauna. The rare, tropical breeze a teasing gift—a sweet whisper in your ear. Miami. Even the brightest sun and neon lights couldn't change it. The place was fucked. Dirty. Corrupt. A nightmare happening in broad daylight.

Pete was on all fours now. His head hung down. A quick cough turned into a dozen and soon he was lying on his side, spittle dripping out of his mouth, his eyes out of focus and his body writhing in the dirt.

He tried to get up, his vision blurring. He got his footing and paused to catch his breath, his body leaning on the grime-covered wall. He tried to concentrate: On his hand pushing himself off the wall and toward the end of the alley. On each foot—left, right, left—as he started to walk. On what had led him back here, outside the Gables Pub, bloodied, drunk, and alone.

The night had started off routine. Standard. Pete needed to get out. Do some reading. His friends weren't around anymore. He didn't care. Fuck 'em. He was fine sitting at his favorite bar, reading his dead father's worn copy of *Night Shift*. Shuffling the pages back every few minutes, having forgotten what he'd read, too proud to give up. The pub was on the fringe of what people considered Coral Gables— meaning it wasn't as nice as the mansions and high-rise buildings that meshed with the tiny city's old Spanish décor. Just a few miles from Miracle Mile, the pedestrian-friendly heart of the Gables, the pub felt like another world: dark, dirty, and out of place. Time passed. He had a few whiskey shots to go with his seven or eight beers and felt rough. Not smooth, like he used to feel after a few rounds, when the buzz glowed around his face and made him smile without thinking about it. No, he felt rough and grimy, like bare feet on a dirty sidewalk.

The two guys were big, but not built. Ex-frat boys with nothing to do but get wasted on a Tuesday night. The television perched over the bar was playing Dolphins football highlights from the night before. Jets 35, Dolphins 7. The two guys and their girlfriends were a few seats away at the other end of the bar, cursing at the screen. Pete found what little concentration he had disrupted. He put his book down and scowled at the double date. They shrugged and kept yapping. Pete groaned and ordered another round. Beer and a shot. The whiskey went down warm. He could feel it coating his throat and stomach.

Next thing he knew, he was sitting next to one of the women, his hand on her leg. Where were the guys? He wasn't sure. Whatever. The other girl—chunkier, louder, obnoxious—was yelling something. She seemed upset. Pete swayed. He tried to play off how drunk he was to the girl, tried to make it seem accidental. His hand went too far. She tossed it off. He tried to stand up, one hand on the bar, his other swinging a bottle of Heineken around. That's when he felt a hand gripping his shoulder. He remembered being pushed out the front door and into the street. It was the two guys. He'd thought they had left. Wrong.

Pete remembered mumbling an apology, but that was lost. Lost in the noise of the two guys yelling and lost as he felt himself being shoved into the alley. It was narrow and wet, dark and empty. That's when he felt the first kick to his midsection. He was splayed on the ground, and trying to get himself back to standing only resulted in a weird push-up. The second kick hit him in the face.

Pete now tried to will the memory away but failed. He wiped his wrist over his mouth and found more blood.

He inched down the alley, away from the pub, toward the backstreets that would allow him some semblance of cover from the shame he knew was starting to kick in. He moved his tongue around his mouth, checking for missing teeth. Relieved to find there were no unwanted gaps.

He reached the end of the alley. Pete had parked his banged-up Toyota Celica on the street a few blocks north of the bar, past a small parking lot. It was dark enough outside—a few hours past sunset—that he could limp to his car and not make too much of a scene.

He didn't see any people or cars. Pete let go of the alley wall and began to half walk, half hobble across the street that intersected with the end of the alley. He was out of breath by the time he crossed the street and stopped to lean against the short cement wall surrounding the parking lot.

The sound of an engine cut through the quiet evening.

Pete turned to meet the noise. A van was approaching from his left, the clank-and-growl sound coming from under its hood getting louder as it approached. He stepped back. His first thought was that the two guys were back, this time with wheels. The van was close enough to Pete that he wasn't sure he could risk darting back across the street. He was also unsure he could dart anywhere. His head throbbed and the pain in his side had become sharper. He considered the hospital for a second but pushed the thought out of his mind. He just wanted to get home.

The van was now close enough for Pete to see inside. He let his eyes wander over it, his vision lazy and blurry. As the van came up beside him, the driver came into focus—a tall, thin white man with longish brown hair. Pete couldn't tell much else about him in the darkness. The driver didn't notice Pete, watching the road instead. But then the van stopped for a second. Pete and the driver looked at each other. The driver nodded his head. He thought Pete wanted to cross the small street—which he had, but the arrival of the van threw him off. Pete motioned for the van to continue. At first he'd only noticed the driver, but as the vehicle drove on past him, Pete realized there was another passenger—a teenager, curled up in the front seat. The girl was petite—couldn't be over sixteen, Pete figured—and her hair looked rumpled and disheveled.

Pete stepped back. The evening's silence was replaced by the sound of rubber tires on asphalt, as the van accelerated and was gone.

CHAPTER TWO

HIS HANDS TIGHTENED *on the steering wheel. A bead of sweat formed at the edge of his scalp. The drunk man had caught him off guard, stepping into his path like that. The last thing he needed was to hit a pedestrian and make a scene. No matter. They were almost at the spot. The Voice would be appeased and grow quiet again.*

The girl was splayed out on the passenger side, her head at a weird angle. He noticed the bloody smear at the base of her skull. He hadn't wanted to do that, but she would have fought. She would have screamed. He thought back to a few hours earlier. Dadeland Mall—a giant eyesore located in suburban Kendall in southwest Miami. A giant block of stores and restaurants that looked more like a prison than anything entertaining. He'd followed the girl and her friends. They were window-shopping. Eating at the food court. The usual. He'd wooed her for days via e-mails, Facebook messages, and the occasional text message. His method hadn't failed him. He was cautious.

He turned the van onto the expressway, heading south.

After a while, her friends had left. She needed a ride home. He texted her from the disposable phone he'd purchased that morning.

From *"my friend's phone."* Meet me outside, we can get a soda. *She was hesitant. He watched from the van. The only thing he'd held onto since the darker times. Since New Jersey. Virginia. Georgia. He changed the signage on the side every month or so. Some months he was MONSON ELECTRIC. Other months, it was ANDREA'S BRIDAL.*

He spotted her standing outside of Macy's, near the Parking Lot C, alone. He got out of the van and approached her from behind. He tapped her on the shoulder. She turned around with a start, a confused look on her face.

"Excuse me, young lady?"

"Yes?"

"I'm Steve's uncle. Have you seen him? He said he was meeting a friend."

She looked concerned.

"Oh, well, he said he was going to meet me here," she said, with no prodding.

"That's not like him not to show up," he said, his hands sliding into his jeans pockets. "Weird. I dropped him off here a little while ago."

She shrugged her shoulders and checked her phone. Nothing from "Steve."

"Have you spoken to him recently?"

"Just a few minutes ago."

"Hmm," he said, rubbing his chin. He'd cleaned up a bit in anticipation of the encounter. His longish hair was tied back, his stubble trimmed to a reasonable length. He was as clean-cut as he had to be. "I'm going to take a quick swing around the parking lot and then maybe the other side of the mall. Want to come along?"

She hesitated. It sounded safe; he could see her debating it in her head.

"It's up to you," he said, shrugging and beginning to walk away. "I'm just getting a little worried about him. I can tell him you were looking for him, too—when I find him."

"No, no," she said, speeding up her pace to catch up with him. "It's OK. Let's go."

He'd left a piece of pipe by the front passenger-side tire. As she opened the van door he swung at her skull with force. She let out a slight yelp and tumbled forward. He pulled her up and pushed her into the van, looking around and confirming no one had seen him. He settled her into the seat, positioning her to look like she'd just dozed off. He allowed himself a moment to caress the hair framing her young face.

He turned off on the exit for Campbell Drive.

The girl whimpered. A slow, low moan of discomfort. He realized she would be awake soon and stepped on the accelerator. A little more speed was OK. They were almost there. And then he and the Voice would be sated for a little while longer. He turned the car radio on. The oldies station. The sound of Harry Nilsson's smooth baritone came through the van's scratchy stereo system.

"Remember . . . life is just a memory, remember . . . close your eyes and you can see . . ."

ACKNOWLEDGMENTS

The writing of *Silent City* was a cathartic one for me. I first put pen to page around 2007, homesick and a little aimless. I was a few years into living in New York and had, thanks to my dear friend Will Dennis, discovered a handful of authors that would change my life: George Pelecanos, Dennis Lehane, Laura Lippman and James Ellroy. I found myself completely bowled over by the flawed, human and compelling protagonists I met in the pages of books like *A Firing Offense, Darkness, Take My Hand, Charm City* and more. Not only did these books feel completely real, rife with great stories and sharp social commentary, but each also boasted a unique and equally important setting. The Washington, D.C. of Nick Stefanos would never be confused with the Los Angeles of Lloyd Hopkins.

In terms of the book you're holding in your hands, reading those books sparked an idea of my own: That maybe I could take a stab at this and create my own character, who not only felt real to me — like someone I could have hung out with — but also took up space in my own hometown of Miami.

It started off as a short story, told in the first person with a protagonist I was still getting to know. After a few years and many revisions, it became my first novel — and one of the things I'm most proud of, and thankful for.

Pete Fernandez's first adventure would not be in your hands without Polis Books and its publisher, Jason Pinter. Jason's one of the smartest people I've ever met in the publishing world, and his faith and support have been unwavering. I'm eternally grateful and supremely honored to share the stage with the killer lineup of authors he's gathered at Polis.

I'd also like to thank my all-star agent, Dara Hyde. She's been one of Pete's biggest supporters since the beginning, and I couldn't ask for a stronger advocate and sounding board. This book and its sequels couldn't exist without her.

Thanks to Wayne Lockwood and Codorus Press for giving *Silent City* its first home. Thanks are also due to my friends at Archie Comics and DC Entertainment, the many beta readers who gave notes at every stage of this book's long gestation, my supportive author pals and publishing/press colleagues, my friends (too many to list but I hope by now you know who you are) and family (calling all Seguras, Steins, Steinfelds, Gutierrezes, Rivelas, Bustamantes, Burgos, Fernandezes, Kesslers, Dejus and Rugovas!), especially my parents and my mother-in-law, Isabel Stein, this book's unsung editorial hero.

This book is also dedicated to the memory of my grandfather Guillermo Fernandez and my uncle Francisco Rivela, two great men I will never forget.

My biggest thanks go to my wife, Eva Stein Segura. You make every day better.

Alex Segura
Queens, NY
September 1, 2015

ABOUT THE AUTHOR

Alex Segura is a novelist and comic book writer. He is the author of the Pete Fernandez novels *Silent City* and its sequel, *Down the Darkest Street*, both available from Polis Books. He has also written a number of comic books, including the best-selling and critically acclaimed *Archie Meets Kiss* storyline, the "Occupy Riverdale" story, and the upcoming *Archie Meets Ramones*. He lives in New York with his wife. He is a Miami native.

Visit him online at
www.AlexSegura.com
and @Alex_Segura.